FRIE...
AND
NEIGHBOURS

A heart-warming journey of self-discovery

By

Ruth Torjussen

For Joe and Dan with love.

CONTENTS

ACKNOWLEDGMENTS

Thanks to Helen, Karen, Flis and Steph for your support in getting this book completed.

Thanks to Allan Savory and Jody Butterfield, John D Liu, Walter Jehne, Didi Pershouse, Charles Eisenstein and every other soil ecologist, regenerative farmer, permaculturalist and writer who inspired me through their work and helped me understand the importance of the ground beneath our feet.

CHAPTER 1

The arrival

The fence ran the whole length of the garden, front and back, about 40 metres in all. Jenny stood in the driveway and raised her vintage designer sunglasses to better view it.

She sniffed. What a sorry state of affairs.

A few weeks earlier, the second big storm of the year had battered all but the wooden posts, splitting several sections into pieces and flinging them up into trees, around the garden and across the street without a care. Her husband Lonny had cheerfully rescued every little bit and then reconstructed what was now in front of her, a botch job of a fence wedged in behind a row of newly planted tiny shrubs.

'I'm not buying a new fence, Jen,' he said. 'They're no good for the environment. The old one will have to do till the hedge has grown.'

She looked at the tiny shrubs and said, 'What hedge? I can't see a hedge!'

'You wait, duck, before you know it, that lot will be six foot tall and full of wildlife!' he replied with his usual exuberance.

Lonny's stubborn refusal to upgrade the fence wouldn't matter too much except that new neighbours were moving in any minute and really... well, she wouldn't blame them if they complained. People do have standards after all.

She patted her forehead with the back of her hand before putting her sunglasses back on. This heat was getting crazy. If she stayed out in it much longer she would wilt. If only the new neighbours would hurry up and arrive. She meandered up the drive and casually strained her neck towards the sound of distant traffic. No, there was nothing coming this way.

She turned back to the house where scaffolding had been erected to enable the addition of further solar panels on the roof. Lonny was up there sorting it all out, busy as usual. He caught her glance and leant over the top rail.

'Come on, Jen,' he called, 'come up and see the view.'

She squinted up at him in the dazzling sunshine. At fifty-one, her petite figure hadn't changed much over the years but the lines on her face now suggested more worry than laughter. She put a cautious hand on the scaffolding ladder to feel how steady it was. It felt firm but she resisted. Their three-bedroom semi on the southern tip of Stoke-on-Trent wasn't a big house, but still, that roof was high up and scary. Lonny would be up there for the next few weeks installing the extra panels as part of his ongoing efforts to make the family plot more self-sufficient, ready for when 'it all kicks off'. She tried to be interested in his prepping and environmental projects, but it wasn't really her cup of tea. Plus the scaffolding annoyed her because it made the house look ugly. She had gone to great lengths to choose the right shutters for the front windows, to make the house seem more south of Paris than south of Stoke. Now the stupid scaffolding was covering them all up.

Still, the view from the roof must be good, it must stretch across Manor Lane and Meir Park on the one side and to the countryside beyond on the other. That would be nice. Lonny called her again.

'Come on, duck, you can do it.'

She put her foot on the bottom rung, but the sound of a car approaching distracted her. In Bramfield Drive, a quiet cul-de-sac, any car had the potential to be a bit of news. Sure enough, the engine sounded like it could belong to a van which might mean the long-awaited tenants were finally moving in next door. She would go up on the roof later, plenty of time for that.

After fifteen years of living next door to dear old Myrtle, Jenny couldn't help but feel a rush of excitement at the thought of nice new neighbours moving in. Younger people and hopefully a lovely woman she could be friends with. Just a nice warm female face over the fence, to wave and chat to each day and maybe get a text from every now and then: 'Fancy a coffee?' It wasn't too much to ask was it? She wasn't asking to win the lottery was she?

She peered over the patchwork fence to where the van was coming round the corner and into view. But at the first sight of it, the look of happy expectation on her face collapsed. She retreated into the shadows of the scaffolding in haste.

'Newlyweds' was how the letting agent had initially described the new neighbours, conjuring up romantic images of white weddings and honeymoons, while admitting later that they already had a couple of young children. Well that was par for the course these days, that didn't mean anything. Also they were renting the house off Myrtle's son despite house prices in Stoke being the lowest in the country, but everyone has to rent now and then so that didn't tell her much either. But this filthy old van churning out thick smoke from the exhaust told her a lot more. And this big, thuggish bloke stepping out and aggressively shouting parking instructions to the driver, that told her a lot too.

She peered closer at the driver. A big, fat tattooed woman. Shouting back at her husband and calling him a *cunt*.

God Almighty. That told her everything.

She rushed inside.

In the hallway, away from the dazzling light of the sunny garden, she put a hand on the wall to steady herself as the comparative darkness of inside enveloped her. Another knock back. Another disappointment. Why had she been so stupid as to expect more?

She walked into the kitchen, poured a glass of water from the filter jug and leant back against the units. Her hand was shaking as she drank a few sips. A hideous foul-mouthed woman was moving in next door, it was just typical. She might have guessed it would happen. I mean, could her life get any worse? Could it?

She caught sight of the calendar on the wall and the numerous Saturday night bookings coming up in her role as a Marie Osmond impersonator. Oh God, each one of those was like a booking for a dentist's drill. Clearly it could get worse. In fact, it seemed out of control now, it was ridiculous. She never wanted it to be like this. Trapped in an awful life. In a cage. And now with a pair of gorillas running loose next door.

A notification sounded on her phone and she grabbed it, hoping it was Annie or Kate or Emily messaging to say hello or, even better, that they were coming back to Stoke for a visit.

But no, it was the weather app saying to take care because it was getting hotter.

For God's sake, she didn't need an app to tell her how hot it was. She tossed the phone aside. It brought no relief these days.

It hadn't always been like this though, had it? In what now seemed like a different lifetime, she had been fortunate enough to know many, many happy days. She looked at the numerous framed photos on the gallery wall which stretched across the kitchen diner. Pictures of her and her best friend Sue, and others of her and Annie and Kate and Emily, her friends from the salon. Beautiful women surrounding her, supporting her, loving her, filling every day with laughter. Now who did she have?

Even with the best husband and the most adorable sons in the world, she often felt like this these days. Since Sue died, since the girls had left town, since she was forced to close the beauty salon and become a carer. Since her whole world had turned upside down, since her whole world had turned *ugly*; there was a gaping hole in her life the shape of which was female.

*

Jenny and Lonny would often get stared at when they went into Hanley, Stoke's city centre. Lonny, the handsome youngest son of Jamaican immigrants who had settled in Stoke in the 1960s and Jenny, the daughter of a beauty queen from South Wales, would literally turn heads. Jenny always loved to look her best whatever the occasion; even just a trip to the Potteries Shopping Centre or, these days, the doctor, would see her making an effort. And for her Marie Osmond routine, of course, the curling tongs were on at full throttle. At least they used to be. Maybe it was having such a dishy husband who was eight years younger that kept her on her toes, even though she knew he wasn't the type to stray. Or maybe she remembered the sharp-tongued criticism from her mother if she *wasn't* well turned out, a cardinal sin in her books, even for five year olds. Despite this, Jenny had enjoyed her career as a beautician with her own salon for many years, the girls by her side, her clients looking pampered and fabulous. But eventually, after years of grinding austerity in Stoke, beauty treatments became a luxury and the salon began to suffer. Then there were those incidents with the dreaded Botox. She never could get the hang of giving injections, especially when people didn't sit still.

When Sue was diagnosed with cancer, Jenny used the lack of business as an opportunity to go to Cardiff to be by her best friend's side. Then, as the recession hit and she had to lay off the girls, they had seized the opportunity to break out in a midlife change of direction: Annie went off to university on the south coast, Kate set up her own salon with her husband in Jersey, while Emily hooked up with a champion weightlifter and followed him to Lanzarote.

Jenny knew that a change of career was what faced her too, but coping with Sue's illness left her unable to put much thought into it. In desperation, she ended up joining a care agency because she knew that at least if she was a carer she would never be out of work. Which was true, she was never out of work. Then one day, just after Sue died, she was visiting a bed-ridden old lady with Alzheimer's and had to change her incontinence pad despite telling the agency she didn't really want to do personal care. But no one else was available, they said, so she just had to get on with it. And the old lady wouldn't cooperate. She thought she was back in the playground and Jenny was a young boy trying to pull her knickers down and she fought and kicked with all her might. Eventually, Jenny won and then found herself having to clear up what seemed to be an open sewage works. She cried as she did it. She cried and she thought of Sue and how much she missed her and the girls and the salon and all the glamour and the laughter they used to share. And how they were now all gone and she was left drowning in shit.

Literally.

*

Under the pretext of dusting the bathroom window ledge she looked out of the half-open window, nudged the shutter open a little wider and peered down into next door's garden. At least with the scaffolding up she could be as nosy as she liked because no one would be able to spot her.

The black van, now parked half on the drive and half on the lawn, had destroyed the flower bed border. Unbelievable. Myrtle would have risen up out of her wheelchair shaking her fists if she had seen this. And it seemed the 'newlyweds' had done all their packing using bin liners. One bag after another spilled out of the van. Where was the furniture? It was as though they had moved the entire local rubbish collection. She winced at the sight of all that plastic; Lonny would have a fit.

She could see the woman jumping out of the back of the van, still shouting at her husband. He seemed to have disappeared. Not surprising, who wouldn't? Oh here he was, reluctantly putting his phone away like he had a bet on at the races that was much more important. God Almighty, if looks could kill! Well, their honeymoon was well and truly over, wasn't it? She could hear young children shouting and screaming and hoped there weren't too many of them. Oh Lord, there might be seven or eight. Jenny opened the window slightly wider to get a better view, still straining to see because of the scaffolding planks.

She saw her new neighbour bending over to pick up a few of the bags and noted the unsuitability of the hipsters she was wearing, given the size of her backsi–

A flood of nausea stopped her thoughts abruptly. She realised she had just turned into her mother, the biggest snob in South Wales. Her eyes filled with tears. This wouldn't do, this wouldn't do at all, it was obviously her depression getting the better of her. The depression that had moved into her life after Sue died. She left the window, feeling ashamed of herself.

She took a moment to look in the mirror and tried to force a smile to help shake off the negative vibes. A few moments went by as she tried several times to grin like a Cheshire cat. This tactic usually worked. But not today.

She heard Lonny call from outside.

'Duck? Come and meet Dawn – our new neighbour!'

She stayed quiet. After all, she was in the bathroom. Surely here she could get away with not giving a response? She went back to the window to see if she could see them; yes, there they were, at the fence. Dawn had a huge smile on her face, she obviously liked Lonny. Well, that was no surprise, everyone did.

'Sorry, duck, I think she's otherwise engaged; she'll come and say hello later,' he said.

Don't say that, Lon, she winced, can't you see she's not my type?

Just then, Dawn looked directly up at the bathroom window and saw her standing there with her feather duster, through the half-open pane of frosted glass. She grinned and waved.

Jenny backed away, her face flushed.

CHAPTER 2

Grief

Normally, Jenny forgot her dreams moments after waking. They never made much of an impact. But this particular one did. It was Saturday afternoon, the day after the arrival of the new neighbours and she was having a nap.

In the dream, she was on stage as Marie Osmond singing 'Paper Roses' while the guys – Lonny and The Four Topsmonds – were backstage changing outfits from the Osmonds to the Four Tops. No different to reality there then; this was the act they put on in pubs many Friday and Saturday nights throughout the year and the room was always heaving. At least it was while the men were on stage. But the usual reward for Marie was everyone vacating the room and going to the toilet or stepping out for a smoke. Everyone, that is, except the pub landlord who would take the chance to clear up any mess while the crowd was absent. But in her dream, this clearing up seemed to be never-ending. There was more and more broken glass, spilt lager slops and even pools of vomit appearing and the landlord wanted her to keep singing because he needed a chance to clear it all up. So she had to sing 'Paper Roses' again, and again, and again. She wanted to shout out, 'For God's sake! How long is this clear-up going to take? I can't sing this bloody song forever!' But she couldn't speak. It was as though her good manners had her rooted to the spot and she just had to keep on singing.

Then she saw someone writing a review of her on Facebook, writing it in such a way that she knew Jenny would be able to read it over her shoulder. The review said, '*This Marie Osmond is a joke. She can't sing and she's a little bloody liar!*'

Jenny could smell her mother's perfume and she knew it was her.

When she woke, she felt the urge to find a pen and write it all down. She sat on the bed and wrote a full page about the dream. It felt good to write it all down. She sniffed. She might have known her mother would be in there having the last word.

She had been thinking about her mother a lot lately. God, she was annoying. But then she had always been annoying and it had never bothered her much before. Why should it bother her now?

The sudden sound of loud groaning and furniture shifting came from the other side of the bedroom wall as their new neighbours began to unpack. Jenny realised with a shudder that both houses were the same layout so the room behind the wall must also be the biggest bedroom and the newlyweds would therefore be sleeping in it. A big belch followed by loud laughter from Dawn rang out as though to confirm that thought. Jenny grimaced. Something told her that a belch would be the very least of it.

She tried to get back to her thoughts about her dream and her mother.

As she read through her notes, her eye was caught by a book that lay on her bedside table. *Grief and How to Survive It.* Lonny had got it from the charity shop down at Meir to try and help her after Sue died. She had read it three times now, often with tears in her eyes, so she kept missing important bits of information. For some reason, she felt compelled to open it now.

Her eyes fell on a random passage:

'...*causing all kinds of long-lost buried traumas to dislodge and rise to the surface...*'

Long-lost buried trauma – yes, that sounded like her mother alright.

Sue had sussed Jenny's mother out immediately, of course. She understood that, despite holding that precious title, she never actually had Jenny's best interests at heart. Whereas Sue did. Right from the outset.

Jenny met her best friend on their first day at St Augustine's, a strict Catholic primary school in Cardiff, South Wales. Jenny was shy and didn't like the attention she often received as a pretty little girl with pigtails. Especially from Uncle Pat, the stupid creep. Once she was friends with Sue, she felt safe. Sue was just as pretty as she was, but her clever dark eyes could soon suss out anyone dodgy and she would shout out loudly and give them a good kicking. It was quite funny sometimes. She was like a Wonder Woman from the get-go, Jenny often thought. There was never a time when Sue was not supremely self-assured.

The two little girls, Jenny, shy, white-skinned, one dimple, and Sue, confident, black-skinned, and two dimples, always sat together in class. They would regularly be caught whispering and their teacher, old Fanny Parker, renowned for her girdle-enhanced hourglass figure would call out, 'Jennifer! Susan! You Bold Madams! Be quiet this instant!' The two little girls would try and keep a straight face but fail miserably.

Dragging herself back to the present, Jenny went downstairs. While she made a cup of tea to take out to Lonny in the garden, the photo of her and Susan on the gallery wall caught her eye – five years old and full of mischief. It never failed to make her smile.

Her gazing at little Sue's lovely dimples came to an abrupt end as some sort of loud hammering noise began on the other side of the wall. The newlyweds must be putting up pictures. Or a dartboard perhaps. She tutted. What a shame their houses were joined like this and that they weren't separated by a driveway like they were from their other neighbours, nice quiet Fusun and Ahmed, who had twin babies yet still managed to hardly be heard.

She wondered with dread whether the language from the first day might be normal behaviour for Dawn and her husband. What a terrible influence that would be on the boys. Hopefully, it was just the stress of the move which caused Dawn to erupt like that. Anyway, it wouldn't be long before they were settled in. In fact, they should be settled in already, seeing as they only had to open a load of old bin bags.

In the back garden, Lonny was enjoying seeing Dawn and her two young daughters run around the garden having fun. It had been a while since the house was occupied and he was looking forward to getting to know their new neighbours. He went over to the fence just in time to see the older child use brute force to put the hosepipe on and then quickly ducked as a stream of water blasted past his face, hitting the glass of the French windows.

'Shanelle!' Dawn shouted, embarrassed. 'I told yer, don't spray it over there!'

'Dunna worry about that, duck,' Lonny laughed. 'She can spray all the other windows while she's at it – saves me paying the window cleaner!'

Inside the kitchen, the noise of the water had made Jenny jump as she was making tea. She peered out of the window, now with rivers running down the glass, to see her husband chatting with Dawn instead of telling her off. *Lonny please don't encourage her*, Jenny thought, annoyed at her gregarious husband. She eyed Dawn cautiously and wondered whether she should go and introduce herself but something told her there was a good chance she might get drenched if she did. What a shame that her hopes for a nice friendly face over the fence had been completely dashed. *Typical.*

She quickened her pace. It was fast approaching dinner time and woe betide her if there was nothing on the table. Her sons were in the habit of devouring food, just like their Dad, and even a five-minute wait would bring on a chorus of moaning. She gathered up Lonny's laptop and books and files from the kitchen table and moved them onto the coffee table in the lounge. '*Miraculous Abundance*' was the book on the go at the moment. '*One-quarter acre, two French farmers and enough food to feed the world*' read the tag line. '*The Soil Will Save Us*' was the one he had just finished. Jenny never asked about any of them. She just knew that her husband was consuming knowledge at a rate of knots and churning out permaculture, prepping and environmental projects in a non-stop whirlwind of enthusiasm. If he wasn't in the garden or rewilding the canal with complete strangers, he was out swapping seeds or planting trees. Sometimes it exhausted Jenny just to watch him.

She made a salad and some homemade veggie burgers. She always cooked everything from scratch, just like her father had done when she was growing up. She had loved the nights when he was home from work early enough to make dinner. When it was her mother's turn, she'd most likely get a boiled egg and a bit of lettuce.

'Dinner!' she called out to Lonny in the garden at the same time as the three lads came running in from their friends' house down the road. At eighteen, Ryan was the eldest, the only child of her first marriage to Alan, someone she would really rather forget. Ryan was a quiet boy, never without his acoustic guitar, even though he was too shy to give much of a performance outside the family. His wiry frame, foppish blonde hair and pale skin set him apart from his brothers. Nate came next. He was only fourteen but as tall as his older brother. Nate was into hip-hop, football and girls, although not necessarily in that order. At the moment, he was going through a growth spurt which made him seem enormous; Jenny couldn't quite believe that he was her son – sometimes he seemed like he should be Lonny's brother. Their youngest boy was Solomon, or Solly, who was ten and his mother's favourite, or so he thought. He was currently sporting a huge Afro and refusing to have it cut, which drove Jenny mad.

'Hands. Wash yer hands,' said Lonny as he followed them in and they all clustered around the sink. He sat down at the head of the table opposite Jenny. The boys and their dad began to hoover up their food. Jenny watched them for a moment and wondered about days gone by when people would have waited to say grace and not started until their mother was seated and the whole ambience would have been calmer. Like the Waltons from the TV show maybe. But her four fellas were fast eaters and had almost finished by the time she sat down.

'Wait for yer mum, lads,' said Lonny hastily, although he hadn't waited himself. Jenny felt the wave of testosterone in the room, filling up every nook and cranny. The pictures of her friends on the wall might suggest a lot of women in her life but those days were gone. She had to accept the fact that now her life was all about men and boys. Lonny's talk of growing their own food often lapsed into lads' talk of football, or music where *motherfucker* was a common word, or video games where people were shot and mutilated. She always had to be on red alert for farts and burps and nose-picking and God knows what at the table. Then, when she snapped, she would feel guilty, but really she shouldn't have to. It was just that all of this male stuff was stuff she hadn't got a clue about. She felt like a square peg

14

in a round hole.

'Ryan, after dinner you should tidy your room before Robbie comes,' she said, eager that his nice young guitar teacher would not be put off by the momentous mess on the bedroom floor.

'Robbie doesn't mind mess, Mum.'

'He will when he trips over something.'

'He won't trip over anything.'

'Just do it.'

'Ry,' said Lonny, 'come on, you can do it, it won't take five minutes.' He turned to Jenny. 'So it looks like the newlyweds are settling in, duck. I met Dawn, you should go and say hello.'

Jenny sniffed. The 'newlyweds' were not the type of people she wanted in the next street, never mind next door. She would put off saying hello to them for as long as possible.

'What are they like, Dad?' asked Solly, with his mouth full.

'They're not our kind of people, love,' Jenny said. She didn't want to be snobbish, not least because she intensely disliked her own mother's ridiculous snobbery but some people...

'How can yer tell that, Mum? They've only just moved in!' said Ryan.

'They're probably saying the same about us,' said Nate.

'Have you been reading the *Daily Mail* at work, Mumma?' said Solly, with a look of pained concern.

Lonny winked at her. He had his sons well trained to spot any prejudicial nonsense from anyone, including their own mother. 'That's exactly what I was thinking, duck,' he said.

'She called her husband the C word, Lon!' Jenny snapped. Really, sometimes it was tough enough living with one activist never mind three more coming along in quick succession.

The phone rang and she took the opportunity to leave the table and find a few moments to collect herself. Was she really becoming a snob like her mother? Lonny wouldn't put up with that for one minute. She picked up the phone wondering who it could be. Nobody rang the landline these days so it was probably a scam of some sort.

'Hello?' she said, already feeling that her fuse was short and that anybody ringing from a call centre would feel the wrath of her tongue.

'Hi, Jen,' said a voice. It was Eddie, Sue's husband, or Sue's widower, Jenny thought, giving him his official title and feeling her heart suddenly fill up.

'Hi, Eddie. How are you? How are the girls?'

'They're good thanks, love,' came his voice, kind and gentle as ever, giving no hint of the shock that was to come. 'Everyone's fine.'

'Oh good,' said Jenny, thinking that what he really meant was *as fine as can be expected.* 'That is good. Well thank God you're all over that dreadful flu now so I can come down soon to see you and the girls, I'm looking forward to it.'

'Yes,' he said, 'that would be great.'

She could hear the caution in his voice and when he coughed and cleared his throat she got a premonition that something terrible had happened. 'Is everything alright, love?' she asked. 'Are Amy and Alice OK?'

'They're fine, Jen,' he replied. 'Amy's doing her A-levels next month so she's studying hard. Between the studying and the demonstrations I hardly see her!'

'Yes she sends me pictures of the demos, Lonny's very pleased with her. It's more than the lads are doing! What about Alice?'

'Alice has got the lead in a show in her drama group, *My Fair Lady* I think it is. They'll be touring with it in the summer.'

'Oh bless her!' exclaimed Jenny, delighted. 'That's amazing. Tell her I'm very proud of her. And wouldn't Sue have loved that?'

'Yeah, she loved all those old musicals didn't she?' Eddie said warmly. They both laughed as though it was only when talking about Sue that they felt any relief. I know what you are going through Eddie, Jenny thought. I go through it too every day love. Just hang in there, you have to keep it together for the kids.

'Jen,' he said, breaking through her thoughts of allegiance, 'I've got some good news.'

'Oh yes?' said Jenny, wondering what news could possibly be called good after your wife dies just before her fiftieth and all the family and friends who were planning to attend the birthday party suddenly find themselves at a funeral instead. But then she guessed he was doing the same as her and trying to pretend that life was normal, that life would once again be brilliant like it had been before, when really they both knew that the sun had gone out and it would never feel warm again.

A tear began to form in her eye. 'What good news?'

'I've met someone,' he said and she felt such a kick in her stomach that she thought she might collapse to the floor with the force of it.

'Who?' she asked, hoping against hope that he would say, 'I've met a fantastic electrician, he's a dab hand at solar panels, I was going to tell Lon all about him.'

'Who is it?' she asked again, sharply this time.

'She works at Alice's school. She's one of the teachers, I met her at the parents' evening.'

'And? What? Have you asked her out? Are you going on a date with her?' she asked in disbelief. 'Are you sure you're not rushing into this Eddie? It's only been nine months.'

'We all grieve at our own pace, Jen,' he said, 'it's different for everyone.'

'I know it is but... have you told the girls that you're thinking of dating again?' Her voice began to wobble at the thought of Amy and Alice's faces dropping at their father's betrayal.

'Jen it's been nearly a year now, love,' he said. 'The girls know that I'm doing the right thing, they've told me to go ahead if this is what I want to do. Life is short, we all know that now. The girls will both be gone to uni soon enough and I can't miss this chance of finding happiness again. I know Charlotte is the one.'

'What do you mean?' said Jenny, scarcely able to believe her ears. 'How do you know that?'

'I've been seeing her for a while now, love,' he said calmly. 'I wanted to invite you and Lon and the boys to our engagement next month.'

'Engagement?!' she cried in horror. It hadn't even been a year. Not even one year. What a pig. What a selfish pig. Complete and utter fool and a pig and an idiot and a stupid selfish git.

'Yes, it all happened very quickly. No one was more surprised than me.'

'Really? Well I'm surprised too!'

'She was very good to me after Sue passed.'

'I bet she was!'

'Jen, come on, she's a lovely person, you'll like her when you get to know her.'

'Well I'm not quite ready for that, Eddie,' she shouted at him, causing Lonny's eyebrows to raise just as he reached for more bread and butter. 'Because in my book, that's cheating! And that's not fair! Sue deserves better than that. You can't cheat on her already!'

'It's not cheating, Jen! The last thing Sue would want is for me to be alone and miserable for the rest of my life.'

'No one is talking about the rest of your life! But a few years would be nice! Just to show a bit of respect, that's all she would want.

18

A bit of respect!'

Lonny came over and grabbed the phone off her. 'Hey. Come on, Jen, don't get upset now.'

'Ed, she'll call you back!' he shouted and put the receiver down. The boys had all stopped eating. They had witnessed many moments like this since Sue's death last summer. Just when they thought Mum was getting better, she was actually getting worse.

'Lonny!' Jenny cried, her legs almost giving way beneath her. 'Eddie's getting engaged, I can't bear it! He's forgetting her already!'

'It's alright, duck, it's alright.' He hugged her and kissed her forehead. 'He won't ever forget her but he's moving on and that's what you've got to do now. It's time to move on.'

CHAPTER 3

In the garden

Although the scaffolding was up, there was no action on the roof yet because Lonny was waiting for a friend's help to get the solar panels installed. He had decided against just YouTubing it, which is what he often did when learning something new. In order to be able to sell his electricity back to the National Grid, he would need a proper authorised bod to advise and then review his work. Fortunately, his friend Stella at the allotment was one such bod. So he waited patiently; after all, there was tons to do in the garden. There were a hundred and one seedlings to plant out for a start.

Jenny continued to be annoyed at the scaffolding poles she saw each time she looked out of the window. She was also annoyed at the view of the house from the street. It was a 1950's semi, attached to the newlywed's house on one side and identical to it, both houses painted white over pebble-dash with a small porch covering the front door and a garage to one side. Jenny was proud of the house; they always kept it looking neat, and at this time of year she would normally be planting numerous hanging baskets and pots for the patio as anything to do with flowers was her territory not Lonny's. But there was no reason to bother with this horrible scaffolding surrounding the building. And besides, this year she felt different to other years. This year, flowers wouldn't do anything.

It was the first week of what was forecast to be a very hot early summer. The boys had left for school. Jenny sat in the garden in her shorts and pretty vest-type t-shirt, grabbing a quick half hour in the sun before going to work. She sipped her coffee and tried not to think about Eddie and his new fiancée.

Lonny was working on his vegetable patch, the patch that seemed to be growing and growing as though their back garden was actually an allotment. He had their whole plot divided into zones and had an illustrated map on the kitchen wall explaining what everything was. Jenny knew that the house was Zone 1 and the compost bins and cherry trees at the back of the garden were Zone 4, and the field beyond was Zone 5, even though it didn't actually belong to them; Lonny was possibly going to do a bit of guerrilla tree planting. As for the zones in between, she hadn't really got a clue. It just seemed to be raised beds everywhere with not a spade or fork in sight because Lonny was strictly No-Dig. She knew he had plans for the front garden to be just the same. With ponds. And chickens. And bees. Fortunately, there was still the patio to sit out on and she still had her rose garden by the fence, although he was squeezing a few fruit bushes in there too.

Lonny had become addicted to the garden lately. She needed something like that; some hobby to get her back on track and stop things unravelling completely. In the meantime, she would book another appointment at the doctor's, maybe this time they would come up with something to help her. She reached for her bottle of organic sun cream and massaged a touch more into her long, sleek legs.

From inside the newlywed's house came a sudden blast of music, something pounding and grinding with a bassline that might dig up Lonny's veg patch whether he liked it or not.

21

Lonny looked up at his wife's startled face and laughed. 'This will liven the place up a bit!'

Jenny tutted. Lonny might be cheerful now but that would soon change if Dawn's music carried on blaring all day. But clearly, Lonny was not having the same thoughts. She watched him hail Ahmed, their neighbour from the other side, as cheerful as ever.

'Alright, Ahmed? How's it going, duck?'

'Lonny, I want to put down some raised beds, and I need a bit of advice.'

'Sure man!' said Lonny with a look of delight on his face as though Ahmed had just told him he'd won the lottery or something.

Jenny thought how tired Ahmed looked. This recent hot weather must be keeping their twin babies awake at night. He and his wife Fusun were a lovely couple. Of course, Jenny didn't speak to them much. After all, they probably wouldn't have anything in common. At least, *she* wouldn't have much in common with Fusun, who wore a veil and never wore makeup and had twin babies to look after. But at least they were quiet and respectable, unlike the newlyweds, whom she was beginning to dislike more with every passing day. That morning, she had heard them rowing in the bedroom. She hoped it wasn't to be the first row of many.

Ahmed called out politely, 'Alright, Jenny? Enjoying the hot weather?'

'Yes it's lovely isn't it,' she replied. 'Are the babies managing to sleep in it though?'

He shook his head. 'They couldn't settle at all last night, I hope they didn't disturb you.'

'Don't worry, we didn't hear a thing,' Jenny assured him, 'not like...' she indicated the other side of the fence where hip-hop still reigned supreme. Ahmed smiled at her but it was clear that neither he nor Lonny were bothered enough to complain about it. Steady on girl, she told herself, you're showing your age.

With the music pumping out, lying in the sun was no longer an attraction so she kissed Lonny goodbye and walked the twenty minutes down Manor Lane to Bill's house on the Meir Park Estate.

Bill was an easy client in some ways. Jenny was part of a whole team of carers who were dedicated to keeping this disabled old man living in his own home for as long as possible. She would go in and cook him a proper meal at lunchtime and then maybe help him do his exercises if he agreed to it. A stroke had left him partially paralysed although, in his own words, he had 'got off lightly' because he could still just about walk. Not that he really wanted to walk anywhere except into a pub. His days were spent watching snooker or darts or football or horse-racing, no soaps or drama for Bill. Jenny did his laundry and his shopping and often just sat with him to keep him company. She knew that he had a soft spot for her, which in turn gave her a soft spot for him. Apparently most of the other carers, whom she hardly ever met, were right old battle-axes while Jenny, he often said, was a *real* lady, much like his late wife Nora.

When she arrived at his tiny bungalow, he was in his high-back chair as usual and the curtains were drawn to keep the sun off the TV.

'Bill!' she said, pulling them back with a violent swish. 'The sun is out! Come on, let's go and sit in the garden.'

'What do we want to do that for, duck? The flies'll get us!' His eyes quickly returned to the snooker.

'No they won't,' she replied with determination. 'I'll make a cup of tea and we'll sit out and have it.'

He tutted disapprovingly, but after she had made the tea and was helping him up out of his chair, he asked her with a knowing wink,

'And how's things with you, duck?' He had asked this every day since Sue had died. At least Bill got it, she thought gratefully, he got what she was going through because he was a widower himself, and a real one, not a traitor like Eddie.

'I'm alright thanks, Bill,' she said, helping him stand upright. 'But I've had some upsetting news from Sue's husband, Eddie. He's getting engaged.'

'Bloody ' ell!' said Bill. 'He didn't hang around did he?'

Thank you, Bill, she thought. Here at least she had found an ally. Bill had often said that no one could replace his Nora. Lonny might have said, 'Chance would be a fine thing' and laughed at the old man's steadfast loyalty, but Jenny understood. Some people could never be replaced. End of story.

'Lonny says Eddie is moving on,' she said as they began to walk arm in arm down the tiny hallway.

'I'll bloody move him on if I catch him,' said Bill, knowing damn well that he never had met nor ever would meet Eddie. Jenny patted his hand, grateful for his daft comments.

They sat in the garden for a while. At least outside he would get some Vitamin D, she thought, while noticing disapprovingly that Bill's garden was just an uninspiring concrete yard. 'Why don't I get some flower pots and seeds from Lonny and we can make it a bit prettier out here?' she asked him.

'You can do what you want, duck, but not on my account. I'd rather be inside watching snooker.'

'Well, maybe if it was a little nicer,' she said, 'you would want to sit out here a bit more often.'

'Not me, I don't like the heat.'

'Bill, we should be enjoying it while we can,' she said. 'It's fantastic.'

'Not for the ducks,' said Bill.

Jenny sighed. Was he really such an old misery or was he pulling her leg? She never knew.

'Any doctor's appointments coming up?' she asked him, taking her notepad and pen out of her bag.

'Let me think now, there's ears at the end of the month, then eyes a week on Tuesday, head on Thursday.' He watched her writing furiously into her notepad. 'Then on Sat'day, we got shoulders, knees and toes.' He winked.

She laughed.

After two hours with Bill, Jenny returned home thinking how much his corny jokes reminded her of her own father. Poor old Dad, she thought. She wished she knew a time of day when her mother wouldn't be parked next to the phone, so that she could actually speak to him undisturbed. It only happened occasionally. Still, hopefully they would be back out there for two weeks in August, only a few months away.

She arrived home to find Lonny still working in the garden and Dawn's music still pumping. She stood in the back doorway, hands on her hips.

'Has this been going on since I left?' she shouted over to Lonny. 'What about Fusun's babies? They won't be able to sleep!'

'She's already turned it down once,' Lonny explained. 'I told her off and she lowered it.'

'Lowered it? How can she have lowered it?' fumed Jenny, charging out into the garden and hollering over the fence. 'Dawn! Can you turn the music down please? I can't hear myself think!'

Dawn came down the garden grinning shyly. She too was dressed for the sun in shorts and a vest top. She came over to the fence with her hand outstretched. 'Hiya, Jenny, pleased to meet you, I'm Dawn.'

Jenny stopped abruptly, suddenly aware that she hadn't even introduced herself yet. She put out her hand reluctantly. 'Pleased to meet you, Dawn. I was just going to ask you to turn the music down. I can't take the noise I'm afraid.'

She eyed Dawn's tattoo-covered chest exploding out of her vest and looked down to see that her lower body was similarly busting out of her shorts. Crikey. The elastic waistband looked like it might just snap and ping right across the garden taking the fabric with it. Clearly Dawn didn't realise how big she was otherwise she would cover up a bit more. As it was, there were stretch marks on show everywhere. Dear me. And hairy armpits. Gross. And no doubt hair spilling out of her shorts and all the way down her legs. Jenny strained to see.

Good God Almighty.

Her mind flashed back to the women who sometimes came into the salon, not often because they weren't the type to come regularly, but sometimes it would happen if there was a big enough reason. If they wanted to transform themselves for a wedding or a big birthday, they would ask Jenny to pull out all the stops and make them the best they could be. And she did. She could do it for any type of woman who was willing, she could transform them into something magnificent, she had done it many times. But the client had to be willing at least and Dawn clearly didn't give two hoots.

Dawn blinked and grinned. She had never been so close to somebody with film star looks before, it was mesmerising. 'Of course! I'll turn it down now, duck.'

Jenny left the fence and turned to see Lonny shaking his head. He had spotted her bad attitude even though he was behind her. Was it that obvious? Jenny felt guilty for a moment. She shouldn't be judging her new neighbour too harshly; after all, it was none of her business what she wore, they were never going to become friends, were they? But was she really going to have to put up with seeing her out in the garden all summer screaming at her kids and playing loud music? After the big storms, Lonny had been in a rush to patch the fence back together in time for the newlyweds' arrival. If only she had met them in advance she would have insisted he bought some extra pieces to make it a foot or two higher.

Lonny came up and put his arms around her. 'Stop judging her, duck, she's just the same as you or me.'

'No she flipping well isn't,' she said.

CHAPTER 4

At the doctor's

Later, while Jenny was making a cup of tea in the kitchen, Lonny came in and washed his hands.

'Remember you've got the running club tonight, Jen. I've enrolled you, duck,' he said.

'Oh God!' she winced. She had forgotten about the Stoke Running Sisters. Lonny had spotted them running through Meir Park and flagged them down. She could imagine the scene. Lonny running to catch up with the leader, 'Hold up, duck! Me wife wants to join you. She's depressed!' or some other embarrassing introduction.

'But I've got the doctor's at six!' she said.

'That's alright, you can do both. I'll order the community car and we'll do the doctor's first, then I'll drop you at the Hungry Horse. Don't worry, you'll have plenty of time.'

Jenny sighed. She knew her husband wanted her to build up a new social life, especially now that Eddie had set out his stall and was officially 'over' Sue, but things were a lot harder now that the kids were older. Previously, all she had to do was stand at the school gates and eye up the mums she liked the look of; that was how she had met Niccy, Cher and Tracey, and they had been friends for many years when the kids were young. But those women were long gone. It was going to be harder now. Much harder.

As though sensing her dip in mood, Lonny kissed her and hugged her tightly.

'Come on, duck,' he said. 'We've got to get you back on track.'

The boys came in for an early dinner before football practice. At the table, they argued with their dad about the latest Xbox game, which Lonny insisted they couldn't get until it was available second hand on eBay, there being a strict ban on buying new unless it was from an ethical company.

'You can buy whatever you like so long as it's second hand,' he said. 'This family is not going to invest in the exploitation and environmental bad practice that's behind these products. No, duck, we're not doing it.'

'But Dad, it won't be on eBay for months,' moaned Nate.

'You watch, it'll be on there tomorrow.'

'It won't, Dad!'

'Well if that's the case, it's too bad, but at least you can hold yer head up high. We're not supporting Big Corporate and that's it.'

'How big is Big Corporate, Dad?' asked Solly innocently.

'It's bloody massive.'

'*That's what she said!*' Solly smiled shyly at his brothers who couldn't help sniggering. Even Lonny laughed and shook his head. But Jenny glared at him.

'Young man! You can stop that kind of talk right now!'

'He dunt know what it means, duck, don't worry about it,' said Lonny.

'Yes I do, Dad,' said Solly. 'Nate told me!'

'Nate!' snapped Jenny. 'Would you like to be grounded this week? Because you're going the right way about it!'

She was about to turn away when she noticed Ryan's finger sliding up his nostril in explorative fashion.

'Don't be so disgusting!' she snapped, yanking his hand away.

Upstairs, she reluctantly changed into her running gear which had been gathering dust in a box under the bed. With a bit of luck, she would be delayed at the doctor's and would be able to miss the stupid Running Sisters. She wondered if she would get that nice female GP again, what was her name now? If only she could make friends with someone like that, so attractive and intelligent, and understanding too. But a GP's surgery these days could give you just about anyone. What was she even going to see the doctor for anyway? She hated the anti-depressants she had been given, and had hardly taken them. She just needed some new friends to distract her from missing Sue and the girls, that was all.

The huge GP's surgery in Meir was as busy as ever and every place in the car park was already taken. Lonny dropped her off and then sat listening to a podcast about the importance of rebuilding the soil. As he saw the heavy stream of people going into the building he remembered the times his dad had drunk there in its previous incarnation as the Kings Head Pub. Many moons ago. He wondered if the community and friendships that the pub had fostered were what was missing in people's lives nowadays. His wife for one could do with a bit more company than she was getting.

Inside the surgery, the pharmacist's printer churned out prescriptions non-stop as people queued. Jenny sat in the busy waiting room thinking of what she would say to the doctor. There had been no improvements since her last appointment. She knew that her depression was becoming the new normal and it just wouldn't do. It wouldn't do at all. Sometimes she felt her grief was wrapped up tightly around her, engulfing her like that horrible plastic cling film, it was suffocating her.

'You can see Doctor Parker now, duck,' said the receptionist, interrupting her thoughts. Jenny looked at the clock. Fabulous. The appointment was fifteen minutes late so with a bit of luck she wouldn't get to the Running Sisters in time.

She put her head round the door of the doctor's office and wondered if she was in the right place. He looked about sixteen.

'Hello, Jenny, come in and sit down,' he said in a posh voice. 'How have you been getting on with the fluoxetine?'

'I haven't taken them much to be honest, doctor,' she said. 'I don't like taking tablets. I'd rather get better without them.'

He sighed as though to say, 'What the hell are you here for then?' but managed to tone it down a little. 'And how is that working for you?'

Jenny gawped at him. Was he being sarcastic? She couldn't even tell.

'If you want to get rid of your depression, you need a plan of attack,' he said. 'You need to start doing things – activities that you know will make you feel good. That's the only way to do it without drugs.'

'Yes that's what my husband says. He wants me to join the Running Sisters.'

'Oh yes? Do you like running?' he asked.

'I don't know.' Her chin was beginning to tremble. 'I don't know what I like and what I don't like any more. I'm a different person nowadays so I just don't know.'

'I know that must be what it feels like,' he told her earnestly, 'but I promise you it's only temporary. Psychologists say if we can do the things we loved to do as children it will make us feel a lot happier. Why don't you think back to what you loved doing when you were a little girl? Can you remember?'

No, she wanted to comment, but I bet you can!

She shrugged. 'I just used to play with my friends all the time.' Her eyes began to well up.

Without blinking the doctor reached for a tissue to give her.

'Well, why not try a variety of new things and see what works? It's coming up to the summer term, you could start a course at the local college or volunteer for a charity. What about singing? You could join a choir.'

'I sing already,' she said without a smile. 'I do gigs most Saturdays with my husband and his band.'

'Oh, that's wonderful. What kind of music do you do?'

'I do Marie Osmond's 'Paper Roses'. Just one song.'

'Why?' the doctor asked, his voice croaking a little. 'I mean, erm, why just that one song?'

'It's in the middle of the set while the men change outfits from the Osmonds to the Four Tops, they're called Lonny and The Four Topsmonds, you see. My friend and I set it all up, we thought it would be a good joke. But we didn't realise it would last so long. They're much more popular than we ever expected. It's gone on for years. But for me, it's just one song and you know, people normally use the time to go outside and have a cigarette.'

'I see,' the doctor said, although he looked like he didn't see at all.

'Jenny, have you started your menopause yet?' he asked. 'If so, I'm thinking we could kill two birds with one stone and give you HRT for both your menopause and your deteriorating mental health.'

Jenny sighed. She wasn't going to find any help here. She didn't know why she had bothered coming.

She did feel some pleasure at missing the Running Sisters but it wore off quickly and by the time they got home she felt even worse. I have to make more of an effort, she thought as she sat out with

Lonny on the patio in the evening heat; I have to do as the doctor said and do things that will make me feel good.

She immediately sent a text to Amy, Sue's eldest daughter, who was just about to take her A-levels. '*Good luck for tomorrow my darling goddaughter! I know you'll do brilliantly! Missing you like crazy, get your sister organised and let's please meet up soon! Lots of love xxxx*'

The reply came quickly, '*Thx Jen, yes lets meet up sn, will ask Alice when is best. We are both missing u 2 XXX*'

That worked, now she felt much better. For just a moment. Then the newlyweds' back door banged open.

'Shanelle! Jesus Christ!' roared Dawn as she made her way up to the washing line. 'Pack it in will yer!'

'Oh my God!' muttered Jenny with a face like thunder. 'That woman!'

Lonny sighed and put his book down. He got up and walked over to the fence, no doubt hoping as ever that a bit of encouragement from him would help Dawn rein it in a bit.

'Hiya Dawn! How're you doing, duck? Bit late with your washing today?'

'I know but it dunna matter, it's so hot!' said Dawn, grinning as usual at the sight of her lovely neighbour. 'It'll be dry in ten minutes!'

'No need for a tumble dryer when you live in Stoke!' quipped Lonny, his eyes widening as Dawn began to hang her underwear out on the line. Huge baggy knickers and moulded bras big enough to house a space station.

'Right, duck, I'll leave you to it.' He winked.

'OK, Lonny!' Dawn replied happily. She continued putting out her underwear, clearly forgetting about whatever her daughter had done to upset her.

'Blimey, those bras are a feat of engineering,' Lonny muttered to

Jenny as he returned to the patio. Jenny looked up from her phone and saw them for the first time.

'Oh my God, that is disgusting! Why doesn't she put them lower down where we can't see them? I don't want to see her smelly underwear every time I'm in the garden.'

'Oi, Jen, that's not nice,' Lonny scolded her, shocked and regretting his own comment. 'She's just washed them hasn't she?'

'Yes and don't we know it!'

Lonny sighed. Jenny's constant criticism of Dawn was making him weary. She never used to be like this. She used to be more like him, able to get on with anyone. But recently it felt like he was married to the editor of the *Daily Mail*. He shouted to his sons further up the garden.

'What yer playing lads? Bit of cricket?'

'Yeah,' said Ryan, 'but we'll use the softball, Dad.'

'Yeah,' said Lonny. 'You'd better, I don't want my veg ruined.'

'It's not veg yet,' said Solly. 'It just looks like tiny little weeds,'

'It's veg!' shouted Lonny. 'And it's not just veg! It's our health! It's our security!'

'Yeah alright, Dad,' moaned Nate. He was proud of his father's environmental passions, but really, sometimes he was just an outright nutter. He bowled to Solly as aggressively as he could with a softball and his father's beady eyes on him.

Solly batted the ball across the garden, over the fence and into the huge cup of one of Dawn's bras, where it nestled down and wouldn't come out. The boys gasped.

Then Dawn burst out laughing.

'You got a hole-in-one there, Solly!' she called. Everyone cheered.

'Yes!!' shouted Lonny. 'Yes, yes, yes!!' He chased after his youngest son, picked him up and ran round the garden in jubilation, high-fiving Dawn across the fence on the way, the boys following. Everyone laughed long and hard.

Jenny tutted and walked into the house.

There was no peace for her anywhere. No peace for the wicked.

At that thought she dissolved into tears.

She picked up her phone and the screensaver picture of Sue with her beautiful dark skin, her dimples and her lovely smile looked back at her. She hugged it to her chest.

'I miss you, babe,' she sobbed. 'I miss you so much.'

CHAPTER 5

Marie Osmond

Later that evening, after finding Jenny in the bedroom with a tear-stained face, Lonny lay down beside her and asked her about the visit to the doctor's in more detail.

'Didn't he have any ideas for you?'

'Not really. He was doing his best, but they don't like it when you don't want tablets. He looked about Ryan's age as well. I don't know, Lon, I must be getting old.' She huddled closer to him as he put his arm around her.

'Was that it? Nothing else?'

'Nothing really, except maybe try a college course or something like that. He said I should try and remember what I liked to do when I was a little girl.'

'OK, so what would that be then?'

'I don't know really, I just liked playing with Sue,' she said, sinking quickly. 'Singing and playing.'

'Well, you're already doing the singing, but that doesn't seem to do you much good.'

'I hate it,' said Jenny emphatically. Lonny sighed.

'You know we've got a gig every Saturday from now till the holidays. Are you OK with that?'

'Yes, don't worry, I'm used to it, I just switch off.'

Lonny winced. He knew that despite her thinking she was switching off, the gigs were most likely contributing to her depression.

'You don't have to do them if you don't want to, duck,' he said, trying to help.

'I do. You all need time to change outfits. And the landlord needs time to do a clear up.'

'Yeah, but we could just play the record instead. That would work just as well.'

'Thanks,' she sniffed.

'You know what I mean,' he said, holding her tight.

Yes I do, she thought, feeling worse than ever.

*

The next morning, the early sunshine made her feel a bit better as she walked around the garden with her dainty cup of coffee, watching Lonny doing his twice-daily rounds of checking the young plants. Like any new convert to gardening, Lonny could barely be pulled away from the veg.

'These courgettes are amazing,' he cooed, half to Jenny, half to himself. 'They're like something from out of space.'

'I can't see a courgette there,' said Jenny. 'It doesn't look like a courgette to me.'

'It will do in a few weeks, duck!' Lonny said, undeterred. 'They're coming along great!'

Jenny went back to the patio, thinking of what the young doctor had said yesterday. His mention of doing a college course to help fight her grief and depression had hit a nerve somewhere. She was only qualified in beauty and had often felt a rumbling inferiority complex regarding university and degrees. Not that she would attempt anything like that, but it might be nice to learn something new and hopefully meet some nice people. But what could it be? She spotted a local college prospectus which had been popped through her door earlier in the week and went to pick it up. She looked over the courses, everything from beauty therapy which she already had to politics, beekeeping, foreign languages, economics and researching your family tree. None of those things interested her really, although she knew it was part of Lonny's plan to get bees further down the line. But it wasn't for her. She wanted something that would involve her enough to forget her grief.

She felt a strong urge to feel sorry for herself for not having any friends to attend a class with, but stopped herself wandering off track just in time. She was supposed to be thinking of what she loved to do as a child, not feeling sorry for herself, because that never got her anywhere.

Well, she'd loved playing with her mother's make-up. Obviously that was how she became a beautician. It was a natural progression. Surely there must have been something else she enjoyed doing. Wasn't it just all the normal things that little girls liked? Singing, writing stories, dressing up, playing games. Oh sod it, she couldn't think of anything she liked to do much beyond mucking about with Sue. And anyway, how was this going to lead to doing a course? There were no courses in playing kids' games. Now she felt the urge to toss the prospectus across the patio.

Lonny would pressure her into going to the Running Sisters event next week. Surely she would meet a few nice women there. A few women who hated running, just like her.

She went inside as the washing machine had stopped and she needed to get her Marie Osmond dress ready for tomorrow night's gig. The dreaded gig. Never mind, at least it was money coming in. Not enough money to warrant the abuse she got, but still. She would keep her chin up and get on with it as long as Lonny wanted her to. And she knew he did, despite what he said. What he really wanted was for her to turn it around and somehow get people up and dancing. Maybe she could try telling a joke first or maybe if she had a bit of banter with them, that might do it. But she knew deep down that these good ideas all went out the window once the song started and the crowd surged to the door. Difficult to have banter with people who are running away. It might even turn into heckling. Her heckling them to come back. No, she just had to be tough and hope against hope that it wouldn't last for another four years. God forbid.

She took the strappy pink dress from the washer and went outside. As she hung it on the line she could see Dawn coming into the garden. The sense of disapproval that she previously had for the patchwork recycled fence was now times ten due to her new neighbour. Why oh why wasn't it two foot higher?

'Hi Dawnie!' shouted Lonny from up the garden.

Dawn waved. 'Hi Lonny!'

'Those tattoos of yours'll be getting a nice tan at this rate!'

'I know they will, the weather's brilliant int it!'

'Costa del Stoke! That's what this is, duck!'

Dawn laughed and came over to the fence, putting her hands on the top of it while she waited a few moments for him to come over and chat. Without thinking, she began to jostle the bits of wood patchworked together and promptly dislodged one.

'Oi, Dawnie, what you doing? Watch me fence,' said Lonny, taking the small section of wood back and inserting it into place. 'That's got to see us through the next few hurricanes!'

'You'll be lucky, mate,' she laughed, thinking how lucky she had been in moving next door to such a lovely cheerful bloke. Every time she saw him she felt good. She turned and saw Jenny hanging up her pretty dress and wondered why they didn't enjoy the same friendly banter that she had with Lonny. Maybe she needed to make more of an effort, maybe Lonny would be pleased with her if she did. However, it was a bit nerve-racking 'cos Jenny always seemed to be in a mood. As Lonny went back to his watering, she lit her fag and took a big drag for Dutch courage.

'Hi Jenny,' she said. 'That's a nice dress, are you going to be a bridesmaid or summat?'

'I don't think so,' said Jenny. 'I'm a bit too old for that.' She marched inside and banged the door.

Dawn turned away from the fence, disappointed. She must have done something wrong but she didn't know what. She was just trying to be friendly.

In the kitchen, Jenny was furious. She had been having such a nice quiet ten minutes before work, ten minutes to think about her future, something she rarely got a chance to do and now that stupid nosy cow had ruined it. Oh God. She stopped, ashamed. Something about Dawn was bringing out the worst in her, she realised. She hated feeling such a bitch. Normally though, she didn't have to deal with such people. Oh why was that fence so low? Dawn might be like one of those supermarket checkout girls who thought it acceptable to comment on everything you were buying, from cabbage to tampons. That fence needed to be at least a foot or two higher, then at least she would get some privacy when hanging out the washing.

She left for work and, after a quick elevenses trip to Bill, who hardly noticed her among the click of cue balls, she went on to her second job of the day on the other side of Meir Park estate. Debbie was a local mum in her forties who had MS. She and her daughter Freya needed all the help they could get now and although Jenny wasn't her main carer, she sometimes worked the middle of the day shift to cover shopping, trips to the doctor and cleaning. A bit too much cleaning actually. Debbie was a control freak, something which Lonny suggested was because of her condition. But Jenny didn't think so, it was more likely she had always been that way. Misery.

She was pleased that ten-year-old Freya was there today. She was a delightful little girl, although sometimes overwhelmed by the amount of caring she had to do for her mother. It was during those times that Jenny thought she could help her, cheer her up a little. She was such a little darling, she didn't deserve her life being this tough. Freya opened the front door with a smile and waved to Jenny as she walked up the path.

'Look at your lovely nails!' Jenny exclaimed, spotting the dash of colour like a hawk.

'Do you like them?' Freya asked, showing them off.

'I love them!' said Jenny beaming, going into the house. 'I bet Mummy loves them too don't you, Debs? Aren't they gorgeous? Isn't she a clever girl?'

'Not really,' Debbie replied, 'seeing as I told her the drains were blocked and I needed her to put her hand down into the overflow. There's summat down there, a dead rat or summat.'

Jenny recoiled immediately. 'Have you got insurance for this kind of thing?' she asked.

'What do you think?' said Debbie.

Oh God, it's going to be one of those days, thought Jenny. 'Never mind I'll get Lon to pop round later, he should have an hour free this afternoon.'

Debbie sighed. 'You're so lucky to have a man like that, Jenny. I hope you appreciate him. Otherwise someone else will have him, I know that for sure.'

'Hah! They'd have to get past me first!' Don't even think about it,

Jenny thought. She knew that Debbie was most likely jealous of what fate had given Jenny on a plate as opposed to the fag ends it seemed to be throwing casually in her direction. That should have been me, Debbie seemed to be thinking whenever Jenny walked past. At least that's what Jenny sensed. But Debbie was wrong to think that. After all, she had lovely Freya and Jenny had never got her daughter and it was too late now, as that fifteen-year-old doctor had just reminded her. And just because she had MS, it didn't mean that other people weren't struggling with something that didn't show on the outside. Like Jenny, for instance. Struck down with devastating grief which Debbie knew nothing about. In fact, she knew nothing about Jenny's life beyond the fact that she had a lovely husband.

'The bathroom needs doing,' Debbie called out. 'The toilet's in a right state.'

Of course it is, thought Jenny.

*

She thought of Debbie the following night at the Topsmonds gig when she looked into the mirror in the ramshackle toilet cubicle that was her dressing room. Squashed in and surrounded by mops and buckets and a thousand loo rolls, she thought, if Debbie could see me now she wouldn't be quite so jealous.

Lonny and the guys were in the large function room, which was packed to bursting. There was Jackie, Lonny's older brother, a quiet, dreamy and totally impractical guy, the opposite of her husband. Then there was Godfrey and Viv, Jackie's old school friends who kept themselves to themselves. And finally, there was Charles who was a nice guy and who had a lot of banter with Lonny on stage. Charles was supposed to be Merrill Osmond so he had a fair bit of singing to do himself, whereas the other three just blurred into Alan, Wayne and Jay. No one cared anyway. Lonny as Donny was the main man.

She could hear them singing 'Love Me for a Reason' and she could imagine the crowd of drunken happy women singing along and swooning and reaching out to grab Lonny's leg like they were fourteen again instead of forty-eight or sixty-two. This is what had happened regularly over the last four years and the place was always heaving. In the second half of the show, everyone would dance to The Four Tops' classic Motown songs in an energetic northern soul style, whatever their age and fitness levels. Lonny switched effortlessly from Donny to the Tops' classy lead singer, Levi Stubbs. He had a lot of interaction with the crowd and got them all thoroughly worked up and enjoying themselves. Of course they were all off their faces so that helped.

But in the midst of this great night out, no one would spare a thought for the feelings of the woman singing Marie Osmond's 'Paper Roses'. Instead, they would seize the chance to go outside and smoke or get some air as soon as the first few bars sounded. They cleared out like someone had just dropped a stink-bomb. Selfish drunken swines. Was a gasp of fresh air that valuable when you had only been inside for half an hour of Osmonds' songs?

'Well, what do you expect?' she imagined Debbie sneering at her if she knew. 'Who the hell wants to hear the Osmonds these days?'

So many people that they would almost always sell out, she would tell her.

The irony that these gigs had been her and Sue's idea was not lost on Jenny. The men had been extremely reluctant at first and yet word spread like wildfire and the bookings flowed in. There was often a voicemail message on Lonny's mobile from some northern pub manager looking for 'the black blokes who do The Osmonds' and they were a great success wherever they went. But the days of that initial fun and excitement, when Sue, Annie, Kate, Emily and other friends might be in the audience cheering her on, were long gone. The crowd would then have followed her friends' lead and waltzed around with each other to her song, still laughing and drinking and having a good time. But nowadays, without that lead, they made their own decision to get out of the room as quickly as possible.

The family needed the money, that was for sure. And Lonny wanted her to be involved so she couldn't really get out of it. She would just have to grin and bear it.

She left the broom cupboard and made her way to the wings of the stage as the song was finishing; the hollering and screaming reached a peak and the crowd shouted out for an encore. But the guys had no time for that. They had to change quickly and get back on stage as The Four Tops. So they rushed past her, leaving Lonny to introduce her as 'The one and only, Marie Osmond!'

Then, as the music struck up and she began to sing, the crowd quickly moved outside to the beer garden. Honestly, you could set your watch by it, Jenny thought. Not exactly much time allowed for a joke or a bit of banter. Not really. She waited for the next inevitable occurrence, the landlord coming out with a cloth or a broom just as he had in that awful dream, seizing the chance to clear up a bit before the second half started and the dancing got serious.

'Bring me the brush and shovel Maureen, duck!' he shouted. 'I'll clear up this broken glass while Marie's on!'

No, Debbie, don't be jealous of my life, Jenny thought. *Don't be jealous of it at all.*

CHAPTER 6

Meeting Trudi

By Monday, Jenny was ready for action. Dammit, her life was disappearing before her eyes. She was fifty-one years old and beyond her family and her work as a carer, she had nothing going on. Nothing that she liked anyway, she winced as she thought back to the gig on Saturday night. She had to get her act together. Nobody could do it for her. Lonny was great at encouraging her and he had been as patient as he could be, but this year, with the tidying up after the storms and now the many hours a day in the garden and the solar panels still to do, he was just too busy. No, she couldn't expect much more handholding from him, he just wanted her to get on with it. And that's what she wanted too.

At the newsagents, when she was picking up *The Sentinel* for Bill, she looked at the women's magazines to see if there was anything that would inspire her. There were the usual gossip mags but they were so boring and anyway, Lonny would immediately throw them in the recycling box and give her a lecture.

'Life's too short for that crap, Jen!' he would say, or something along those lines. Might be better to go for sewing or interior design or crosswords; she was interested in all of those things, but none of them were touching the right spot. It would have to be something new.

'Can I help you, Jenny? What are you looking for?' said the newsagent proprietor Mrs Holdcroft, who seemed to be a similar age to Jenny and yet made everyone call her by her full name. She had been very kind to her once after Sue died, when she caught her crying near the boiled sweets. After that, Jenny had presumed she would be informed of her first name so that they could perhaps spark up a friendship. But she had presumed wrong and 'Mrs Holdcroft' it remained.

'I want to do a college course, Mrs Holdcroft,' she said. 'I just don't really know what I'm interested in.'

'Well, dear,' said Mrs H, 'it's about time you found out!'

Back at home, Jenny grabbed the prospectus for the local college again. Enrolment was this week but she felt a sudden urge to get there quickly and sign up for something before she changed her mind. She would go this afternoon. After a quick visit to Bill, she only had a two-hour shift with her lovely elderly client Joyce with Alzheimer's, so she would go right after that and sign up. She didn't know what for. She would just sign up for whatever sounded interesting. Do what the doctor said and sign up for whatever took her fancy. She liked this idea. She wanted to learn something new. And it would be a perfect way to make friends.

She set off for Joyce's in what was her lightest mood in a long time. She would try and make this a good day; the continuing sunshine after so many weeks of wild crazy weather would surely help. She walked to Joyce's large old house on Manor Lane where she would overlap with Hannah for half an hour. By some mistake in the care agency's timetable, both carers were there to get Joyce showered and fed and her housework done, whereas normally one of them would be sent and would have to struggle on her own. This was the highlight of Jenny's working week. Hannah was a pretty, thirty-something single mum who worked like a Trojan to provide for her two children. She was a positive, happy person and Jenny always felt better for seeing her. She liked to imagine becoming good friends with Hannah one day even though she was probably almost twenty years older than her. But did age really matter much these days? Did it?

'Hannah, how about you and me going out for a glass of wine one evening?' she asked. 'It would be nice to get out, away from all this hard work, wouldn't it? I find all this care work is driving me to drink!'

'Oh God I'd love to, Jen, but I can't 'cos of the kids,' Hannah replied, carrying on making the bed furiously and not looking up for one second. She was always in a hurry, racing from one job to the next. 'You should do what I do, hon, I just get a bottle from *Aldi* and it lasts two nights – so much cheaper than going up town. They do a lovely organic wine, Jen. You like all the organics don't you, duck?'

'Oh yes I do, that's a good idea,' said Jenny, turning to face Joyce as she buttoned her blouse and practically burying her head in the old lady's chest to hide the tears that were forming. For goodness sake, why was something that had always been so easy now so hard? School, college, the salon, her sons' school – everywhere had been a seemingly endless supply of female friends, they were queuing up to be pals with her and Sue. Queueing up.

'What time is it?' asked Joyce.

'Twenty past eleven, sweetheart,' she said, thankful for the distraction.

'What time is it?'

'Twenty past eleven.'

'What time is it?'

'Twenty past –'

'Joyce!' Hannah shouted, 'that's enough, duckie! Come on, let's go

47

make a cup of tea!' She handed a pillowcase to Jenny as she passed. 'You finish up the bed, Jen, I'll go and do lunch.'

Jenny clutched the pillowcase and took a moment to breathe. God she was useless, she couldn't even cope with an old lady with dementia.

She looked around the large room, eager for a distraction of some sort, a distraction from the horrible negative thoughts which had arrived back in her head so quickly. She didn't want to register at the college while she was feeling so desperate.

On the wall nearest the large bay window were some photos she had never noticed before, photos of Joyce with her sons when they were little boys, with her late husband, on a stage with an orchestra, looking beautiful behind a radio mic, in a line-up of dignitaries shaking hands with the Queen.

What?

She looked closer. Joyce had obviously been some kind of singer. Some kind of great artist. She felt a tug on her heartstrings. She was a singer too, a totally under-utilised one at the moment, but she knew she had it in her. Everyone had always praised her singing, it was only since 'Paper Roses' that it had all gone pear-shaped. Hopefully one day she would be singing what she wanted to sing.

So it looked like she and poor old Alzheimer's-stricken Joyce had something in common.

She went into the kitchen where Joyce was still asking what time it was. 'Hannah, I just noticed those photos in the bedroom. Was Joyce a singer then?'

'Yes she was, she was a great singer back in the day, classically trained an' all,' Hannah nodded knowingly at Jenny as though this feat was only one step removed from being an astronaut.

'Shall we tell Jenny what a lovely voice you had, Joyce? You sang at the Royal Albert Hall didn't you, duck? And you sang for the Queen for her wedding anniversary, didn't you?'

'Did you, Joyce?' Jenny asked, searching for a flicker of memory in the old lady's eyes, a flicker of knowledge that once, on a grand stage and dressed in satin and diamonds, she sang like a nightingale for the Queen. But there was nothing.

'What time is it?' said Joyce.

*

Lonny had some fruit trees to pick up from the organic nursery out at Madeley, so he ordered an electric van from the community car club. Jenny cadged a lift to the college and told him all about Joyce's glamorous past on the way.

'Imagine that,' she said, 'singing at the Royal Albert Hall, Lon.'

'What a shame she can't remember it,' Lonny said.

'Well, you never know, maybe she gets a moment every now and then.'

'You're a great singer, Jen, maybe there'll be singing classes at the college you could join. You know, musical theatre or summat.'

'No, I don't think so, Lon.'

'Well, what about beekeeping then?' he said, not for the first time. 'That would help me –'

'No.'

'What about making sauerkraut, fermenting stuff? We're going to have ten tons of cabbage by –'

'Oh no, no! I was thinking of something more like pottery, something with my hands.'

'Oh yeah?' said Lonny. This was the first time he had heard of an interest in pottery.

'Well, I don't know,' Jenny said as the van began to approach the college with its glistening roof of solar panels and brand-new vertical

49

garden walls. 'I just want to make some friends really.'

'That will happen in good time, duck. Just focus on finding the right course for now.'

He dropped her in the college car park and Jenny noticed how busy it was. She got a sudden rush of panic that there might be some urgency to this that she hadn't expected. Everyone in Stoke might be trying to better themselves. What if demand outstripped supply and she was left with just classes in metalwork or something? She braced herself for the fight to get into the best class, whatever it may be.

The foyer was heaving with people who looked similarly braced and it was difficult to see where she should go. There were numerous hallways leading off with one room after another after another. It was a maze. She spotted someone at a reception desk near the bottom of a rather grand and ornate staircase. Having an eye for such stylish things, Jenny looked at it admiringly while she waited for her turn.

'Can I help you?' asked the receptionist.

But Jenny said nothing because in that moment she saw *her*.

The woman descending the grand staircase was of a similar age, maybe a little younger, it's always difficult to surmise when someone is so well-kempt. Her long fair hair reached down her back and curls tumbled and fell over her slim shoulders. She was wearing a gorgeous utility jumpsuit in khaki. It looked like Anthropologie's best or possibly Joseph or Whistles, thought Jenny, thinking of the second-hand designer bargains she scoured eBay for. The woman's jewellery was funky, nothing boring here, her bag big, slouchy, immaculately worn leather. Her face was beautiful in a conventional way but there was something about her smile and her blue eyes that was quirky, interesting and kind. She was simply and utterly fabulous. Fab-u-lous.

Jenny's heart began to pound. This is why I am here, she thought, watching the vision of loveliness make her way downstairs. The universe must have arranged it for her. Maybe even Sue in heaven had arranged it for her.

'Are you looking for something in particular?' the receptionist asked, slightly cross that this woman didn't even have the courtesy to look at her.

'Yes I am,' said Jenny, still gawping at the woman. She noted that she was scouring the reception area, most likely looking for where she should go to enrol, just the same as she was. She was so elegant and gracious, she was smiling at everyone, and then she saw Jenny and smiled at her too. Jenny smiled back, delighted, and the woman arrived at the desk just as the receptionist was giving up on Jenny with a shrug.

'Hello,' said the woman in a voice like soft velvet, 'I'm looking for the creative writing course. Can you tell me where to go please?'

Quick as a flash Jenny jumped in. 'Oh that's the course I'm looking for too! I can't find it either! I've been looking all over.'

'Yes, so have I!' said the stranger, reaching out and giving Jenny a brief touch on her arm.

'It looks good doesn't it?'

'Doesn't it?!'

The receptionist looked back and forth at the two women who seemed unable to take their eyes off each other.

'It's something I've always wanted to have a go at,' Jenny found herself declaring.

'Well, when you think about it,' said the woman, 'you were probably very good at writing stories at school, but without the right encouragement, we just stop doing it don't we?'

'Yes, we do!' said Jenny. 'You're absolutely right!'

The receptionist sighed and rolled her eyes as though she hadn't got time for this nonsense. 'The creative writing course is on the second floor, room twenty-four. Next please, thank you!'

Jenny and her new friend were caught off guard by their brusque dismissal and grinned at each other as they turned away.

'By the way, I'm Trudi,' said the woman.

'Pleased to meet you, Trudi, I'm Jenny.'

They walked up the stairs together and along the corridor, talking as naturally and as easily as if they were old friends. Just a simple conversation and a simple walk, but for Jenny it was quite a moment. A peak moment. She felt a happy relief that she hadn't experienced in a long time.

Once they'd found the room, they chatted to the teacher, Celia, who spoke enthusiastically about the class. She told them how it would inspire their inner writer, increase their confidence and unleash their creativity. Or something like that. Jenny was finding it difficult to focus on anything that wasn't Trudi. But she heard the last bit when Celia said what a wonderful experience it would be for them.

Yes, it would be wonderful, thought Jenny. Doing anything with Trudi would be wonderful. They walked back to the foyer and out into the car park, talking about their hopes for the course; Trudi speaking passionately about books and poetry, Jenny winging it about a long held desire to write stories whilst saying honestly that she would be very nervous about it all.

'Oh, so am I,' said Trudi. 'We might both be completely useless, but the important thing is we have a go.'

'That's all we can do,' agreed Jenny.

Then, just before they parted, Trudi said something so utterly fabulous that Jenny nearly wet herself.

'I'm so glad I've met you, Jenny. As much as I'm interested in the course, I'm also doing it so that I can make new friends. I've only just moved into the area and I don't know anyone yet.'

'Oh, you poor thing,' she replied, managing to control her excitement. 'I know all about that. Don't worry, it won't take you long to settle in.'

She knew then that what she had first sensed when she saw her descending the stairs was true. It was *her*.

The waiting was over.

It was her new friend.

Come at last.

She remembered meeting Lonny's old Grandma in Jamaica when they were on their honeymoon. At the sight of her grandson and his bride, the old lady had thrown her hands in the air and shrieked, 'Hallelujah! Praise God! Praise God! Thank you sweet Jesus!!!'

That's exactly how I feel now, Jenny thought.

She went home with Lonny's Grandma shrieking Hallelujah in her ear.

CHAPTER 7

Two cowboys

On the bus coming home from college, Jenny ran over what she had hastily signed up for.

'*Want to have a go at creative writing in a supportive environment?*' the blurb read in the prospectus. Not that I was ever aware of before, she thought. Oh my God, a course in creative writing. When she hadn't really written anything since she left school, beyond shopping lists and birthday cards anyway. And maybe the odd advert for the salon. '*Starting to sag? Don't worry, come to Jenny & Friends, we'll perk you up a bit!*' She had run those adverts in *The Sentinel* for years, but they stopped working in the end. Women these days didn't want a bit of perking up, they wanted a lot. Bloody Botox. Anyway, what did it matter if she had no experience? If Trudi had signed up for car mechanics she would have done that too.

She giggled out loud and didn't care about the looks of the young couple opposite. She gave them a huge smile and they hastily turned the other way, embarrassed. Hah. No doubt they thought she was a middle-aged woman who had had one too many and was on her way to meet her toy boy. Maybe they thought she was thinking of what she and the toy boy would get up to. But no, actually, this was going to be something much more substantial. This was the beginning of a real friendship. She just knew it. And bit by bit, week by week, over time, but hopefully not too much, she and Trudi would become closer.

She sighed happily and unconsciously began to tap her thigh to the beat of a loud blast of rap from a car at the traffic lights. When the course started, they could have tea in the break or coffee after class, or they could arrange to spend a few hours in the library helping each other write poetry or whatever. At least *she* would need help from Trudi, she wasn't sure how much help she could offer in return.

She arrived back in Bramfield Drive in the late afternoon and felt the whole world to be a different place. The cherry blossom trees were in full bloom, flowers were bobbing in the breeze and the smell of dinners cooking made her ravenous. She heard classical music playing and smiled as she walked past the home of Mr and Mrs Stevenson, an elderly couple who clearly must be stone deaf as they always played their music so loudly. But it was often Beethoven or Mozart, stuff her dad used to play, so she never minded hearing it.

The fierce heat was continuing despite it being still early in May and she thought of the potential for another long hot summer ahead. This year she wouldn't be in such a terrible state. She would be able to have days out and little trips to Wales to the seaside. With Trudi. Well, obviously it would be with the family sometimes, but other times it might be just her and Trudi.

She opened the front gate ready to go in and see Lonny. She would be able to give him some good news for once. Poor Lon, she thought, he doesn't half have to put up with a lot and he never complains. She smiled at the thought of telling him she had found a new friend. A beautiful woman who looked like she had just stepped out of a magazine. Trudi.

Suddenly, the front door of the newlyweds' house opened, and a large bin bag of rubbish was hurled out of it and across the garden into the middle of the lawn. The lawn that old Myrtle and her gardener had worked so hard to maintain, thought Jenny with a grimace, and now it's completely ruined. At least the disgusting van had been returned to whatever museum it came from, but really, was it too much effort to walk down the drive and put the rubbish in the bin? Might use up a few calories too. The door slammed shut and she could hear Dawn shouting at her kids and her husband too no doubt. The lads had mentioned hearing them arguing again the other night when she and Lonny were out at the gig. *Newlyweds*. Hmph.

Lonny had come to the front door to greet her with a kiss. He smiled as she nodded towards next door.

'Have you seen that? She thinks the garden's a landfill.'

'They're just settling in, duck, give 'em a few weeks.'

A few weeks won't make any difference, thought Jenny as they walked into the kitchen, Dawn's type are in a perpetual state of chaos. No doubt there would be fifteen bin bags strewn across the grass before long, attracting flies and foxes and God knows what, just like there was on the day they moved in.

Still, she remembered, no need to think of Dawn now, there was someone else she would much prefer to think about.

'Lon, I met a lovely girl at college. We've both signed up for the creative writing course.'

'Writing?' said Lonny. 'What happened to pottery?'

'Oh no, it's too messy. I saw Trudi and we got chatting and she said she was going to do the writing course and so I thought I would too. We spoke to the teacher and she said it was all about just having a go.'

'Great! So what are you going to write then? Stories?'

'Yes, stories and essays and poetry.'

'Poetry? Wow!' Lonny was gobsmacked.

'It's alright, it won't have to be in Russian or anything!'

'I know, but that's amazing, duck, well done.' He gave her a big hug. 'Look at you! A writing course! Well done!'

'Thank you, darling!' said Jenny happily, as though she had just completed the first year. She suddenly felt weak at the knees at the thought of it. Stories, poetry, *words*.

I'll be alright so long as Trudi is there, she told herself.

They walked out into the garden to potter around a bit before dinner. Lonny loved to potter, he was always doing something and rarely sat down to watch TV. In the winter, when Jenny religiously watched *Strictly Come Dancing*, he used to come in from playing footie with the boys and lie down on the sofa with his head in her lap. 'Wake me up if there's a tango,' he would say. Occasionally she could talk him into watching a good drama but since he 'woke', environmentally and politically speaking, he would often prefer to read or study, sometimes late into the night. 'We weren't put on this planet to watch that bloody box!' he would shout at them all. 'Or that box either!' pointing to the ceiling to signify the Xbox upstairs.

That evening, she wasn't interested in anything on TV either, she was happy to sit out in the garden and listen to Lonny talking about what he had been planting and where the new seedlings were going to go.

'This time next month, that lot will be two-foot tall,' he said hopefully, pointing to the aubergine and tomato plants which he had put out earlier than usual due to the weather forecast. Jenny smiled and held his hand. She would often zone out when he talked of gardening and his plans for transforming their 'homestead' as he called it.

'I thought a homestead was a little farm,' she had commented the first time she heard him use the expression.

'You work with what you've got, Jen,' he replied. 'Doesn't matter if it's just a balcony, you work with what you've got.' She was mildly interested but it had become a habit for her eyes to glaze over as she thought of Sue and how much she missed her. Thanks to Trudi, today was the first day in a long time when there was something hopeful filling her thoughts.

The next day was Tuesday, always a busy day as she had Bill and Debbie for three hours each. Then she would rush home to make dinner for the boys as Lonny had his regular permaculture meeting in the local pub. She had gone once last year under his encouragement to get out of the house after Sue died, but the only women there were typical hippie gardeners, white women with dreadlocks, so she backed out gracefully. Not my kind of people, she had thought, presuming that they might also be thinking the same about her. So she never went again, although Lonny would always come back energised and with plenty to talk about. According to him, it wouldn't be long before the whole of Stoke was getting in on growing their own food and regenerating the land. She sometimes thought of the women with dreadlocks, Stella and her sister and their friends. Maybe she should have tried to get to know them a bit instead of letting her mother's voice dominate. God Almighty, it was her mother's snobby voice wasn't it? This last year it just kept showing up. Sometimes she shivered to think of the woman she was becoming.

'That's yer depression talking, Jen!' Lonny would shout when she told him her thoughts. 'You shouldn't give that attitude the time of day!'

The morning got off to a bad start when she was serving breakfast to Bill and mentioned the creative writing course. She had already felt her mood drop a little from the ecstasy of meeting Trudi the day before and it plummeted when he queried grumpily: 'What the hell have you got to write about?' almost as though if she were writing then she wouldn't have time to come and visit him.

'As much as anyone else,' she snapped because, of course, this was at the back of her own mind, as the start date of the course loomed. What on earth would she write about? But, she reminded herself frequently, the point of going to college was to become friends with Trudi, writing stories and poems was a secondary affair, nothing else. She knew that she should also look for other classes to go to or things to do, as she doubted that writing would be that interesting. Maybe the trick was to appear to be interested, to kid yourself, she thought, looking at Bill who acted as though he was so committed to snooker and darts, yet would be up like a shot if anyone offered an invitation to go out for a pint. Well, if it had to be a pretence for her too, she didn't care, it would be worth it in order to become Trudi's friend. Dammit, she didn't care if she absolutely hated writing, so long as she could finish one term in the class, that was all she needed. One term would be enough time to become good friends with Trudi.

She walked Bill down the corridor to the bathroom and plonked him on the loo for twenty minutes as she did every morning. She went back to the kitchen and washed up the breakfast things, his daily egg and toast and the first of many mugs of tea, and then set up the ironing board to iron until she would hear him call out, 'Duck?' Then she would go in and wipe his bottom if necessary and help him off the toilet and wash his hands.

Waiting for his call and ironing a load of raggy tea towels so that they would fit flat in the drawer, she looked out of the window at the peace and quiet and boredom of Meir Park Estate. She spotted something on the pavement and went up to the window to take a closer look. Was it a dog? It was some kind of animal anyway.

She slipped out of the house and walked up the path to

investigate. An old dog lay exhausted in the heat, her belly panting and tongue hanging out. Jenny bent down to stroke her for a while; poor old creature, she really shouldn't have chosen the middle of the pavement to sleep, there was no shade there.

'Silly doggy,' she said. 'What are you doing out here in this weather?'

She went inside and, before Bill could make his demands, she took a bowl of cold water out to her. The dog didn't have a name tag which made it difficult for Jenny to do much more. She just hoped she would have the sense to move into the shade.

Later, she made her way to Debbie's on the other side of the estate. She dreaded Tuesday visits because Freya wouldn't be home from school yet and Debbie without her young daughter was ten times more difficult. Would today be any different? She doubted it, but at the same time she hated feeling so badly towards a woman with multiple sclerosis.

The door was already open as usual. Jenny walked in and the two women eyed each other with hard, grim stares, like two cowboys before a shoot-out.

'Hi, Debbie,' said Jenny, knowing that this would be met with nothing more than a sniff. 'How are you today?'

'Not too good,' said Debbie just like she always did. 'What you looking so chipper for?'

'Well,' said Jenny, not wanting to tell her about Trudi or college because she would go and say something sarcastic and bloody well ruin it like she always did, 'I've just found out that old Joyce, you know Joyce with Alzheimer's, was once a great singer who sang for the Queen at the Royal Albert Hall. Isn't that fabulous?'

'Hmph! Well I'm glad she got chance to live her dream cos I certainly didn't,' said Debbie.

'Well you know what they say, Debs, it's never too late.' Jenny looked under the sink for the rubber gloves.

'What an absolute load of crap!' Debbie swung her wheelchair around and accidentally knocked her mug of tea over. 'Oh shit! Shit! Shit! Shit!'

Jenny rushed over. *Really, would this woman ever be in a good mood?*

'Never mind! I'll clear it up, don't worry, go on, go and watch some tele.'

'I don't want to watch tele.'

'Well, just move so that I can clear up the mess please, Debbie!'

Debbie glared at her and angrily wheeled herself out of the kitchen.

Later, when she was walking home, Jenny wondered if she had been too harsh with her. After all, she was disabled. She didn't know what it was about Debbie, but she was hands down the most difficult person she had to care for.

She remembered women like this at the salon, women who were so difficult they had to ban them sometimes. She thought back to a client who was always drunk and emotional, sometimes happy, sometimes sad, it could go either way. Regardless, she was a pain in the neck and always had a strop when it was time to pay. Then there was that other one who used to gossip incessantly about her neighbour until one day a relative of hers happened to be in the chair next to her. The fight that ensued took them both through the front window and the place had to be boarded up for weeks. God Almighty, she thought, some people just don't know how to behave.

On her way across the estate she passed a small children's park and thought she saw Freya's pretty little face among a group of girls. She walked up to the gate and called over.

'Hello beautiful girl, how are you?'

Freya smiled. She must really love being praised like this thought

Jenny, God knows her mother won't be doing it. She walked into the playground.

'I'm alright thank you, Jenny. Did you go to Mum's today?'

'Yes I did, I was there just now. Does she know where you are, Frey?'

'Yeah I told her I would be playing out with my friends after school.'

I don't blame you, thought Jenny, I wish I could tell her that.

'It's OK, my nanna is coming over soon.'

'OK, love.'

She saw that the swing next to Freya's friend was empty. She walked past the bemused little girls and sat on it and, as the spring sun beat down on the cherry blossom trees, she swung as high as she could.

As she swung, a memory of her and Sue when they were of a similar age to Freya and her friends, flashed into her mind. They were on a bus coming home from school. Top deck at the back. Sue had a can of coke and was shaking it like crazy so that it would fizz up and then she would shower it out of the window onto unsuspecting pedestrians. What little monsters they were. But one day was the best of all. Sue squirted the coke out of the window and it landed on a man in a suit with a carnation in his lapel, on his way to a wedding perhaps or some other posh do. In any case, he got drenched and he turned and shook his fist up at the top deck as the bus went flying by. It all happened so fast, it was over in an instant, but they laughed so much they thought they would die.

Happy days, she thought as she swung back and forth, *happy, happy days.*

CHAPTER 8

The first class

A few days later, and much to Jenny's delight, she had a Zoom call with Emily from the salon at 8am when the boys had just left for school. It turned out that the weightlifter guy Emily had followed to Lanzarote was a bit too kinky for her liking, so she was planning to return to Stoke shortly. Perhaps as soon as a couple of weeks' time.

'Oh, please come as quickly as you can!' Jenny begged, somewhat giving away how desperate she was to have some friends around her again. She had known Emily for over ten years; it would be amazing if she came back.

'Yeah I'm coming, Jen, don't worry,' Emily replied, flashing her long red nails across the screen as she pulled her blonde hair back from her face.

'You're looking really good, Em!' laughed Jenny. 'That kinkiness must have agreed with you!' Both women laughed raucously.

'You don't want to know, Jen. I'm reluctant to tell you, 'cos once told it can't be untold!'

Jenny screamed with laughter, her eyes widening. 'Oh no, no, what a nightmare! You must tell me all about it when you get home.'

'I will,' said Emily, blowing kisses at the screen. 'Love you loads, hon, see you soon!'

'Love you too, darling, I'm so pleased you're coming home,' said Jenny. 'Bye bye, bye bye, bye... bye.'

Jenny had a funny way of always getting the last 'Bye' in any conversation. She sat there, basking ecstatically in the good news of Emily's return. This was surely a sign that things were finally looking up. Lonny came in.

'How's Em?'

'She's coming home, Lon! I can't believe it, I'm so happy.'

Lonny bent over and kissed her.

'That's good news, duck, int it? Can you come and help me in the garden for a minute before you head off to Bill's?'

Jenny followed Lonny out into the sunshine. That evening, she would have her first creative writing class and would see Trudi again. She felt a newfound confidence that with Emily's return she at least had one good friend now, so she wouldn't be exuding the air of Jenny No-Mates when talking to Trudi. It was all coming together.

She helped Lonny move the polytunnel over its frame, but he still wasn't happy with it, so Ahmed came over to help. Fusun was out in the garden putting the washing out nice and early. Jenny waved to her cheerfully, still basking in the glow of Emily's call.

'You can get a couple of washes out on a day like this, Fusun!'

'I know, I love this hot weather.'

They both smiled and there was a moment when Fusun clearly thought a conversation might begin, but Jenny walked quickly back to her patio. She liked Fusun, the little she saw of her, but the religious garb she wore was a block to getting to know her more. Surely, if you always wore a long dress and hijab you were only interested in certain things, things Jenny knew nothing about? She sat down, stretched her legs out in the sun and wriggled her toes. Things had definitely improved now, she could feel optimism in the air and it felt just as good as the morning sunshine. She closed her eyes and put her head back to drink in the warmth.

A door crashing open on the other side of the fence meant the newlyweds must have woken up. Jenny reluctantly opened her eyes. Dawn could soon be heard in the garden with the children, children who were certainly old enough to go to nursery where they could be listening and learning from a lovely young teacher who didn't swear at them every other minute.

'Shenice?! What the fuck are you doing?'

For goodness sake! Jenny looked towards the fence, where she could see Dawn's angry face.

'What the fuck, Shenice?! What yer playing at?!'

'Oi, Oi, Oi, Oi!' Lonny came marching down the garden. 'Dawnie, Dawnie! Come on! You can't be using that language in front of your daughter, duck. How old is she – four?'

'Nah she's only two, she's big boned.'

'Well, either way, come on, come on now.' Lonny and Dawn faced each other over the fence. Jenny looked up the garden towards them, knowing what would happen. Lonny would work his magic on her, just like he could with anyone. 'We want to make these gardens nice for all of us to hang out in over the summer don't we? We can have barbecues and the kids can play and we can all grow lots of veg and plant some trees and all us neighbours can get on and be friends. Wouldn't that be great, duck?'

Dawn found herself smiling shyly and nodding. She had loved Lonny since she first saw him and he had winked at her and said, 'Hiya, duck, welcome to the neighbourhood.' She wasn't sure about Jenny though, so far she seemed a bit of a snob. But Lonny was lovely. He was fucking great.

'But no swearing,' he said. 'We can't have that, Dawn, can we?

Not with young kids around.' He was holding her hand over the fence, shaking it to encourage her. Dawn was beaming, enjoying his undivided attention.

'If you get upset, duck, just do what I do – run into the bathroom, lock the door and let it all out in there.'

'Alright, duck,' Dawn chuckled. 'I'll try.'

'I know you can do it, Dawnie, you're great you are!' She chuckled some more and then he pulled her head towards his to whisper something in her ear. 'You're *fucking* great!'

Dawn roared with laughter as Lonny winked and left her and came down the garden towards the patio.

He sat down beside Jenny. 'I had to say something, duck, we can't have that going on all summer.'

'You realise with all that talk of barbecues and good times with the neighbours that she's now thinking she'll be invited round here.' Jenny shuddered at the thought.

'No, I meant, you know, when everyone has their own barbecue.'

'That's not the way it sounded, Lon. It sounded like there'll be one big barbecue and they're all invited.'

'Well, is that such a bad idea?' said Lonny, much to Jenny's dismay.

'It's a terrible idea.'

'Well, I haven't seen much of him, but I like her, I like Old Dawnie.'

'Yeah, you'll like her till she calls you a C-U-N-T,' Jenny muttered furtively before breaking out in a snigger alongside her husband. Lonny was pleased to see his wife on good form. He reached out for her hand and kissed it. She leaned in to press her cheek to his while they continued to giggle.

'Oi! None of that nonsense!' They turned to see Dawn at the fence wagging her finger.

'Oh for God's sake, we need a higher fence, I can't bear it.'

Lonny leant back in his chair, laughing quietly.

'I'm serious, I can't stand it, flippin' newlyweds.' Jenny got up and went into the house.

She arrived at Bill's a bit later than normal, the combined annoyance at the heat and Dawn making her walk more slowly, even though it was downhill.

She could see him twitching the net curtains looking out for her. There wasn't much that happened on Bill's street that passed him by, at least not unless it was during the snooker final. Just as she was about to walk down the path, she saw the same old dog she had seen previously, lying out in the sun again, but this time in a different place. Jenny wondered why she wasn't choosing somewhere in the shade, this heat would be the death of her. She stroked the dog for a while and tried to entice her onto the grass of Bill's front garden where she might be able to pick up a tiny bit of shade from the house. But the dog wouldn't move so she called the local PDSA to report it. Better safe than sorry.

Inside, she told Bill about the poor animal but he didn't want to hear about dogs; his bad leg was swelling up in the heat and he couldn't focus on anything else. He wanted ice packs and sympathy.

The day stretched out in front of her; her shifts were always slightly different, usually two or three hours each, but she rarely had all three clients on the same day. The mundane work would always be the same though: cleaning, personal care, cooking, listening to Bill and his daft jokes or poor old Joyce and her nonsense and then on to Debbie, who was bound to have saved something awful for her to do.

What a misery that woman is, thought Jenny later, as she made her way across the estate towards Debbie's. Oh God, why was she feeling so much negativity again, being so horrible to a sick woman in a wheelchair for goodness sake? This morning had started so well with Emily's call, then that stupid heifer over the fence had put her in a bad mood again. Why was she letting Dawn affect her like this? She shouldn't rise to it, she should just ignore her.

When she got to Debbie's, her supermarket delivery hadn't arrived so Jenny was sent to stock up on supplies, which was far preferable to cleaning the bathroom again. That bathroom was as clean as a bathroom in a five-star hotel. She wondered if Debbie had cottoned on that Jenny was using a natural bicarb and white vinegar mixture that Lonny had made for her instead of the chemical sprays that the supermarket sold. He had told Jenny that on no account was she to use any of that toxic crap, breathing that in on an almost daily basis would be poison. No doubt Debbie would have a strop if she found out, but once she knew it was Lonny's idea she would melt. She knew Debbie had a massive crush on him.

Finally making her way home in the intense heat, she noticed a tight knot in her stomach and wondered if she was nervous about meeting Trudi again at the class this evening. Trudi on her own might not be nerve-racking, but Trudi in the writing class was another matter. Jenny's mind raced ahead to a scenario where the teacher was asking her to leave the class because she wasn't of a good enough standard. At the same time she was praising Trudi for being brilliant. I have to make the most of these early lessons, she thought, before everyone realises I'm no good at it.

In the bedroom, she touched up her make-up despite knowing that the heat would make it all run off her face. It was the principle that mattered. She had to make an effort for her new friend. She had to at least try and look her best. She thought of her nails, she hadn't had the chance to do them for a while, there didn't seem much point with the kind of work she did. Well, it was too late now, she would do them tomorrow.

'I'm off to college then, Lon, wish me luck.'

'Alright, duck, are you OK getting the bus?'

'Yes of course.'

He pecked her on the lips and smiled at her. 'Sock it to 'em, Jen.'

Jenny looked bemused. 'I just want to see Trudi really.'

'Well, there might be some writing to do at some point, duck.'

'Yes that's OK, in a few weeks, once I get the hang of it.'

On the bus, her nerves gave way to excitement at the thrill of this new venture and her success at finding a new friend so early into it. She found herself smiling at her fellow passengers and when she got off she shouted 'Thank you, driver!' loudly instead of muttering it like she normally did. She had forgotten all about Dawn now, this was Trudi territory. Hallelujah! This was what it was all about from now on. Moving one step at a time in the right direction away from her anxiety and depression. She thanked the universe for letting her meet Trudi in the foyer on enrolment day. Two minutes later and she would have missed her and maybe signed up for something terrible with a bunch of people she had nothing in common with.

She walked into the classroom fifteen minutes early and chose a seat in the middle, second row back. The teacher was bound to expect answers from people in the front row and she didn't want to be expected to contribute, feeling as ignorant as she did about the subject matter. She put her bag on the seat next to her and would only lift it for Trudi. There were two older ladies at the back. Jenny clocked them: retired, bored, boring. She was going to tell herself off for being so rude but she couldn't be bothered, she was far too excited about seeing Trudi again.

The teacher arrived and the room filled up one by one with a variety of adults eager to try out their writing skills. Still no Trudi.

'Good evening everyone,' said the teacher. 'My name is Celia and I'm here to lead this exploration into unleashing your inner writer. Shall we begin?'

In a sea of eager students, Celia noticed Jenny glancing at the door.

'Jenny, is everything alright? Do you need the Ladies?'

'Oh, no sorry, Miss,' Jenny said, acutely embarrassed. 'I just thought Trudi would be here by now. My friend Trudi who registered with me.'

'Ah yes, Trudi. I think she sent me an email,' Celia looked over her notes. 'Yes she won't be in this week unfortunately, but she will be here next week.' She noticed Jenny's face drop like a ton of bricks.

'Didn't she let you know?' she asked.

'Oh, I must have missed her message. Never mind.'

Celia continued with her description of the class and what the students could hope to achieve over the coming term. Jenny's eyes glazed over as she tried to suppress her disappointment. Another long week of waiting to see Trudi, how annoying. Especially as she had been picturing it all so clearly, sitting by her side in class, having coffee together, maybe meeting her husband in the car park afterwards. Then, after a few weeks of this, they could start visiting each other's houses. The two men were bound to get on, everyone got on with Lonny. She would have to make sure her house was on top form by then, the boys managed to keep it in a constant state of mess, but the houseplants and the garden would win anyone over, everyone loved their garden. Hopefully the scaffolding would be gone by then too. She wondered what Trudi's home would be like. It was bound to be gorgeous and classy. Maybe there wouldn't be any mess because she might not have children, or maybe one teenage daughter. Maybe. And a lovely labradoodle dog, something like that, something fluffy and gorgeous. Maybe Trudi's teenage daughter would take a fancy to Ryan and they would get married in a few years and that would mean she would always be related to her. They could share looking after the grandchildren, they could have lots of parties and family events, barbecues in the summer and Christmases together round the fire –

'Jenny? Do you understand?'

'Oh! Yes, Miss!'

'Shall I go over the details again?'

'Erm, yes please, Miss.' Jenny blushed.

She tried to listen properly this time as the teacher explained their first assignment – to examine the different roles in their lives and write about them. For example, Daz, the serious young man with a beard, might be a son, a husband, a lover, a student, a friend. Celia asked Daz what the most important role in his life was and Daz said immediately, 'I'm a lover and a poet, Celia, I don't know which comes first.'

Celia smiled and said, 'OK, Daz, that's wonderful. You don't need to concern yourself with the order necessarily, just focus on what each role is and what it means to you. For instance, how you come up with your ideas for poetry, how and when you write, your influences, that kind of thing.'

She stressed that they should write a bit on each role they had in life, and not leave anything out if possible. She gave them a tip that what might feel like the most difficult area to write about may provide the best material.

Jenny gulped. Oh God, this was her worst nightmare. What a ridiculous subject for an essay. She had expected it to be 'A day in the countryside' or something like that, not this kind of intrusive nonsense. What a nosy parker the teacher must be. Was this even legal? It would be hard enough to write anything given that she hadn't done it since she was a little girl, let alone this personal stuff. Oh well, she would just have to put it all on hold until she saw Trudi next week and they could discuss it together. She could think about the roles in her life, but she certainly wouldn't start writing anything, she didn't know how. Celia came past her desk and Jenny wanted to tug at her sleeve like some shy seven-year-old and say 'Miss, aren't you going to tell us how to do it?' but she managed to stay quiet. Surely it didn't matter that she didn't get it all quite yet. After all, Trudi had missed this class so she wouldn't get it either.

CHAPTER 9

Matt at Aldi's

That Saturday, Lonny and the three boys and some of their mates walked down to the sports fields as usual for Kids' and Dads' footie. There would be far more kids than dads of course but Lonny didn't mind. He had been doing this gig since Ryan was knee-high to a grasshopper. Growing boys and girls needed to run around just the same as growing plants needed water. He was hoping that enough people would turn up in this heat so that he wouldn't have to be both ref and goalie like he sometimes did. That would be a bit too much running around on a day that was forecast to hit 38 degrees.

Since being made redundant four years ago, Lonny's normally ebullient mood had become even more so. He loved his life. He loved that he had found his calling and that he had a chance to make a real difference in the world. How ironic that he discovered this love for the land just at the final countdown. His own garden might not make that much difference, but he knew he was one of hundreds of thousands, maybe millions of people going down a similar route and demanding the end of the pesticide-riddled monocrop era that had ruined the soil and left it unable to function and draw down carbon like it should.

Now he was eagerly looking for opportunities to get more

involved. There were lots of positive, planet-loving people out there doing great things. Just recently he had heard of Ecosystem Restoration Camps where you could volunteer to work on the land in many different areas of the world. There was a camp in Spain that he fancied taking the lads to. It would be a brilliant experience for them, they would realise that the future didn't have to be doom and gloom. He wondered about making this their summer holiday this year. He didn't know if Jen would fancy coming with them or if she would stay with her parents at their villa. He had tried to get her interested in it all; in permaculture and in the different regenerative farming practices that were springing up everywhere, but she had spotted some of the hippie women at the allotments and it had put her off. Crikey, she was a lot more like her mother these days.

After an exhausting game of footie, the hot sun was still cracking the pavements and Lonny, Ryan, Nate and Solly made their way home, a few friends in tow as ever.

'Did you see this, Dad?' said Ryan, reading some news on his phone as they walked. 'It says Stoke is no longer in the top ten worst places to live in Britain! Wow! It's gone down to number 22!'

'Blimey that's a drop int it?' said Lonny, sweating in the heat. 'Not sure how I feel about that. Suppose it's cause for celebration.'

'I don't think I've ever known it be outside the top ten,' said Solly.

'Not in my lifetime anyhow,' said Nate.

'Mine neither!' laughed Lonny.

They took a detour to see Matt from the allotments. Matt was the assistant manager of the local *Aldi* which, along with *Tesco*, B&Q and the other usual suspects, sat on the Meir Park shopping estate next to the A50. When Lonny first met him, Matt had just a small allotment, now he was the proud owner of a two-acre smallholding out at Leek.

They slipped through the gap in the hedge and across the car park to where Matt was having a cigarette break. He was down to two cigs a day now. He would have his last smoke on the day he moved into the smallholding.

Solly looked up at him shyly as they approached; he thought his Dad was strong, but this guy was a *monster*.

'Yo' 'raight, Matty, duck?' Lonny said slapping him on the back and shaking him firmly by the hand.

'How's it going, Lon?' said Matt beaming.

'Good, duck, good.'

'How's the garden? Have you got your tomatoes out yet?'

'I got all the nightshades out last weekend. I hope I don't regret it.'

'You won't, mate, it's forecast to carry on for at least a month.'

'Seriously?'

'Yeah... and reaching 40 degrees they reckon.'

'Crikey,' Lonny winced.

'It's the people in hot countries I feel sorry for,' Ryan chipped in. 'They must have reached 50 degrees by now.'

Lonny shook his head. 'People can't live in that heat. It's madness. No wonder everyone's trying to come over here.'

The two men noticed the anxious faces of the lads and felt obliged to change the conversation.

'How's Jenny? I haven't seen her lately,' said Matt. 'Is she feeling any better?'

'Nah, Jen's not on top form these days.' Lonny stopped suddenly. He wished he could confide in his friend, but he couldn't say a lot in front of the boys, who were all looking at him as though they too were waiting for an answer to that question. 'It's a one step forward, two steps back kind of thing.'

'Well she lost her best friend, it takes time to get over something like that,' said Matt, now regretting the switch in conversation as he saw the boys' even more worried faces.

'I know, I know.'

'She says she'll never get over it,' said Solly.

'That's just what she thinks now, duck,' said Lonny firmly. 'She's not going to be depressed forever, you don't have to worry about that.'

'She'll find some new friends before too long, lads,' said Matt.

'Yeah, yeah, trouble is she's her own worst enemy sometimes,' Lonny couldn't help blurting out.

'How d'you mean?'

'No one's good enough.'

'She likes a woman called Trudi though,' said Solly.

'She met her at the creative writing class,' Ryan said.

'She's supposed to be a right looker!' said Nate.

Matt raised his eyebrows and grinned. 'Who? Trudi? Ooh she sounds nice dunt she! Is she single? Do you know which *Aldi* she shops at?'

'She sounds a bit more Waitrose to me,' Lonny laughed.

Matt snorted. 'Come off it, they all come here with their Waitrose bags.'

Lonny chuckled, but he was eager to move things along, he had a question for his friend. 'Matty, what's this I hear about a new cafe which will only use local produce? Stella said you knew the woman in charge. Will they buy stuff from people who grow at home? I can't afford to be registered organic but that's what it is and I'm going to have tons of veg if this weather carries on.'

'Yeah, she's a friend of a friend. It's a great idea, like a food club to regenerate the land and the people. They'll do fermented foods and drinks and everything.'

'Great, they want cabbages for sauerkraut then, right?'

'Everything as I understand it, Lon. It's a good opportunity for us growers. I'll send you her email.'

*

Jenny had finished work when Lonny and the boys returned; a quick breakfast and bathroom visit at Bill's was all she had to do at the weekend and she felt lucky today that the garden was quiet so she could lie out on the wooden sun lounger undisturbed. There was a gig tonight at a pub down in Stafford and, as usual, she felt weary at the thought of it.

She looked at the notepad on her lap. At the top of the page she had written: wife, mother, carer, *singer*, *friend*. Once she had put a stop to Marie she would no longer be a singer. As for friend... how would she be able to write this last chapter or paragraph or whatever it was called? She couldn't. But how could she miss it out? The teacher would think she had no friends; Trudi, more importantly, might read it and think she had no friends. Well let's face it, she didn't have friends at this moment, not nearby at any rate. But that hadn't always been the case. She could write about Annie and Kate and Emily and of course she could write about Sue. She could be honest and write about how much her death had devastated her. But that might take up the whole essay. She looked up as Lonny and the boys opened the front door and came into the house, Lonny walking straight through to the garden to check where she was as normal.

'Hiya, duck,' said Lonny, giving her a kiss on the lips. 'How was Bill today?' He sat down beside her and picked up his permaculture magazine and reading glasses.

'Oh, same as ever,' said Jenny, 'very happy being miserable.' They both chuckled. Ryan asked Nate if he wanted to play cricket.

'In a minute,' said Nate. 'I gotta pee first.'

'Make a donation, Nate!' Lonny called to his son, in reference to the watering can in the bathroom that was collecting urine to fertilise the plants.

'Yeah alright, Dad,' muttered Nate, used to this by now.

'Hi Mumma,' said Solly, flopping onto her lap and giving her a big hug, his Afro practically covering her face.

'Hello my big boy,' said Jenny, trying to get his hair out of her eyes.

Solly sunk down so that his head was snuggling against her chest. This heat was making him tired and listless; he nuzzled back and forth.

By now, Lonny was deep into the article on food forests, but after a while he looked up over his reading glasses.

'Oi, Sol.'

'What?'

'Stop nuzzling yer mother. Get off her chest.'

'Why?'

'Cos that's for babies and toddlers. You're too old for nuzzlin'.'

'I onna, Dad.'

'You are.'

'Onna.'

'Are!' Lonny glared at him. Solly reluctantly climbed off his mother but still hung on to her neck, nuzzling her head now and sniffing her hair. Over the years, Jenny had got so used to being mauled on a daily basis that she hardly noticed him being there, she was still looking at her notepad, trying to think of what she could write in her essay.

'Mumma, remember when you had that nice shampoo, the one that used to smell dead good?'

'Hmm? Oh yes, I remember. The coconut one.'

'Yeah, it was dead nice wasn't it?'

'Yes, it was beautiful. How funny that you remember it.'

'I always remember that smell,' said Solly, running his fingers through his mother's hair and sniffing it as though he hadn't yet given up all hope of finding it. 'I really loved it. Really, really loved it. Mumma, can I ask you a question?'

'Yes of course, darling,' said Jenny, intrigued.

'Why don't you use that shampoo any more? Can't you be arsed?'

Jenny sat bolt upright and pushed him away. 'I beg your pardon, Solomon Lonsdale!'

Lonny looked up over his reading glasses. ''Ey, 'ey, 'ey! Watch yer language!'

'Arsed inna bad language.'

'Yes it jolly well is!' said Jenny emphatically, wondering if her new neighbour was already exerting a bad influence on her sons from over the fence, so soon after arriving. Actually, there was no wondering about it.

'Tinna, Mumma.'

''Tis,' said Lonny. ''Tis in this house at any rate!' He winked at him. 'Go play, go on!'

'See, Lon, that's Dawn's bad influence taking effect already!' said Jenny, glaring over the fence to the newlyweds' empty garden.

But the thought of Dawn being a bad influence didn't cross Lonny's mind and he was tempted to tell his wife to give it a rest.

Instead he returned to his magazine and continued to read the article on food forests and how fruit bushes and nut trees and vines will grow well under the canopy of the larger trees so that there is something edible and useful growing at every level, even the ground. At the same time, the forest would be regenerating the soil and drinking in carbon. Flippin 'eck, he wished he'd known this stuff eighteen years ago when he first bought the house. A tree takes a long time to grow and if he'd got them all in the ground then, they would all be eating apples and pears and cherries as well as walnuts and hazelnuts and even almonds possibly. Almonds! Wow. In Stoke! And all of it drinking in carbon all day long. And they'd have all that shade from the larger trees which, if this heat was the new normal, they would badly need. As it was, he only had the dwarf apple and pear trees which were trellised up the fence on Dawn's side and hopefully would help keep that section of it standing when the hurricanes returned.

Still, as the Chinese proverb goes: '*When's the best time to plant a tree? Twenty years ago. When's the second best time? Now.*'

'Jen,' he said, 'I'm thinking all the gig money for the next couple of months should go into setting up a food forest in the front garden. We've got to do it quick, duck, we've got to get those trees in the ground. Can you keep doing Marie for a while? I don't want to rock the boat and change anything. You're on all the promotional stuff now, so we might as well keep going till Christmas, yeah?'

'Christmas? Lon, it's only May! That's ages away.'

'I know, duck, but we need the food forest. And I've still got the pond to do, and then the bees and the chickens. It all costs money you know.'

'OK then,' she said. 'I don't mind.'

'Are you sure?'

'No,' she said, trying to smile. 'I'm not sure at all.'

'You'll be alright, babe,' he said. 'You're a great singer.'

'Thanks, hon.'

'You are, Jen.' He winked at her.

I just wish I could sing a different song though, she thought.

CHAPTER 10

Pain

'Mavis duck, there's some vomit at the back! Clear it up while Marie's on!' yelled the portly pub landlord, taking advantage of the fact that the dance floor was empty.

Vomit? That is disgusting, Jenny thought. Although clearly not quite as disgusting as 'Paper Roses' seeing as it was that which, as per usual, had cleared the floor so abruptly. She looked through the open doors to the beer garden, which was absolutely heaving with drunken people who were happy to be outside and away from her.

I don't want to be in here singing a stupid song on my own, thought Jenny. I want to be out there having fun with people.

Then she thought, no I don't, I don't want to be out there either.

She wondered if she would ever find her place in the world again or whether she would always feel the odd one out. Oh God, what a drama queen she was sometimes. Not seeing Trudi at the writing class had really set her back again. It was so hard to try and stay positive when nothing was going her way. Earlier on, she had stood in the wings and watched Lonny singing 'The Twelfth of Never' as drunken women who were old enough to be grannies screamed out his name. She wished she could be more like her husband, he looked so at home on the stage; there was no hesitation in his voice, no embarrassment that he was pretending to be a fourteen-year-old white boy from Utah, when he was a forty-two-year-old black man from Stoke. He just sang every word like he meant it while at the same time knowing it was all a big joke which the whole audience was included in. The only time in her life – outside the home – that she had anywhere near that confidence was in the salon.

And that seemed like a long time ago.

This had got to end, Jenny promised herself as she sang, her lovely voice getting more feeble by the minute. My life has to change. If I don't change, I will never have a friend like Trudi. And I will be letting Sue down. Sue always used to be there to take charge whenever things got really tough. But Sue wasn't here anymore. And Lonny was doing his best but he was too busy saving the world. She knew he was frustrated with her, he wanted her to hurry up and get back on track and get involved with the environmental activism which he believed to be so crucial.

'We need you on board, Jen,' he had often said to her this last year. 'You can't opt out, duck. The time is now. We rise together or we all sink. That's it.'

When 'Paper Roses' was finished and the men had returned to the stage as The Four Tops, she lingered for a while in the wings and watched them belt out 'The Same Old Song', which never failed to get everyone on the floor for some serious dancing. While Lonny didn't quite have the amazing vocal talent of Levi Stubbs, he always looked like he was having the time of his life singing this classic Motown song.

She stood behind the velvet curtain and remembered the first time they met. It was at Sue and Eddie's first home. After a few years as a plumber in the army, Lonny had returned home to Stoke and immediately bought a house, despite being a young man on his own.

But the sale had been a nightmare, so in the meantime he had toured the UK staying with mates like Eddie who needed some work doing. Sue liked him a lot and asked him to put a new bathroom in, which happened to be at the same time that Jenny was staying there. She had been in hospital for three weeks and was recuperating under Sue's watchful eye. She was on the sofa watching daytime TV with Ryan, who was just a baby, when Lonny came marching in. He always moved quickly, he had enough energy to light up Blackpool Tower. Of course he was only twenty-four at the time whereas she was thirty-two and already feeling a lot older.

'Hiya, duck!' he said. 'How're you doing? Sue said you've been in the wars, in 'ospital and everything. Just to let you know, I'm here to put a new bathroom in so there'll be a bit of drillin' and such like. But if it gets too much just shout. I'm to look after you, Sue says. She's got me doing two jobs for the price of one!'

'She's clever like that isn't she?' Jenny giggled shyly.

'You can say that again! She haggled with me for half an hour on the quote for the bathroom. Half an hour! I couldn't believe it. I said to her, "Duck, while you're doing all this talking the price is going up!"' He laughed and winked at her.

Then he played with Ryan and he popped in throughout the day to see how she was and to bring her a cup of tea or a sandwich. By the time the bathroom was finished, Jenny was smitten. She found out that his name was Simon Lonsdale but that everyone had always called him Lonny, the only person who didn't was his brother Jackie. 'Simon' didn't suit him at all, but 'Lonny' did, it suited his gregarious personality.

Thinking back, Jenny was more convinced than ever that Sue had deliberately engineered their romance. Because when the bathroom was finished, several other jobs magically appeared, some of which

Lonny wondered why the heck Eddie couldn't do. But Eddie and Sue were both out at work of course. They both worked at the council offices in those days and there was a nursery that Sue took Amy to. So they were out all day and she and Lonny seemed to be in all day.

It took many months though; after what she had been through with Alan, she had thought she would never trust another man. But Lonny exuded trustworthiness, he was a gentleman. He was a loud, funny, ridiculous, adorable gentleman. And she could see right into his twenty-four-year-old mind; she could see that he was determinedly working out how to marry this thirty-two-year-old woman and help bring up her baby as his own. Thinking about how he would get the money, where they would live, how it would all work out. She could see in his eyes that he was trying to figure out the equation. He didn't make a move until he was sure he had it all figured out, because he didn't want this to be casual; he knew he wanted to marry her and be with her forever.

When they finally got together, she heard all about his equation which was basically man + woman + kids (living in Stoke) = fifty per cent cheaper than anywhere else. By then, she was used to his strange accent, and the fact that he was so young didn't bother her at all. He was more responsible at twenty-four than Alan had been at thirty-six. He was great with people too, he was grounded and reliable and solid, whereas she often felt like the proverbial candle in the wind. Especially these days.

As the song finished, she watched Lonny and the guys enjoying a bit of banter with the audience. They were laughing and joking and having fun. Things which sometimes seemed as alien to her as time travel. Then they began singing the Four Tops' song, 'Reach Out, I'll Be There', which always sent everyone wild, and it seemed like the whole audience were jumping up and down as one unit, reaching out with arms outstretched.

I want a lovely life again, she thought as she left the wings and made her way back to the broom cupboard to change. I don't want this loneliness anymore and I don't want to be a carer wiping an old man's bottom and I don't want to be Marie Osmond singing 'Paper Roses' while someone is clearing up vomit.

Somewhere deep down inside her, she knew that a change was already underway.

CHAPTER 11

A date is set

The next day, she found Bill on bad form. He had news to deliver. The dog was dead. Killed in the heat. The PDSA were far too busy so some bloke at the council had to come and remove the body.

'That'll be me they're removing soon if this weather dunt break,' he said.

'Bill, you're in the shade with plenty of water to drink!'

'It dunt make any difference. I can feel it, I'm on the wane. It's sapping all me energy. And I'm not a bloody dog, I hate water! I want tea!'

Jenny rolled her eyes and patted his forehead with a cold flannel. 'Hold your horses, I'll get you some tea in a minute. And you can't go leaving us before the snooker final. That will mean you've watched all those matches for nothing.'

On the way home, she passed Mr and Mrs Stevenson's house just along the street. They were playing a mournful cello concerto and, as usual, the windows were open and the music was filling the air.

Poor old dog, thought Jenny, feeling pretty weary herself.

Back in her room, she tried once again to start her essay. She had been thinking of her mum again, God knows why, maybe it was just the fact that she knew this essay had to be written and there had to be a chapter or a paragraph at least titled 'Daughter'. When she had her own children, she realised that her mother must have been some kind of narcissist, the way she treated her. Everything had to revolve around her, she was so self-centred. Which all made for quite a dysfunctional childhood. Then of course there was Uncle Pat, her mother's older brother, who used to touch her up when she was little under the guise of being chief babysitter. That went on for a few years. Until one day there was a birthday party and Sue was there. She soon sussed the old creep out. 'Keep your hands to yourself, buster!' she shouted at him, to the shock of the adults in the other room, before giving him a good hard kick in the shins. He never touched her after that. Sue had saved her despite being only six. Her mother had been furious about that episode, but furious with her and Sue, not with her brother! If it wasn't for Sue, she guessed her mother would have gladly swept it all under the carpet.

No, this 'Daughter' chapter was going to be difficult to write. Maybe she would have to just focus on Dad.

In the end, she decided she wouldn't write anything until she had seen Trudi at the next class; after all, if she didn't turn up twice in a row then most likely she wouldn't be doing the course at all so why bother? She felt devastated at the thought of not seeing her again, it just didn't bear thinking about. She put her notebook away; she wasn't going to get any writing done today. Instead, she caught the bus to the town centre to visit a new preloved clothes store at the market.

She welcomed the opportunity to get away from the house. The scaffolding made her feel like she was living in a cage. And if she was out in the garden, she knew it wouldn't be long before she would see either Dawn or Fusun putting washing out or drinking tea. Then she would feel a veil of guilt and downright irritation fall over her. Why couldn't she have neighbours who had more in common with her?

She sometimes felt as though her house was getting crushed between the weight of two dominant forces. Of course, Lonny could more than hold his own, he was a character the whole neighbourhood knew and liked, but Jenny felt herself becoming more insignificant as each day went by. Sometimes she felt overwhelmingly unimportant to anyone, although she knew deep down that this wasn't true. Trudi would provide the help she needed to turn this around, but it was all moving so slowly. One class a week and then she might not even show. It was so frustrating.

In the Potteries Shopping Centre in Hanley she passed a pop-up store selling Neal's Yard Organic skin care and thought she would treat herself to a new lipstick, a nice bright one for summer. She stopped to look at the colours and the saleswoman welcomed her, telling her she had beautiful skin and asking what make-up she wore and recommending new products before Jenny had even answered.

Jenny didn't really want this hard-sell nonsense. She couldn't stand it. Her eye had been caught by a woman going up the escalator, a woman with long wavy fair hair. Could it be Trudi? No it wasn't, of course it wasn't, that woman wouldn't even come up to Trudi's armpits. Oh God, it was so difficult to remain positive when –

'– a marvellous experience, a real fun time for you and your friends, dear, and there are two spaces left this month!'

'Sorry?' she looked down at the leaflets the woman had shoved into her hand.

Host a Neal's Yard Organic skincare party in the comfort of your own home. Spoil your friends with the ultimate personal pampering and shopping experience.

'How many friends do I need to book one of these?' she asked cautiously.

'As many as you like, dear! If you have a large lounge, I can handle up to thirty. The more the merrier!'

'I was thinking of something a bit cosier, just a few of us.' She saw the woman's face falling and hastily added, 'My living room isn't that big, I'm sorry.'

'Well, that's alright, dear, the smaller events are often the best. I can give more one-to-one skincare consultations. Just so long as I make my required commission,' she winked, 'I don't mind at all if it's just seven or eight.'

Seven or eight? Surely that was doable? She could invite Trudi and get to know her better. Trudi would love a little party like that, she was sure of it.

Her eye was suddenly caught by a poster for a cancer charity, Macmillan Nurses, on the wall of the stall. They were the same nurses who had looked after Sue in her final weeks. The woman noticed her glance.

'And ten per cent of all profits this month go to our chosen charity, Macmillan Nurses. So you can be helping a good cause while you're enjoying yourselves.'

Jenny felt her heart pounding. It was a sign. A sign from Sue that she approved of Trudi and wanted Jenny to be friends with her. Oh my God. Her eyes began to water.

The woman must have noticed her reaction because all of a sudden she took Jenny's hand and patted it.

'Does this charity mean something to you, my darling?'

'Yes it does. They looked after my best friend when she passed last year.'

'Oh well then,' said the woman, 'you know what this is?'

'A sign?'

The woman nodded. 'Absolutely. Is this your first do since she passed on?'

'Yes,' said Jenny, wiping away a tear.

'Well, there you are! It's a sign that she approves heartily, my darling. Otherwise you would have walked on by and not stopped. Two minutes earlier and you wouldn't have even seen the poster because it wasn't up. How about that then?'

'Yes, yes, I think it is a sign. Thank you.'

Jenny's mind went into overdrive. Hosting a party was all very well, she used to be the Queen of Parties at one time, this was one hundred per cent her domain. But who could she invite besides Trudi?

Don't panic, she thought as her heart beat even faster. Calm down and think. Emily would be home soon so she could come, Hannah from work would surely come, plus herself and Trudi, that was four. Surely she could find three or four more women to ask?

'Shall we get a date in the diary?'

'Yes,' she stammered, feeling both thrilled and terrified. But it was a good idea, she needed to see Trudi and get to know her outside the stress of that damn writing course. She needed to nab her while the iron was hot, so to speak, she might not get another chance. 'Yes, yes please, let's get a date organised.'

The date was set for the end of the month, that would be plenty of time. And this kind of thing was what she used to do in her sleep, a party with lovely food and drinks and women talking about anything and everything while under the pretence of beautifying themselves. Sue knew this, she knew a party like this would be just what she needed. It was a project, an important project for her, a lot more important than that stupid essay, which was so difficult to even start. She took a deep breath, it was going to be fantastic, she just knew it.

'We'll have a wonderful time,' said the woman as she wrote out the booking form. She signed her name Cheryl and added a big kiss. 'Look at you, such a beauty, and I'm sure you've got some equally gorgeous friends. When you look as good as you do sweetheart, it makes my job a lot easier!' She laughed. 'I'll email the invitations to send out. You don't have to do anything except the food and drink, I'll take care of everything else!'

Jenny beamed, already planning that Lonny could take the boys out to the cinema or out anywhere, she didn't mind where. Did she have ink in the printer? She thought she did, in which case she would race home and print out those invitations immediately and give one to Trudi at the next class. Oh, it was so exciting. Things were moving now, things were happening, thanks to Sue. She had shaken off that claustrophobic feeling of being surrounded by people she didn't like and she was taking charge of her own destiny. She deserved to have some lovely friends, she always had them before and now she damn well would again. Yes indeed, happy times would return and Sue would approve. After all, Sue had orchestrated the whole event. She knew Lonny and everyone else would most likely say this was a load of rubbish but she didn't care. Sue would want her to be happy, she would know that she wasn't trying to replace her, she was just trying to get on with her life and manage as best as she could and to do that, she would need some nice women around her.

Nice women, like Trudi.

CHAPTER 12

The Running Sisters

The next day, Ryan confided that his dad had been in touch and wanted him to go and spend a fortnight in Spain with his new wife and her kids. Jenny preferred to let Lonny take charge of these conversations as she got too upset at the thought of Ryan being forced to see his dad. She always jumped to the conclusion that he was being forced anyway.

'Do you want to go, Ry?' Lonny asked him.

'I don't mind going for a weekend... two weeks is too long though.'

'It's way too long,' Jenny muttered.

'Why does he hardly ever get in touch and then when he does, it's two weeks on holiday with a big swimming pool, big beach, big this, big that?' Ryan asked. 'He always has to be the Big Man doesn't he, Mum?'

'Yes, he does, love, that's exactly –'

'Alright, alright, let's calm it down a bit,' said Lonny hastily. He tried to represent the male perspective, so many of his friends being divorced now, even though he knew Alan wasn't like any of them. They were nice blokes, but Alan had been a right piece of work.

'Remember, he is your dad, duck. In his own way he loves you I'm sure, he's just not very good at expressing himself.'

'He's not my proper dad though, you're my proper dad, I've seen you every day since I was a baby, you look after me, you're the dad I love.'

'Ah bless you, Ry.' Lonny reached out and grabbed Ryan's arm. 'Come 'ere for a cuddle.' Ryan immediately looked bashful and tried to pull away, half-heartedly giggling.

'Come 'ere I said!' laughed Lonny. He hugged him and kissed his cheek several times. 'I love you just the same as Nate and Solly. There's no difference to me, duck.'

'I know,' he said, 'Thanks, Dad.'

Lonny suggested taking Ryan down the country towards Hereford or somewhere, to a service station where Alan could pick him up and take him back to Cardiff for a weekend. He had dealt with Alan many times before, once or twice a year since Ryan was young, because Jenny wouldn't speak to him. Alan had certainly been a disastrous husband but still, you have to respect the fact that he is Ryan's birth father, Lonny thought, remembering what the judge had said in the custody case. He always treated Ryan well, and Ryan didn't seem to mind a couple of days with him every now and then. On the phone, he told Alan that Ryan didn't want the fortnight as it would be too long away from his brothers and his mates. A weekend would be better. They arranged to meet the following Thursday afternoon, as Ryan always had a free day at college on Friday. Lonny groaned, thinking of the traffic, but Friday would be even worse and at least the club car was the latest electric model and would safely get to Hereford and back without any issues.

Jenny kept going on about the details of the trip and what a pain it was for Ryan to have to spend a whole weekend with people he hardly knew. Whenever Alan got in touch it upset her, Lonny knew that, but he also sensed that she was trying to distract him from something. He looked at the clock.

'Hey, duck! Tuesday, 6.30 – Running Sisters!'

Jenny groaned; she had hoped he'd forgotten but it looked like there was no chance of that. Still, it might be a way of meeting a couple more women she could invite to the party. She only needed a few more. With that in mind, she hurried to get changed.

Lonny was going out to a meeting about the new food club cafe so he accompanied her down Manor Lane and across the estate towards the starting point at the Hungry Horse pub, trying to gee her up as to the social advantages of running in a friendly group like this. She hadn't mentioned the party to him yet, she wanted a confirmation from Trudi first otherwise she would cancel it. So it all seemed a bit of a dream at the moment. A happy dreamy cloud in her head, whereas her body felt sick to the stomach, what with Ryan hearing from his father and her having to go running on the same horrible day.

'Just chat while you're running, duck,' Lonny said, as though he were explaining school etiquette to a reluctant four-year-old. 'Find out who you get on with and who you don't. Then, when you've been going for a few months, you can invite some of them back for a barbecue or a party or summat. Me and the lads will clear out for the evening and you and the women can do whatever you want to do.'

I'm not waiting a few months for a barbecue, thought Jenny, I'm not even waiting till I can chat and run at the same time, 'cos that might take till Christmas. I'm getting my own party organised and all I need are two or three extra people to attend. And that is my sole reason for turning up at this stinking, rotten event.

'I hate these stupid running sisters!' she whimpered as they neared the pub and spotted an abundance of Lycra-clad ladies. Oh God, she wished there was another way of finding women for the party –

surely there was a way that didn't involve getting out of breath?

'Jen, there's fifty women 'ere, all wanting to be friends with you. What's the blinkin' problem?'

'They're not my type!'

'How d'you know?'

'They're runners, Lon!'

'So?'

'So I'll have nothing in common with any of them!' she said, aware that they were getting closer to the starting point.

'Jen, pack it in! That's enough! Stop being your own worst enemy!'

'I'm not though!'

'You are! You can run really well. Remember when you used to run at the gym?'

'That was ten years ago!' she hissed.

'That doesn't matter at all,' said Lonny, as though he were a sports specialist who trained hundreds of middle-aged women every week. 'You used to be a good runner! It will come back to you, your body will remember!'

'My body does remember, that's why it wants to vomit!'

'No it doesn't, you'll be fine.'

'Oh Lonny, don't go, I need the toilet, I just need the toilet –'

'No you don't, Jen, you went right before you came out.'

'But I want to go again now!'

'No you don't, it's an illusion!'

'What?'

'Your body's playing tricks on you, just ignore it.' He pushed her forward into the crowd of women.

'Oh God!'

'Gemma, so nice to meet you finally. Welcome!' said an athletic-looking woman in her twenties, coming over to shake her hand.

Jenny was about to correct her but found that it was too late as all the other women flooded round her and Lonny was suddenly nowhere to be seen. Oh God, she was so unfit now, what was she going to do? Just because she hadn't put on any weight in middle age it didn't mean she was fit. She was unfit. Totally and utterly.

'Ladies, are we ready?' said the athletic woman who, Jenny noticed, had a rather threatening red whistle on a chain around her neck. 'Helen is in front and will show you the route. This week we'll follow the bee corridor all the way around the edge of town, OK? No stopping to pick the flowers please! And no sprinting either, just a steady jog. Please say hello to our newbies, Gemma and Louise –'

'It's Jenny actually,' she said, forcing a smile. She looked around at the many new faces and tried to forget the toilet and instead wondered which women she would be inviting to the make-up party. 'Hello everyone!'

'Jenny? Oh that's strange, I thought we had a Gemma starting this week.'

'We have,' said someone else. 'My friend Gemma from work, she'll join us at Rough Close.'

'Oh, OK. Who are you then, Jenny?' said the athletic woman, as though a potential lapse in security had occurred and she would have to blow her whistle. 'Have you filled out the application form online?'

'Yes. No. I mean I don't know, my husband just brought me down here.' Oh God what a stupid thing to say, what an idiot she was sometimes. She could see all the women turn away and begin to stretch or talk among themselves as though not wanting to associate themselves with someone who couldn't do the simplest thing without their husband's help. The only one looking at her with any kindness was the other newcomer Louise, an obese woman who looked like she could do with some support. *Don't look at me, love,* Jenny thought, *I can't give you any help, I'm hardly standing upright myself.* She looked around for Lonny but he was hurrying away in the distance. *Oh, crikey.* At least Louise looked like she might be even worse at running than she was.

*

But that wasn't the case at all. Louise actually wasn't half bad at running and as for the rest of them, well, they disappeared so fast there was no time for any kind of communication at all. Jenny gasped for air as she jogged painfully behind Louise who was impressively managing to conquer the uphill of Manor Lane without too much ado. Jenny's heels were beginning to rub and she thought she might have the beginnings of runners' nipple, something was irritating her inside her bra that was for sure.

Surely I can't go straight home, she thought, as she passed the turn-off into Bramfield Drive, trying hard not to scratch her breasts in public. That would be so pathetic. And there might be an opportunity to speak to someone at the end. Dammit, she needed those two or three extra women for the party. Sue had set this up for her. Now she just needed to pull it off. Besides, what would Trudi say if she walked in and there was hardly anyone there? What would Cheryl, the party organiser, say? She was as nice as pie when she was booking the event, but if she didn't make any commission, she'd have the right hump. She looked like she could be quite a tyrant that one; the last thing Jenny wanted was for Trudi to feel pressure to buy something, or to have Cheryl getting in a bad temper and getting heavy about it all. God Almighty.

She tried to think positively and to imagine Trudi in the living room having a fantastic time, surrounded by other lovely women: Hannah hopefully and of course Emily, who would no doubt be entertaining them all with her sexually adventurous tales. They would all be screaming with laughter. But who else would be there? Oh

God, she had to find some more women to invite, she didn't really need to know them that well, if she could just catch up with some of these runners she might be in with a chance. They would be going downhill soon, surely then she could catch up.

She arrived at the roundabout at the top of the hill at Meir Heath and followed Louise down the other side towards Rough Close on the road to Stone. A car beeped loudly and she thought instantly, get lost you bastard!! before realising that she was staggering all over the middle of the road because going downhill was proving to be almost as difficult as going uphill. Her legs were so wobbly she couldn't control them. And she couldn't even see Louise now. Which way had she gone?

Reality set in. She would never catch up with the other women in time to have a conversation. Her face would be purple and she wouldn't be able to talk and anyway, they all thought she was a fool for saying her husband had brought her there. What was the point? She could hardly breathe. Oh God, maybe she had a hole in her heart. She couldn't take it any longer. She needed help. Help.

'Help!' she cried as she stumbled through the doorway of the Rough Close Tavern and collapsed on the floor.

Bar manager Lauren looked up from pouring a pint of ale.

'Bloody 'ell, duck! Are you alright?' She rushed over to help the stranger up off the floor but Jenny didn't want to move.

'No, I just need to rest!' she cried. 'I just need to rest!'

'I know, duck, but you're in the doorway there! There'll be people coming in and falling all over yer!'

Jenny managed a reluctant shuffle towards the jukebox.

'She's in shock,' a voice advised.

'Give her a large brandy!' said someone else.

'Yes please,' she whimpered.

*

She got home at about the same time she would have if she had run the five miles with the Running Sisters. Noticing how flushed and red she looked, Lonny applauded proudly as she walked through the door, but then, when he went to kiss her, he jumped at the smell of booze on her breath.

'How'd it go, duck? Been celebrating your return to running?'

Jenny tutted. 'You could say that.'

'Did you meet anyone?'

'Yes. A woman called Lauren.'

'Yeah? Lauren. Is she nice?'

'Yes very nice. And very kind.' Her lip trembled. Lauren had sat at the bar with her for an hour listening to her tales of woe covering everything from Sue's death to having to wipe Bill's backside for a living. Jenny hadn't mentioned being so deprived of friends, but maybe some things were so obvious they didn't need mentioning. Maybe as a long-standing bar manager, Lauren had enough perception to see right through her. In any case, she would probably never see her again so it didn't matter. She would certainly not be running again anytime soon.

'Go on...'

'She reminds me of that darts player who won the World Championship. The bald one,' said Jenny, who was an expert in these things thanks to Bill.

Lonny raised his eyebrows. 'Great!'

Exhausted, but proud that she had at least made an effort, she showered, changed into a summer dress and sat out on the patio with Lonny, surveying the garden. It was the boys' cooking night and they had made a veggie chilli when they got in from football, then hurriedly gone back out again. In this hot weather it seemed like they were out all the time.

'That's the way it should be,' Lonny said when she voiced her concerns. 'I'd be more bothered if they were stuck in their room in this weather.'

Jenny nibbled on a dish of the chilli which had one flavour – heat; she winced and put it to one side. She wished she could have a dish of whatever Fusun and Ahmed were cooking. It smelt divine.

'Oh man,' said Lonny. 'Come on, Jen, you've got to make more of an effort with Fusun – her food!'

'It smells gorgeous doesn't it?'

'Let's invite them over next week sometime, then they'll have to invite us back.'

'No,' she said, not really knowing why, except a fear that if Lonny started insisting on her being friends with Fusun it might be Dawn next. God Almighty. She winced at the thought of it. No, she would do things her way. By hook or by crook she would have this make-up party and invite her kind of people to it and she would get to know Trudi a little more, and lovely Hannah from work would come too, and Emily would be home soon and back on the scene. She would have friends that she could be proud of, friends who she would want to spend time with, friends who would drag her out of this depression she was in. She knew Lonny didn't seriously expect her to become best mates with a younger woman who was busy looking after her twin babies. He just wanted them to be able to hang out in a neighbourly fashion like he did with Ahmed. To make the most of the things they might have in common: being a mother, cooking, hating the newlyweds. Maybe she should make an effort with Fusun. Maybe she could try a bit harder. But not just yet. No, the party was all that mattered now and very soon she would be printing off the invitations and handing one of them to Trudi at the creative writing class. She couldn't wait.

CHAPTER 13

The invitation

After another day of blistering heat an unexpectedly cool breeze blew through the car park of the community college and seemed to welcome Jenny with its soft caress. She had looked forward to this evening so much that she was even pleased to be seeing Celia the teacher again, and the retired ladies and that funny earnest young poet with the beard and all the other people she had met last week and hardly taken any notice of. She smiled graciously at everybody, while still marking her territory with her heavy handbag – she didn't want anyone encroaching on Trudi's seat beside her.

As the clock ticked towards six o'clock, she grew anxious – surely Trudi couldn't not turn up again? That would be ridiculous. Then a flood of people arrived all at once and the chairs began to fill up. Who were these people? She didn't remember there being so many last week. Celia was scouring the room for places to make sure everyone would have a seat. She began bossing people about and moving people around. Then she told the poet to shift into the space next to Jenny and she was forced to move her bag to the floor. Dammit! This was outrageous! A flash of anger swept across her face, which seemed to worry the poet a little. He looked a bit red-eyed today, a bit on the edge, so Jenny backed down from having a strop.

Even she knew that poets were sensitive types. Anyway, Trudi would be coming in soon with her lovely smile and she wanted to be calm and collected and to greet her with an equally lovely one.

And then, finally! In walked Trudi, looking absolutely gorgeous. A waft of roses filled the air, and what a beautiful tan; oh God, she was divine! But she wouldn't be able to sit any closer, the class was full to bursting.

Forced to sit right by the door, Trudi searched the room until she saw Jenny and then waved and smiled and mouthed, 'Hi!'

Jenny waved back, her other hand gripping the invitation which she would give to her at the end of the class. The stupid class. Never mind, she knew Trudi was interested in it so she would give it a shot. She would try to find something good about it. Despite not being able to sit next to her new friend, she settled down for the lesson feeling as happy as she had in a long time.

But the ninety minutes passed really slowly. Celia was giving them all sorts of exercises and reading materials and then, before she knew it, Daz the poet was reading out his latest efforts about his boyfriend – how he had found him and loved him and now lost him. Jenny winced, thinking that perhaps one day this would be her having to read out her own pathetic attempt and she wouldn't be able to get out of it because Trudi would be waiting to hear what she had to say. Oh dear God, this would soon be her, she couldn't bear it. She felt that the poet was watching her to see what she thought of his words. What did she think? She didn't know what she thought. Was it good or bad? How on earth would she know, she'd only been in the class five minutes.

In embarrassment, she looked out of the window and up at the ceiling and down at the floor as the poet's lament continued on and on.

'Before the times of old I knew you, before the frozen kiss of yesterday's yearning...'

Suddenly there was a screech of chair legs and Trudi stood up, mouthing 'Sorry' to Celia who looked at her watch and nodded 'OK' to Trudi.

What was this? What was happening? Trudi was leaving early and Celia must have known about it and yet she hadn't said anything to Jenny. Bitch. She wasn't having this. She wasn't going to wait another goddam week. Not on your life.

She stood up hastily, her chair also screeching on the floor tiles. The students who had all been looking at Trudi were now all watching Jenny as she bombed across the classroom towards her friend.

'Trudi, Trudi, I just wanted to give you an invitation to a party. Get the date in your diary, I'm sure you're very busy,' she whispered.

'That I should be the chosen one, that I should be the one your sinuous limbs reach for in the night...' Daz droned on with determination.

'Oh yes, absolutely!' whispered Trudi taking the invite and looking at the date. 'I'm pretty sure I can do the thirty-first. Count me in! Thanks so much, Jenny!' She reached out and gave her a quick hug and then turned and crept out of the room. Jenny waved and then turned and crept back to her seat. But really, there was no point in creeping. The poet had stopped speaking, Celia was looking cross and the whole class was smirking.

But Jenny didn't care two hoots. She had done it. She had invited Trudi to her home. The party was going ahead!

*

At home, she could barely hide her elation as she told Lonny of the plan. He nodded, pleased to see her so happy.

'Sounds great, duck!'

'It will be great won't it, Lon? It will be fantastic. And it will be the start of the new me. No more moping about. I know I've got to get out there and get on with my life, I know it's what Sue would have wanted.'

'It is, darlin'. So, who's coming besides Trudi then? Anyone I know?'

Jenny's face dropped a little but she said determinedly, 'The make-up lady says it has to be at least seven people including me. I'm not sure who I'll invite yet though; obviously Trudi, and Emily should be back home by then, maybe Hannah from work, she's a lovely girl.' She came to a grinding halt.

'What about Lauren from the Running Sisters?'

'Oh no, she's not the type, she wouldn't be interested. In any case she works in the evening, she's manager of the Rough Close Tavern.'

'She could get the night off.'

'No she couldn't.'

'Course she could –'

'No.'

Lonny sighed and thought hard for a few seconds.

'Hey, here's an idea, how about we get Jackie and his new girlfriend to dinner? Then if you like her, you can invite her.'

'Oh, Lon, that's a great idea! Have you met her? What's she like?'

'I dunno anything about her except she hates fish!'

'Oh that's so funny!' Jenny squealed with delight. Lonny's older brother Jackie, one of the Four Topsmonds, seemed to have had a crush on a work colleague called Miranda for ages; she must be wonderful. How exciting to meet her at last! She wrote her name down on the list as though it were a given. 'I can do a veggie lasagne or something just to be on the safe side.'

'No I'll do it, duck, leave it to me. I'll speak to Jackie and try and get them round on Wednesday night. You concentrate on your party,' said Lonny.

'Thanks, love,' she said and hugged him tightly. Things were looking up.

*

The next morning when the lads had gone to school and she could enjoy a nice cup of coffee in the garden before work, Jenny began to think about food and drink and possibly redecorating the living room before the day of the party dawned. She prided herself on her sense of style for interiors, the same way she did with her clothes, so everything was looking pretty good anyway, but maybe a new coat of paint on the walls would be a good idea. Just to freshen it up. Maybe she could do it on the weekend, after the dinner with Jackie and Miranda.

She mused that it was strange how the guys from the band hadn't provided more partners that she could be friends with, but Jackie and Charles were divorced and rarely dated now, and Viv and Godfrey were married but didn't socialise at all, they had grandkids that they helped to look after and anyway they lived up Burslem way, at the top of the city. She hadn't seen their wives for ages. She often thought that Viv and Godfrey didn't want her to be part of the gigs. She took an equal cut for one song, which perhaps wasn't fair, but they couldn't argue because Lonny was the boss and he said they should all have equal money. Maybe they would be happy if she quit. And she would quit one day soon, she knew it. Once Lonny had got his food forest or whatever it was. She didn't want that weird dream coming true and have to sing that dratted song forever. There was another gig coming up at the weekend, but it wouldn't bother her half as much now that she had the party to look forward to.

Lonny was further up the garden giving the small plants support sticks as they were already shooting upwards at a rapid rate. In theory, as it was only mid-May, a lot of the seedlings should still be in the greenhouse, but he had planted them out because the greenhouse was now like an oven. And the cucumber, squash and tomato plants in particular seemed to love being outside, they were growing inches every day. Plus the soil hiding under many layers of mulch was dark and much richer than it had been. Lonny was mesmerised. It was the first year he had grown things from seed, previously he had bought established plants from a garden centre, but this year was different and it was making a big difference to how he felt.

'Wow, look at you, look at you. You are amazing, you are doing so well,' he muttered to each one of them.

Suddenly Fusun's babies begin to cry next door. The kind of grating cry that might well go on for a while. And it was both babies. Jenny could see Lonny stand up and wince. Poor Fusun, she knew Ahmed was out at work. God knows how that poor woman was coping on her own with twins, it was hard enough one at a time. It doesn't bear thinking about, she thought, as Lonny came down the path towards her.

'Jen, the babies. Listen to that noise!'

'I know, poor Fusun, I don't know how she does it.'

'Why don't you go and give her a hand? I can't cos Ahmed's out, it will make her feel uncomfortable. She might be feeding or summat. Go on, go and give her a hand.'

'I can't, I've got work in half an hour –'

'Half an hour will do it, duck! Only takes ten minutes to settle a baby.'

'Lon, I can't go in there and say let me help but I've got to go soon; that's not helping at all!'

'It's better than nuthin', duck.'

'No it isn't, it's a wind up, offering help and then taking it away.' Really Lonny was too much sometimes. He could be such a bossy boots.

'I just want to help her,' he said. 'That noise would drive anyone mad.'

106

'Well put earplugs in then, she'll be less stressed if she knows they're not disturbing us.'

Lonny snorted and went back up the garden. At that moment, Dawn's music with its loud drum and bass began pumping out as though she too had heard the crying and this was her way of handling it.

'Oh my God!' Jenny sat up.

'See, that I can deal with,' laughed Lonny.

Jenny grimaced: crying babies on one side and horrible music on the other. The next thing she knew, her patio was being showered by sand and bits of gravel. A small stone landed in her coffee and splattered it across her t-shirt.

'Dawn!' she jumped up and hollered across the fence. 'Can you control your child please, I'm being showered in stones here!'

'Shenise!' Dawn roared up the garden. 'Stop it! Stop it now, yer little shit!'

'Dawn!' yelled Lonny. 'Watch yer language!'

Dawn's unruly face appeared at the fence. 'Sorry, Lonny,' she said. 'Sorry, Jenny.' But Jenny could only scowl. That fence needed another foot of wood on top of it. At least a foot, maybe two feet if it wasn't too expensive. She would tell Lonny that it had to be done. He wouldn't be happy but she would insist. Those shrubs were growing far too slowly. She had hoped they would be like the squash or the tomatoes, shooting up inches each day, but every time she looked at them they looked exactly the same.

Good grief, she thought, it comes to something when it's a relief going to work. I hope it's not hot on the night of the party. I hope it's cool enough so that Trudi and I can be in the living room and get some peace from this chaos.

She went inside and banged the door.

CHAPTER 14

The fence

The next morning she was up and at the fence with a tape measure. Another two feet should do it. It didn't have to go all the way to where the raised beds were, and the front garden could do without it too. But it was absolutely essential for the patio and the clothes line and her roses and everything near the house. And she didn't want it to be trellis either. It had to be proper fencing that would totally block *her* out.

Lonny watched her from the kitchen window. Bloody hell, it was only 7am and Jenny was already outside measuring the fence. He would have to think of some way to talk her out of this, but he hadn't slept well last night and he felt too weary to tackle it all at the moment.

Some nights, the enormity of the challenges facing humanity left him unable to sleep. What would happen to the lads? In ten or twenty years, the world would be an unrecognisably brutal one if things didn't change soon. Some days, when he saw them together with their mates on skateboards or playing footie or on the way home from school, big gangs of testosterone-driven teenagers giggling about who they fancied or slagging off teachers, he wondered how it had come to this; that they had been handed such an insanely bleak future, screwed over by the elite of previous generations who had trashed the planet in their rapacious drive for profit. Greedy, predatory men. Or was it the greedy, predatory capitalist system? Either way, it was all done so that a few idiots could sit in their ivory towers and look down on everyone else. But what use was that when there was no soil left to grow food and no water left to drink?

It was just after seven and he was sweating already. This heat was crippling and it was going to get a lot worse. It was already happening in the southern hemisphere, people were dying in huge numbers. People who had farmed the land for generations were forced to flee, they couldn't feed themselves. Refugees on the move, millions of them, because industrial agriculture had ruined the land. The soil, the place where both water and carbon should be stored, the miraculous, life-giving ground beneath us had been destroyed and left unable to function. Why wasn't anyone talking about it? Regenerating the soil was the answer to climate change, it was the answer to desertification, it was the answer to the destruction of the ecosystems, it was the answer to everything but it still wasn't mainstream, it was crazy. Maybe it was too late anyway, the weather was getting so extreme the planet must surely be fucked. He wiped a tear from his eye, he had to shift this feeling of being overwhelmed before the day started.

He thought of all the good stuff happening on the ground. Every day he heard about something amazing, some new invention, some different way of doing things that didn't exploit the earth or the people. And every day, permaculture and regenerative agriculture and renewable energy and tons of other exciting stuff were becoming more accepted. And on a local scale, things were seriously picking up, he had already leant a hand to the rewilding of the canal and the creation of the bee corridors and community veg gardens in many different areas. There was no doubt about it, there was plenty of good stuff happening. But would it be enough?

He made up his mind. He would definitely take the lads to the Ecosystems Restoration Camp in Spain in the summer where they could spend a few weeks volunteering. There was a webinar coming up where he would find out a bit more of what would be expected of them, but he was sure it wouldn't be anything too difficult. Of course, the heat might be a problem. But he wanted the lads to meet other people like him and Matt and Stella; to know that there were people all over the world who were eager to make things work for their generation and not just carry on protesting, or worse, act like nothing was happening. He needed to do it for his sake as much as theirs.

He made two cups of tea and took them outside and put them on the patio table. He walked over to Jenny and hugged her for a good while. He felt like Solly, he wanted to nuzzle into her hair or chest and lie there all day.

'You didn't get much sleep did you, babe?' she said. 'Why don't you go back to bed for a few hours before you go to B&Q?'

'Nah I'll be alright.'

'We need about two feet times five sections, Lon.'

'Do we? OK, duck.'

Just then the newlyweds' door opened with a bang and Dawn and the kids came out with their noise and cigarette smoke, announcing that the day had well and truly begun. Jenny immediately broke off from the hug and went indoors.

Lonny sighed; this was getting ridiculous. He went over to the fence, forcing a smile and a cheerful word.

'Hey Dawnie, you're up nice and early. You're on it aren't yer? You're on the case!'

'I dunno about that Lon, I just couldn't sleep in the heat!' She beamed, pleased that she was seeing her favourite man so early in the day. He always had something nice to say to her even if he was telling her off.

'How's Mark doing? I haven't seen much of him since you moved in.'

'Oh, he's alright, he's at work most of the time, he dunna hang around with us much. Careful, Shanelle!' she yelled up the garden. She sipped her coffee and took a drag on her first cigarette of the day, being careful not to blow any smoke in Lonny's direction.

'Is he interested in gardening? I'd be happy to give him some advice if he wants to grow some stuff.'

'Oh, he'd never do anything like that, Lon, he's not interested. I wouldn't bother him anyway, he's a right ignorant twat. He's a racialist and everything.'

'What?' said Lonny, shocked. 'You serious?'

'Yeah, unfortunately. But I'm not though,' she laughed nervously. 'It's just him, he's from a stupid family, they're all dead thick.'

'Yeah but Dawn, you've only just married him, you're newlyweds!'

'I know,' she said. 'It's shit int it?'

'Well, if it's shit, why the hell did you do it?'

Lonny's direct question unnerved Dawn a little. 'I dunno,' she said, the smile disappearing off her face, suddenly aware of how what she had just said would impact on her lovely neighbour.

'Yeah you do,' said Lonny, 'you must do.'

Dawn wiped her eyes hurriedly. 'I'm in a lot of debt Lon. I thought if I change my name and move, they won't be able to find me.'

'You can change your name without marrying anyone!'

'Can yer? Oh well, I didn't know that.'

'It doesn't work anyway, duck, it might buy you a few months but they'll find you in the end. Bloody 'ell, you're in a right mess aren't yer?' He patted her on the arm.

111

'Yeah I am,' she sniffed.

'Is he the girls' dad?'

'Yeah.'

'Well he's going to be around for the next fifteen or twenty years then, int he?'

Dawn looked as though she was thinking about the long-term implications for the very first time.

'D'you love him?'

'Nah I hate him.'

'Do yer?'

'Yeah, sometimes.'

'Well you're sending out mixed messages aren't yer, duck? You can't marry someone at the same time as hate 'em.'

'I just did,' she shrugged and then giggled, trying to lighten the conversation. Lonny didn't smile.

'Don't worry, Lon. He's a dickhead, but he's alright sometimes.'

'Is he? Glad to hear it, duck!'

Dawn laughed, hoping everything could now go back to normal.

But Lonny's face looked like it couldn't.

*

Matt was in the office when he saw Lonny and the boys cutting through the hedge. He finished his phone call and pulled the blinds back a little. As ever, Lonny was walking. If he wasn't walking, he was cycling. If he wasn't cycling, he was driving the electric community car. He used his own petrol car so infrequently that Matt had almost forgotten ever seeing him in it. He admired Lonny, he walked his talk and one day, hopefully in the not too distant future, he would be able to do the same. His little patch of land up in Leek was calling him.

He took his afternoon cigarette and went outside, grinning as he saw Lonny getting accosted by an old man.

'Here, Lonny, I hear they've outlawed those rotten pesticides! Well done, duck, well done!'

'Ta, duck,' laughed Lonny. 'But it wasn't just me, it was a big campaign. The whole country came together for that one. Very impressive wasn't it?'

Then a young grandma came up with her grandchildren in a double buggy.

'Hi, Lonny, I thought the pesticides had been made illegal. Why are they still using them then? It's absolutely outrageous!'

'It is illegal in this country now, duck, but the supermarkets are getting round it by importing food from abroad.'

'It's a loophole, int it, Dad?' chipped in Solly.

'It is, it's a loophole, but they're being sued right now and they're gonna lose big time, so don't worry about that.'

'Big Corporate never take any notice until people start suing them do they, Dad?' said Ryan.

'But why do they even do it when they know it's so harmful to the environment?' asked the woman.

'It's greed, pure greed,' said Lonny. 'That's what we're up against. It's the same as any fight anywhere. It's the people against Big Corporate, the people against the system. It's not farmers, they're just doing their job.'

'Well, I'm ashamed to say I never took any notice of things like this until my grandchildren were born. But from now on, if there's anything I can do to help, just let me know.'

'The best thing you can do, duck, is to grow your own food. That is the single most radical, most transforming thing you can do. And if you can't do that, then get a delivery from your local organic farmer. We've got to start putting the planet first and growing stuff in a way that improves the soil instead of destroying it. Good soil stores carbon for millennia! So it's a win-win situation. We need more soil with more plants growing in it, drinking in all the carbon in the atmosphere and giving us food at the same time! We're gonna get a green roof down here at *Aldi* aren't we, Matty? And plant a lot more trees and let the wild grasses grow. We've got to do that everywhere we can, across the whole country.'

Another woman was passing by, walking slowly to listen to what he was saying. Several other people were wandering over in their direction too.

'I've only got a tiny garden,' said the younger woman. 'There's no room for a veg patch.'

'Even if you've just got a little yard out back, you can grow summat,' insisted Lonny. 'Come on, let's all get on board, we can do this, let's help each other! Let's get everyone involved! There should be community gardens on every corner, in every school, every street, every town centre, we should have green growing on the roofs, on the walls. Fruit and veg growing everywhere that everyone can just help ourselves to, just like we do with blackberries in the summer. It's win-win! Good for the land and good for the people!'

'Yeah, but they'll make a law against it, Dad,' said Nate.

'What if they do?' roared Lonny, having fun now. 'We'll tell 'em to stick it where the sun don't shine! The government is supposed to be working for us, not the other way round!' Everyone screamed raucously.

An old lady grabbed his arm. 'I remember you Lonny, you're the man who helped my daughter re-wild the canal,' she said.

'Yes I am, duck, hold up, let me guess – are you Margaret's mum?'

'Yes, yes, duck! She said you were a tremendous help, said she couldn't have done it without you.'

'Ah bless her, duck, but that's not true. It's not about me or Margaret or any one person in particular, it's up to all of us now, everyone's got to get involved. We've got a lot to do, you know.' He winked.

One of the younger mums suddenly turned on Matt. 'And we should dig up these supermarket car parks too, we don't need 'em anymore! Well not this size anyway, you could have a bloody wildflower meadow here instead.'

'Yes!' said everyone. 'Much better.'

Matt put his hands up in defence, laughing. 'I agree with you, duck.'

'Brilliant idea,' said Lonny. 'Brilliant. How about we reduce all car parks across the country by fifty per cent! Matt, give her your boss's email address. Get a petition started and put it on social and I'll sign it and spread the word, duck.'

The boys looked on admiringly at their dad, giggling at the enthusiasm he had whipped up in the crowd. Eventually, when the people dispersed, Matt got a chance to hand over the contact details of the local leaders of the food club cafe.

'Cheers, Matt,' said Lonny. 'If this works it could be great.'

'How's Jenny doing?' asked Matt, taking advantage of the fact that the boys had wandered off.

'Ah, she's still not herself, duck, she's taken a dislike to the new neighbour and wants me to make the fence higher to block her out! I'm on my way to B&Q.' He nodded to the huge DIY store across the industrial park.

'That doesn't sound like Jen. She used to get on with everyone.'

'Not these days, it's like being married to the editor of the *Daily Mail* or summat, she's finding fault all the time.'

'She's depressed,' Matt shrugged. 'Grief can do funny things to you.'

'It can, duck.'

'What about her new friend Trudi?'

'Yeah, she doesn't find fault with her that's for sure. She's arranging a party so she can get her round to the house and you know... get to know her a bit better.'

'Oh yeah? What kind of party? They need any nice looking single blokes?'

Lonny laughed. 'Nah man, it's just for the ladies, some kind of make-up party, a woman comes round and dolls everyone up and then they buy stuff, that kind of thing. It's not for a couple of weeks.'

'You have to get her back on track, Lonny, she's your rock.'

'I know but it's difficult, it's like she keeps taking one step forward and two steps back.'

Solly had drifted over from the older boys towards his dad and Matt to gawp admiringly at the latter's muscles. Matt winked at him.

'Time for a haircut, Solly?'

'No, tinna.'

'I think it is.'

'He won't let anyone do it except this woman in Birmingham,' said Lonny, grabbing a chunk of Sol's Afro. 'Look at that!'

'Drastic action is called for,' teased Matt.

'No, tinna!' yelped Solly.

'Tis!'

'Tinna!'

'I've got clippers at home, I'll do it,' said Matt.

'No!' said Solly, running off.

The two men turned to each other pleased to be able to continue their conversation.

'Keep going, Lon,' said Matt. 'History favours the man of action.'

Lonny grunted. 'Don't talk to me about history. That'll make us all depressed.'

'So, where're you going now? To buy fencing?'

'Nah, I'm going to get a quote just to pacify her, there's no way I'm actually going to do it. I'm not interested in building bigger fences.'

*

Jenny was just about to put some tester paints on the living room wall when Ryan's guitar teacher Robbie stopped by to drop off some guitar strings. His new girlfriend, young and pretty and heavily made-up with spider-style fake lashes, heavy brows and glossy lips stood by his side. Jenny was instantly mesmerised.

'Sorry, Jenny,' said Robbie politely. 'This is my girlfriend Chloe. You haven't met her before have you?'

'How could she have met me before? We've only been going out a week! Oh he's a daft pillock!' Chloe said, fortunately with a lot of warmth.

'Hello, love,' Jenny said. 'Pleased to meet you. I must say I like your make-up, isn't it glamorous?'

Chloe blushed and beamed; this was clearly the ultimate compliment. 'Oh my God, Jenny, I absolutely love make-up! Oh my God, it's the real passion in my life, int it Robbie? I told him but he dunna really understand, but there's nuthin I would rather do than make someone over. I'm going to be a proper make-up artist, I'm going to go to college and study it. I'm going to set up me own YouTube channel and do makeovers on people and get thousands of subscribers and put it on Instagram too. I've already got me own Instagram account, I've had it fer ages, sum of 'em on there are dead crap, but some of 'em are good and I'm learning every day and you know the style I like to do, Jenny? It's kind of like art on yer face, like a beeeautiful scene of nature, like a pond wi' ducks or summat like that, like a dolphin in the ocean or summat –'

'On your face?' Jenny managed to interject.

'Oh yeah, it looks brilliant, dunt it, Robbie? Oh, he dunna know, I dunno why I'm asking him!'

'Come on, duck, stop blathering,' said an embarrassed Robbie.

'Oh shurrup, shurrup, I wunna be long, I'm just tellin' Jenny that it's absolutely amazin' and you should go on YouTube and search for face-painting with make-up, it's absolutely amazing, absolute works of art they are, Jenny and that's what I wanna do. I wanna be the Michelangelo of Stoke or summat like that. Works of art, but for faces, just for faces.' She ran out of breath and had to gasp for air. Jenny seized the opportunity.

'OK, I'll have a look on YouTube! Thanks Chloe, lovely to meet you. I'm sure I'll see you again. Bye-bye now, bye-bye. Bye-bye.

She shut the door.

God Almighty.

Although many would have presumed Jenny to be an extrovert, she was actually a hard-core introvert who was exhausted by people such as poor Chloe. What a shame she had that unstoppable gob on her, she thought as she collapsed into a chair. She could have invited her to the party otherwise.

After some rest and recuperation, she arranged the dining area nicely, ready for the visit from Jackie and his new girlfriend Miranda. She still had time on her hands so she tried out a few tester paints on the wall so that she could do a quick refresh the weekend before the party with Trudi. She was pretty sure she wanted the Farrow and Ball Hardwicke White, a kind of classic beigey grey, which would look spectacular with the white mantelpiece and cornices. Lonny had put in a wood burning stove a few years ago, but just lately he said he wanted to rip it out and put in some kind of rocket heater, at least that's what she thought it was called. Apparently it was much better for the environment and was a lot cheaper, but she hoped he wouldn't get round to it anytime soon, she loved her stove. When Trudi was visiting in the winter it would be nice to have it lit and have the room all cosy. Sue was the only person who was even better than she was at making a house look lovely; she had got most of her stuff from auctions and car boots. Either that or she had got Eddie to make something from scratch. She was so stylish. She wished she could ask her opinion on the paint colours. Inside her head, Jenny asked, 'What colour shall I go with babe? Hardwicke White, Old White or Shadow White?'

'Why are you asking me, darlin'? You've already made your mind up!' came the reply. Jenny smiled.

She dusted the photos on the wall and looked once again at those dimples that she loved so much. There will be no grey hair and wrinkles for you Sue, she thought, your beauty will never fade. 'You took my breath away sometimes, you were so perfect, like a proper princess weren't you?' she muttered as she dusted, noting that, strangely, she was feeling happy to be spending time with her, just to be looking at Sue's face again bought some level of joy. And all thoughts of fences and snobbishness vanished and her heart was open and kind and loving.

Then came the stab in the heart and the torturous twist that she had to cope with every day. She was still here in this world but Sue wasn't, she was gone and she would never see her again. The pain gripped her yet again, her heart closed up tight and she felt bitter and fearful and alone.

CHAPTER 15

Invasion

At five to seven, Jenny remembered something in the nick of time.

'Oh my God!' she squealed and rushed into the downstairs toilet to quickly pull Lonny's sign off the wall – '*Don't waste your pee! Make a donation into the jug (female) or watering can (male). Regenerating the soil sponge will help restore ecosystems and drawdown carbon. (And don't make a mess lads!)*'– and remove said jug and watering can. She didn't want to put Miranda off at their first meeting!

Lonny stood at the front window as Jackie parked his car in the mostly empty road. Or tried to at least. Back and forth he went, as cautious as ever, and all the time using more petrol. Lonny snorted as the manoeuvring went on and on.

'You've got loads of room!' he shouted out of the window.

But Jenny wasn't concerned about Jackie's parking, she wasn't concerned about Jackie at all. She peered nervously into the front passenger seat. Finally, Miranda got out of the car, a lovely looking forty-something woman, dressed in the bold, primary colours of the season. Her first thought was, ooh she looks nice.

But at the same time she heard Sue's voice in her head, laughing: 'Looks aren't everything you idiot!' and a tight knot formed in her stomach.

Through the years, she had met Jackie's various wives and girlfriends and knew that he attracted women who walked all over him. He was a softie after all. And he could dither for England. He needed to stand up to people, Lonny was always telling him, but he never seemed to listen. He was fifty-two now, nine years older than Lonny, and after three divorces, he should presumably be getting better at choosing the women in his life. He deserved to meet someone nice who showed him a bit of respect and didn't try and pummel him into submission. Would Miranda be the one? And, more importantly, would she be number five on Jenny's party list? As she came down the path, hand in hand with a loved-up Jackie, the chances were looking good. She might have a new friend by the end of the evening and a new sister-in-law possibly, before too long. How exciting.

Lonny spotted the eager look on his wife's face. 'What d'you think?'

'She looks lovely!'

'Yeah, so did the others,' he said and went to open the door. 'Hiya, duck!'

He was grabbed by a pair of bejewelled hands and kissed firmly on the lips. Jenny smiled – Lonny never kissed anyone except her and the boys and his mum, but Miranda wasn't giving him any choice. He would have hated that.

'What a beautiful face! Just like your lovely brother! And yes, I can see the resemblance! I can, I can!'

'He's going grey though,' said Lonny wiping his mouth.

'No you daft apeth – Donny Osmond! I can see it!'

'Oh, yeah well, should have gone to Specsavers –'

'Hahahaha. Oh, he's a funny man as well, fantastic!'

'Miranda, this is my wife Jenny –'

A slight tension was palpable the second that Miranda laid eyes on Jenny, but Jenny was far too welcoming to pick up on it. She was over the moon at the possibility of getting to know Miranda. So over the moon in fact that it made her seem a little starstruck.

'Hello, Miranda, lovely to meet you at long last. We've heard a lot about you from Jackie over the last few months!'

'Oh really, he's been talking about me has he? Well I can't say I'm surprised, I always knew he fancied me.' She winked. 'I tried to hold out as long as I could, I wasn't sure about him to be honest. I thought anyone who's been married four times before –'

'Three times, duck,' said Jackie.

'Three times and a long live-in partnership, duck, that's as good as a marriage to me.'

'It's all in the past though,' said Jackie, looking rather uncomfortable.

'The dim and distant past, duck!' Lonny jumped in to help his brother. 'No need to bother about that now. What's important is that we have a lovely evening, int it? Now then, who's ready for a nice cold glass of prosecco?'

'Oh, yes please, I'm always ready for that!' Miranda looked around the room and clocked the gallery of pictures and the many houseplants and flowers and colourful rugs picked up at auctions, charity shops and car boots over the years. Jenny smiled and hoped she would get a compliment for her good taste, as she usually did from anyone coming into the house for the first time.

But no, not on this occasion.

'How are you enjoying the heatwave, Miranda?' Lonny asked as he poured the wine.

'Well I've had air con fitted and that's made a heck of a difference, Lonny. I thoroughly recommend it. You haven't got it have you?'

'No, we certainly have not,' said Lonny.

'Shame. Oh well, I hope I last the evening,' she said, fanning herself.

*

It was a little later, when they were eating the first course of stuffed mushrooms and salads, that Lonny began to realise what they were dealing with. Amongst his circle of friends, the drive to stop climate change and the destruction of the ecosystems was a never-ending conversation, leading to never-ending action. He didn't really know many people who didn't think this way – surely everyone with a brain in their head thought this way?

But when he apologised about the annoying plastic seal wrapped around the top of the second bottle of wine, explaining that he normally managed to get home-made stuff from his friends Stella and Jeff but they had run out, Miranda dismissed it.

'Oh, don't start about the plastic, Lonny. Honestly, the amount of fuss they make these days. It just goes on and on doesn't it? What a lot of nonsense!'

'You're right there, duck,' agreed Jackie.

'Well, it needs to go on and on, that's the only way they take notice,' said Lonny, shocked. 'Think of all the damage it's doing. It's poisoning the oceans, it's part of the reason we've got so little fish these days.'

'Well that doesn't bother me one little bit, I don't eat the slimy stuff,' Miranda pulled a face. 'I can't even bear a mention of them.'

'I told you she hates fish,' said Jackie, looking cross with Lonny for bringing them up.

'Yeah, but even so, the ocean is of paramount importance, it's a –'

'Don't worry, Miranda, tonight's menu is entirely fish-free!' said Jenny, trying to keep things pleasant.

Miranda glared at Jenny for mentioning the 'f' word and ignored her comment. She turned to Lonny. 'So long as it's still blue when I go to Tenerife I don't give a hoot!'

'We'll be there in a couple of months, just you wait and see!' Jackie winked and put his arm around her.

'Ooh, are you taking me on holiday? You lovely fella!'

Jackie grinned, triumphant.

'I thought you said you were skint,' Lonny said to his brother.

'Haven't you heard of credit cards, Lonny?' laughed Miranda.

Lonny tried to suppress a wince as he turned away. There would be no prizes for guessing that his brother's new girlfriend would be walking all over him soon, just like the others had done. What a fool he was. What an absolute bloody prat.

Meantime, Jenny was mirroring Miranda's healthy thirst. She didn't often drink much alcohol, but sometimes needs must. She poured herself another large glass while she tried to figure out the effect that Jackie's beautifully turned out new girlfriend might have on Trudi if she came to the party. Miranda would be perfect if she would just be a little quieter and a little less opinionated. As it was, she seemed to have an emphatic opinion on just about everything, like now for instance.

'Don't bother with those Four Tops songs, Lon! Take my advice, duck, stick with the Osmonds, you'll go much further!' Miranda waggled her finger at Lonny.

'It's the Four Tops that keep me going Miranda; if it was just the Osmonds. I wouldn't do it.'

'Nonsense! Everyone loves the Osmonds, the Four Tops, well – your average person has never heard of 'em.'

'What?' said Lonny. 'The Four Tops are Motown, duck! Motown! Everyone knows the Motown classics!'

'Do they?' Miranda shrugged.

Jenny jumped in to rescue her. She didn't want their guest getting the hump so early in the evening, although it was beginning to feel like the kind of evening where somebody would get it, that was for sure.

'I think it's us women who love the Osmonds, isn't it, Miranda? Who didn't love Donny when they were a little girl, hey?'

'Personally, I'm not old enough, duck, but I know what you mean.'

'Oh well, I'm not old enough either, it was my friend's big sister who got us singing his songs,' said Jenny.

'Yes, and that's why those gigs are a good idea, because all you older women are still carrying a torch for him!'

As Jenny was reeling from this, Miranda continued, 'But as for Marie, it's a shame int it? Jackie told me all about the abuse you get at the gigs. Sounds awful, duck. Some people just don't know how to behave, that's all I can say.'

'Oh well, it's not that bad.'

'Is it true that someone spat at you once?'

'I never said that, duck, where d'yer get that from?' said a worried Jackie.

'Well you must be thick-skinned, jolly good, you need to be sometimes don't you?'

Jenny tried to avoid Lonny's eye. He was nudging her foot under the table. He had probably made his mind up about Miranda by now, but she hadn't, she needed more time. It was pretty clear things were not turning out as she had hoped, but dammit, she needed to fill up her guest list for the party. What was wrong with this woman, why couldn't she just be nice? Maybe she was nervous, after all she was meeting Jackie's brother when they hadn't been dating that long. Or maybe it was the booze. Maybe if she kept her on alcohol-free wine for the first few glasses? She could keep a separate stash in the fridge just for her, she could syphon it into an empty bottle of proper wine so that she would never know. She made an excuse to get the next course from the kitchen and Lonny quickly joined her.

'Bloody 'ell, she's something else int she?'

'She's a bit nervous I think,' Jenny whispered back.

'Nervous? I'd say it's more than that, duck.' Lonny racked his brain for something positive to say before conceding, 'I've got a bad feeling.'

'Well, we have to make an effort; look at Jackie – he's smitten!'

So when she got back to the table with a big tray of home-made veggie lasagne and Lonny's garlic sourdough bread, she redoubled her efforts.

'Have you got any children, Miranda?' she said, thinking that this should be safe ground. After all, a yes or no answer should suffice.

'Oh no, no, no! I made that decision when I was younger. If I want to keep this –' she motioned to her trim but unremarkable body 'in good shape, the last thing I need is kids. Oh no, all those stretch marks and saggy boobs! You've had three haven't you, duck? Poor old Lonny, that's all I can say!' She laughed loudly.

'Miranda,' said Lonny, stepping up to the plate, 'when your wife's given birth to your children, you love her body even more, you're not bothered about a few stretch marks.'

'Oh he's good, he's good, what a gentleman!' She turned to Jenny and mouthed, 'He's such a liar, your husband!' and laughed loudly again. Like a machine gun going off, Jenny thought.

'Actually, I got back in shape in no time,' she smiled through gritted teeth.

'That's right, you did, duck,' said Lonny. 'All that running.'

Jackie was helping himself to a supersize plate of lasagne. 'And what about Sheila? She lost a load of –'

'Who's Sheila?' demanded Miranda.

'Me ex-wife number three, duck.'

'So? What about her?'

'Well, she lost six stone after the twins were born and she was more fit at forty than she was at twenty fi –'

'Excuse me, Jackie, do you mind? Show me some respect! I don't want to hear how fit your blinkin' ex-wife was, do I?'

'Sorry, duck, I was just sayin' –'

'Well, don't!' She raised her eyebrows to Lonny and Jenny. 'Ex-wife number three – bloody hell fire! All I hear about are his exes.'

'Trouble is, there's a lot of 'em,' quipped Lonny. 'He dunna do much else besides get married!'

He nudged Jenny's foot under the table. 'She was nice, old Sheila, wasn't she? Nice – but a bit of a cold fish.'

'Yes, she was a cold fish, I remember.'

Across the table, Miranda squirmed at the word 'fish' and Jackie opened his hands in annoyance.

Lonny took a momentary pleasure at their joint discomfort and thought hard of other phrases which involved the word 'fish'. It might be the only way to bring the evening to an early close.

Jenny was growing increasingly nervous. This dinner party was proving to be quite unlike any other she had ever given. Or attended for that matter. She felt shy and awkward in front of Miranda. She had rather hoped that she might warm to her and that by now they would both be giggling about embarrassing fashions they used to wear or Netflix series they had seen or silly things that men did or children or pets they had or... anything really. Instead, she felt a very strong urge to hide under the table until she had gone.

Appearances could be so deceptive. Just like Storm Helen had appeared to be nothing much initially, just a bit of a breeze; but then, when she went out to lock the garage door, the wind was smashing up the fence and it had picked her up and pinned her against it like she was just one of Solly's soft toys. Nothing of any weight or substance, just a scraggy thing to be picked up and flung somewhere.

And now there was something that felt similarly disruptive right across the table. She tried hard not to let the disappointment show on her face. But what a shame it was. And what a waste. Miranda had looked so lovely when she walked down the path. If she could just get her on the right track somehow, a track where she was comfortable, where she could show her best side, where she could show what a nice person she was. But the rate she was going, this seemed nigh on impossible.

'What about this Citizens Assembly nonsense then?' Miranda said, already beginning to slur her words. 'Can you believe it? The cheek of people thinking we should listen to them. It's completely outside the government you know, it's not even legal! I don't want some old grandma or a bunch of kids down the road making decisions on my behalf, I want the men who have been trained to do it!'

'They're the ones who created this bloody mess!' said Lonny, gobsmacked.

'Well, maybe it's not a bad idea to involve the kids down the road!' said Jenny, realising that if she didn't at least join in the conversation she would never be able to steer it in the right direction. 'I mean, it's their future isn't it?'

'It's my future I'm bothered about, duck, I don't give a flying foxtrot about theirs! Seriously, what would they do for the rest of us beyond bringing down the price of glue! I mean, for Christ's sake guys!' She laughed again. Lonny winced.

'No, tinna like that, duck,' he said. 'Kids these days are different −'

'You must be thinking of your old glue-sniffing mates at Longton High,' grinned Jackie, nudging Miranda's arm.

'What are you on about? I never went to Longton High.'

'Didn't yer?' he said, before realising. 'Oh sorry, duck, must have been someone else.'

Miranda raised her eyebrows and tutted. 'To get back to my original point, Lonny,' she said, her finger prodding the table. 'What we need is a return to the old days, the real old days when Great Britain meant something in the world. Now, I know you don't like all this posh lot in government, but one thing you can say for them is that they are certainly trained on how to run a country, they learn it all at their boarding schools you know.'

'I'll tell you what they learn, duck,' said Lonny, beginning to lose it, 'how to loot and plunder and exploit the planet, that's what they fucking learn! And they're not allowed to leave school till they've got a Grade fucking A!'

'Lonny, stop swearing!' said Jenny.

'This whole system,' said Lonny, finding it difficult to stop, 'is built on colonialism, and colonialism was never the good old days by any means, duck. People suffered. Big time.'

'So what if they did? It's ancient history. It's got nothing to do with nowadays.'

'It's got everything to do with nowadays, duck! Everything. Here, let me lend you one of me books.' He stood up and walked over to the bookshelf, wiping the sweat from his brow on the way. God, the stress of it – and they were only an hour in. If he'd known such a fascist was coming to dinner – a fascist and a bloody fool – he would have gone up the allotments. He thought of the solitary magpie which had swooped down into the front garden before the visitors arrived, possibly a signal from Mother Nature of the impending invasion of an alien force. After all, Mother Nature always gives warnings if we look for them. Like the cows turning their bums to the east and lying down in unison when the bad weather comes in from that direction. Or the bees and butterflies not visiting their usual plants when a storm is due. Or flowers smelling stronger before the rain. Of course, he hadn't thought to take any notice of that magpie and now it was too late. The evening was still young and there might be several torturous hours to go.

'Sit down, Lonny, I don't bother with books,' said Miranda. 'I don't need any books to tell me what to think. I can find what I want on the internet. Jackie says you're a big one on climate change as well. You shouldn't be so gullible, you should think for yourself like wot I do!'

'A flood, two hurricanes and a heatwave this year and it's only blinkin' May!' Lonny shouted. 'People are dying in the heat!'

'Well they should have air con fitted then shouldn't they?' she chuckled and winked at him as he sat back down.

'More carbon emissions!' said Jenny, trying to muscle in.

'Most people can't afford to have it done anyway, duck,' said Jackie, helping himself to a huge wedge of homemade garlic bread and devouring it in one bite.

'Well, they can do what I do then and put it on the old credit card! Seriously, Lonny,' she said, 'there's nothing wrong with having a heatwave every summer. What's not to like?'

'It's not as simple as that, Miranda –'

'Some people are so skint they can't get credit though,' insisted Jackie. 'It's all the damage from austerity int it?'

'Oh please, there's always plenty of money around for those who don't mind a bit of hard graft. Recession or no recession, there's more money around today than at any time in history. Fact! More millionaires and billionaires than ever before. Int it marvellous?'

'I wish I were one of 'em,' grinned Jackie. 'I'd buy a big yacht and whisk you –'

'What's bloody marvellous about it?' said Lonny, hastily swallowing his food and banging down his fork. 'How about we have less billionaires and more black rhinos? That'd be a lot more marvellous.'

'Would it? Are you sure?' Miranda laughed.

'Money's not wealth, duck! What good is money if all the ecosystems have gone and you've got no clean air and no water and no soil to grow food in? It counts for nothing!'

'I've lived in Stoke all me life, Lonny, bit of pollution never did me any harm! We're made of stronger stuff you know, we're not a bunch of wimps –'

'Well, I'm not anyway,' said Jackie flexing a bicep. 'Feel that.'

Miranda touched his arm. 'Ooh very nice!' and that machine gun laughter went off again.

'Now then,' said a flustered Jenny, 'is everyone ready for dessert?'

*

'Fuckin' hell!' muttered Lonny to Jenny in the kitchen. 'I'm flagging. I dunno how I'm going to get through this.'

'Come on, we have to find a way of getting on with her,' said Jenny. 'Just stop talking about the environment!'

'I can't do it!' he hissed, grabbing another two bottles of wine.

*

'Hey, Jen, tell Miranda about your party,' said Jackie as his sister-in-law dished out home-made fruit crumble and posh ice cream.

'Oh!' said Jenny, taken by surprise and dropping the serving spoon.

'Si said you were having a little party to try and make some new friends,' said Jackie, continuing to put his big foot in it.

131

'Oh no, no, no,' she said, mortified. 'It's not like that. It's just a little gathering.'

'Oh, that's right,' said Miranda, looking up from her phone. 'Your best friend died didn't she, duck and you haven't got any others. Sorry to hear that.'

'Well, it's not really like –'

'She does have other friends, but they've all moved away,' said Lonny, glaring at his brother. 'Doesn't matter, there's plenty more fish in the sea int there, duck?'

'What did I tell yer? I said don't talk about fish in front of Miranda,' muttered Jackie, glaring back. 'Yer keep talking about fish.'

'So, what about the local women?' asked Miranda.

'They're not my type really,' said Jenny, beginning to wish that the ground would open up beneath her.

'Oh no? Hmm.'

'I have tried,' she assured her.

'Have you? Right. So, what's this party going to be like?'

'It's not a proper party really, it's just a little gathering,' said Jenny. 'It's Neal's Yard Organic skin care and make-up. They give you demonstrations and you can try out all their products.'

'Oh, don't waste your time with them, duck. Organics is just an excuse to charge a few extra quid.'

'That ain't true,' said Lonny. 'Organics is for people who don't want to be poisoned by Big Agriculture.'

'Oh Lonny, don't go falling for all the spiel! I'm disappointed in you!'

'The soil is dying, duck. Pesticides kill the soil. And they're killing us too!'

'Well I don't see anyone dropping down dead after they've eaten dinner.'

'No, but haven't you wondered why everyone is fucking ill? Diabetes, obesity –'

'Lonny stop swearing!' said Jenny.

'Don't be so daft, those people just need a bit more self-control,' said Miranda.

'We're being poisoned!' Lonny hollered across the table. 'Slowly poisoned by industrial agriculture! And they're killing the soil too!'

'Heavens above!' Miranda cackled. 'What's the answer then? Would you rather we didn't eat?'

'I'd rather we ate stuff we grew ourselves or we bought from local farmers who are trying to regenerate the soil and save the planet. That's what we need, not the crap that's sold us by the money men. The stinking rotten money men in big corporate agriculture!'

'Oh I do like a passionate man!' She winked at Jackie. 'You never told me your brother was like this, he's a bloody dynamo int he?'

'Bit too much of a dynamo if you ask me,' Jackie commented quietly. 'We're not farmers you know Si, we dunno what you're on about. Bloody soil.'

'Ignorance is bliss Miranda. Ignorance is bliss!' Lonny shouted one last time. He felt weary. Fucking 'ell, his brother was a clown. Couldn't he see that this woman was ridiculous? He wiped his brow. This heat was ridiculous too. And now he was ridiculous because he'd been sucked right into an argument instead of rising above it. He realised he couldn't rise above it anymore, time was too short. He poured another glass of wine as though the only way out of the situation was to drink more.

'Remember you're driving Ryan down south tomorrow, love,' Jenny said.

Lonny snorted. 'I onna doing that. We'll get the train.'

Having exhausted Lonny, Miranda finally turned to Jenny. 'Why don't you just have a normal party, Jenny? Have you got bad skin?'

'Not that I'm aware of,' said Jenny, a little sarcastically, looking at her bare arms.

'What about rashes, have you got any rashes?'

Lonny roared with laughter.

Jenny turned to him. 'Lon – have I got rashes on my body?'

'I can't see for your stretch marks, duck, bloody stretch marks all over the shop.'

'Is that true, Lonny? See, I was right wasn't I? I'm always right!' squealed Miranda.

'Fucking 'ell!' said Lonny, barely under his breath.

Jackie was still thinking about the previous conversation. 'Maybe it's those pesticides making you sick, Miranda, 'cos you often have time off work don't yer?'

'I do not! No more than the next person anyway. Who are you – bloody HR?'

'Well no, I was just saying –'

'Well don't!'

Good job the crumble is on the stodgy side, thought Jenny in the silence that followed, at least when people are chewing they can't shout at each other. She thought again of the nice barely worn patch of rug under the table. It seemed to be calling her, enticing her down there; maybe if she pretended to drop something, just a spoon say, perhaps with some crumble on it so there would be some mess to clear up. Then she could pass a few minutes doing that. Maybe even drag it out to ten or fifteen. Of course, she might get accidentally kicked in the stomach but that was preferable to –

'By the way, Jenny duck,' said Miranda, 'a word of advice about making new friends.'

Jenny stopped chewing.

'Now, I'm just saying this with your best interests at heart. I know a lot about these things, 'cos I'm studying psychiatry online –'

'Don't you mean psychology?' Lonny asked, his eyebrows practically reaching his hairline.

'Yes that too, Lonny, it's all of 'em put together.'

'All the psycho stuff,' said Jackie, chewing his pudding.

'It's a proper course is it?' asked Lonny, trying to keep a straight face.

'Yes, it's a three-month intense one.'

'Intense?'

'Yes, very.'

'It's hard work int it, duck?' said Jackie.

'You can say that again.'

'You put a lot of effort into it, don't yer?'

'Well I don't mind putting a lot of effort into it, I don't mind that at all,' said Miranda, beginning to run out of patience. 'It's only three months and then I'll be qualified.'

'Go on, what qualification is that then?' asked Lonny, pouring himself another drink.

'It's a certificate.'

'Print it off yourself?'

'Oh no, no, they post it to you, Lonny, it's all framed and everything.'

'She's dead clever you know,' said Jackie admiringly.

'She must be,' said Lonny.

'Anyway, Jenny –'

'She knows whodunnit before the crime's even been committed –'

'Does she?' said Lonny. 'That's amazing that is!'

'She –'

'Christ Almighty! Will you let me speak please, Jackie!' Miranda tutted, her eyes rolling for the tenth time that evening. She turned back to Jenny with an attempt at a charming smile. 'I was just going to suggest, love, that if you're trying to make new friends and you're not getting anywhere –'

Jenny tried to swallow but couldn't.

'If you're not getting on with people, if you feel like there's no connection, if you're turning up your nose at this one and that one and the other one and you're finding that no one's good enough, then you might need to work on developing your social skills, duck. Just a suggestion. I've noticed them sadly lacking tonight. You're not really a people person are you?'

Jenny slumped back in her chair. She felt like fainting or bursting into tears – but no, she wouldn't give the cheeky bitch the satisfaction. She took a deep breath instead. God Almighty, would this evening ever end? Right now, she was sure she would be having more fun sitting opposite Dawn and that was saying something.

The thought made her suddenly burst out laughing.

'What's so funny?' demanded Miranda.

Jenny ignored her and turned to whisper in her husband's ear. 'I was just thinking we'd be having a better time if we'd invited Dawn!' she giggled.

Lonny smiled and hugged her. 'That's right, duck, we would.'

CHAPTER 16

In recovery

The next morning saw Lonny sprawled in a helicopter position across the floor and Jenny sleeping scrunched up on the sofa. As the early morning sunlight poured into the room and they began to stir, Jenny remembered that it was a Thursday and a school day and the boys would be down shortly. She groaned and stretched and thought of the lesson she had learnt, which of course she knew anyway: Don't judge a book by its cover, dumbo! Miranda was so sunny faced and pretty and well dressed, but that was all just a trap to lure you in. Underneath the shine lurked a bloody fascist, as her Dad used to say about Thatcher. But at least they had got rid of her quickly. When Miranda grabbed Lonny and tried to tango him round the lounge, Jenny had shoved her favourite fish cook book in front of her face until she ran screaming from the house, and then, when she was safely out, had slammed the front door with even more gusto than she did with Dawn out the back.

God Almighty, what an evening. They must have crashed out straight afterwards. She looked at Lonny beginning to stir on the floor. It had been a long time since she had seen him that drunk. His throat would be hoarse today. Still, it had seemed like the only option at the time.

She drank a large glass of water and then went upstairs to shower. As she was washing, she thought of the party list. She was back to just three guests: Trudi, Emily, Hannah and herself. It obviously hadn't worked out with Miranda but thank goodness she had found out what she was like in advance. Still, the fact was that she had to find three or four more women from somewhere. She must remember to ask Hannah at work today, they would only overlap by five minutes but that would give her enough time. The Neal's Yard lady had said she wanted at least seven. Obviously she needed some commission. Maybe she could explain that there would only be four, but that they would all buy a lot; she could always rely on Emily to buy something, she always had money. But then again, Hannah was always broke and she knew nothing about Trudi's finances; she dressed really well but it might all be second-hand stuff from eBay just like her own clothes. No, she needed more women at the party. Maybe she should ask Trudi if there was anyone she might want to bring. But she had already said she didn't know anyone and anyway that would mean her attention would be with her friend and not Jenny, it would spoil the dynamics.

She got out of the shower feeling worse than when she had got in. She had intended to shave and trim her body hair but she didn't feel up to it. Quite frankly she didn't feel up to anything. She noticed her eyes were beginning to tear up again. Partly from the stress of last night – what a waste of time that had been – and partly due to her being so stupid as to let all her friendships drift away over the last few years. She hadn't made any effort to bring in new blood and now it was all coming home to roost. She might miss this chance with Trudi because if she got wind that she was Jenny No Mates, she would dump her like a ton of hot bricks – no one likes a loser. She stumbled into the bedroom and began to sob, huddled in her wet towel on the bed. This hangover wasn't helping either.

Lonny came in with his own sore head. 'What's up, babe?' He lay down on the bed and put his arm around her.

'I don't know how I'm going to make it to seven people, Lon,' she sobbed. 'Trudi will see that I've got no friends and she'll think I'm a loser.'

'Bloody 'ell Jen, how old are you? Twelve? It's just a stage in your life cos of circumstances. You've always had tons of friends. You shouldn't worry, you'll make tons more.'

'But the party's in less than two weeks!'

Lonny groaned. 'Duck, calm down. I need to get over having Laurel and Hardy for dinner. I can't think straight.'

He turned over with a sigh and was out for the count. It was lucky that he could get some more sleep as he had to escort Ryan to meet his dad in Hereford later. He would need to be on the ball for that. Jenny wished she could sleep too but she had to get Ryan's bag organised and the lads off to school, and then there was Joyce to deal with later this afternoon. She didn't think she would take her out anywhere today; she was exhausted and time with Joyce could be massively challenging at the best of times. She often talked complete nonsense for hours. Not nonsense that you could ignore, but nonsense that asked questions, demanded answers, disputed answers, argued about nothing and repeated, repeated, repeated. God it was exhausting, but it was only three hours and sometimes she would be quiet the whole time. Let's hope today would be one of those days.

She remembered she had a Zoom call with Amy and Alice later that morning. That would be lovely, it was always a pleasure to see her god-daughters. In the meantime, she had to get the lads off to school quickly so that she could start the big clear up after that awful dinner party.

Downstairs, Ryan looked like he hadn't slept either. He was a quiet boy and whenever a visit to his real father beckoned he seemed to disappear further into himself. Jenny hugged him. 'Alright honey? Are you up for this? You don't have to go if you don't want to, you know.'

'I do really, Mum.'

'No you don't. We can just say you're sick.'

'No, it'll be OK, it doesn't happen very often. Is Dad feeling alright after last night?'

'He needs a bit more sleep I think, and you'll be getting the train, he won't be fit to drive.'

'I'll look at the times online,' he said.

'Have you cancelled Robbie for this evening?' she asked him.

'Yeah, I messaged him,' he replied.

She kissed him and hugged him and, as she often did when he was making this trip, worried that she may never see him again. It was a bit of a wild stretch of the imagination, but she couldn't help it. She just hated him having to do this. After all, she had split with Alan when he was a baby, how could there be a father–son relationship? It was a farce. Lonny was Ryan's dad now, it was Lonny he loved.

'What did you think of Miranda, Mum? Is she coming to the party?'

'Over my dead body,' Jenny said grimly.

Ryan laughed and picked up his guitar to strum. Nate came down in just his pyjama shorts. He hitched up his leg and farted loudly. Jenny gave him a glare; she wasn't in the mood for this.

'Mum! Can I have toast?'

'Yes you can, love, the bread is in the kitchen!'

'Aw Mum!'

He collapsed on the sofa in fake agony, hands swiftly delving into his pyjama trousers for a comforting grope.

'How are you going to be a great footballer when you've got such a bad case of lazyitis?' Jenny said, yanking his hand out. 'Leave it alone!'

'I anna got lazyitis, I'm just starvin'!'

Solly sauntered in, sleep in his eye, thumb in his mouth. He plonked himself on the floor in front of the tele and immediately his massive Afro blocked the screen.

'Mum!' shouted Nate. 'Sol's hair needs to be cut, man! I can't stand it.' He tried to shove his brother out of the way, but Sol fought back and soon it was a scrap.

Jenny snapped; her headache was getting worse. 'Come on, Solly move yourself! Look at that hair, it's way too big, it's absolutely massive!'

Solly swung round. 'That's what she said!' he said and burst into hysterical laughter.

'I beg your pardon!'

'Sorry, Mumma!'

'What have I told you about these stupid jokes? They're not funny you know!'

'They are, Mumma!'

'They are not, they're disgusting! And now Solly has picked them up from you Nate, I hope you're pleased with yourself!'

'Tinna my fault!'

'Yes it bloody well is!'

She stormed out to the kitchen and started banging pots around. God Almighty, how much easier it must be having a little girl like Freya who would get up and do a bit of crayoning in the morning. She eventually managed to pack them off to school, hurrying them all out of the door, and giving Ryan an extra hug and telling him that Lonny would meet him in the school car park at lunchtime.

She tidied the kitchen and put the dishwasher on from last night. She couldn't believe that they had been so drunk they had left it all overnight. Her mother would flip if she could see the mess. She looked out of the window and saw Dawn over the fence. Her neighbour didn't look too happy this morning but at least she wasn't shouting at her kids. How funny that she had ended up thinking that an evening with Dawn would have been preferable to that bloody obnoxious Miranda. What a truly awful woman she must have been to make her think that!

After an hour or two of clearing up, Lonny had gone off to meet Ryan and Jenny was ready for the call with Amy and Alice. She had managed to keep in regular contact with them since Sue died, but was always longing to see them more often and hug them and feel them in her arms and smell their hair and their cheeks as she kissed them. It was the closest she could get to her friend and she could eat them alive, she loved them so much.

'Hello, my darlings,' said Jenny as the two girls lit up her screen. 'You're getting more beautiful every day I swear.'

They talked for a good while about A-levels and studying and friends and boyfriends and their plans. Then eventually, when the time felt right, Jenny asked them about the elephant in the room: their father's engagement. There was a pause.

'I just want him to be happy really, Jen,' said Amy. 'He was terrible after Mum died, he just went to pieces and we thought we wouldn't be able to leave him at all. I expected to have to defer college for a year to look after him. I mean, he was so depressed he hardly got out of bed. He couldn't go to work, he couldn't do anything.'

Jenny's face softened a bit as she heard this. They hadn't really mentioned this before. So he had been grief-stricken then. Good.

'Charlotte is a lovely person. I think Mum would approve of her,' said Alice.

'And it lets us off the hook a bit because it would be terrible if we

142

had to worry about him being lonely and isolated when we were away at college.'

'I suppose so,' Jenny said reluctantly, humbled by the maturity of both girls. 'But I'm still surprised that it happened so fast.'

'Our grief counsellor says men often move on a lot quicker than women. They can't cope otherwise, they just go to pieces.'

'Well, women go to pieces too,' said Jenny, slightly peeved, 'but we still have to get on with things.' She broke off as her voice got choked. Damn it, she didn't want this to happen in front of the girls.

Sure enough, Amy started to cry. Alice handed her a tissue.

'Oh, I wish I could see you girls, I can't bear it any longer, I just want to give you both a big hug. That's what we need isn't it?'

All three sobbed for a moment.

'Let's meet up. I'll take a day off work,' said Jenny, trying to get them all back on track. 'I'll come down on the train. We could be out all day, we won't have to bother your dad.'

They arranged to meet the following week, just before the party, Jenny noted. Still, the party itself wouldn't take much organisation, all the work was in advance, wondering who on earth would come.

Later that afternoon, when she was with Joyce, a sudden thought dawned on her. Maybe the girls could come to the party? They could come up on the train and stay for the weekend. Trudi would no doubt make a fuss over the teenagers, they were such lovely girls. So would Hannah. And of course they knew Emily well from the days of the salon when they would visit with Sue. Emily would be all over them. And that would bring the numbers up to six which would be a lot better.

At Joyce's large house on Manor Lane she found her clearly getting restless. Her Alzheimer's meant that her anxiety levels were often high and today was one of those days.

Jenny cut some flowers from the garden, which she handed her to smell while she went to get a vase from the kitchen. When she got back, Joyce was eating the flower stalks like they were celery sticks. Oh crikey.

'Where are the candles?' she said as she munched. 'I've got to light the candles dear, where are they?'

'I'll light the candles later, Joyce,' Jenny said, wrestling the flowers off her. Joyce was Jewish and often made reference to the tradition of lighting candles at dusk on Fridays, the day before the Sabbath.

'You can't light them, dear!' she said, affronted. 'I have to light them.'

'Oh yes, sorry, Joyce, I forgot.'

Joyce eyed her suspiciously. 'Who are you?'

'It's Jenny, Joyce,' she said. 'I'm your carer.'

'Carer? I don't need a carer! Who are you? What faith are you?' She spoke like she was the prosecutor asking the key question in a major trial. 'Answer me!'

Jenny sighed. She knew where this was going. 'I'm not really anything, Joyce, but my family were Catholic –'

'Catholic?' Joyce shrieked. 'Roman Catholic? Oh I am so sorry, dearie, I didn't know! What a shame for you, what a shame!'

'It's alright, Joyce,' Jenny laughed. 'It's no big deal, I never think about it.'

'Oh, but if I had known I could have done something to help!' she said, having returned to her funny high-pitched voice. She turned to an invisible person sitting on the other side of her. 'She's Catholic! Isn't that a shame?'

Jenny laughed and patted the old lady on the hand. Joyce was much funnier than the boys' daily rendition of '*That's what she said*', even if she didn't mean to be.

'Shall we try some singing, Joyce? What about 'Somewhere over the rainbow'?'

'What about it?'

'I thought you might like to sing it with me.' Jenny began to sing the song. Joyce watched her for a moment before turning back to the invisible person on her left. 'She's Catholic, isn't that awful!'

Jenny giggled again and carried on singing, patting Joyce's hand as she did so. She went back to her idea to invite Sue's girls up for the make-up party. She would phone them once she got home. The thought flashed through her mind that it may cramp her style having them there when she was attempting to make a new friend in Trudi. They might think that she was trying to replace their mum, just the same as Eddie had. But no one could ever do that, it wasn't possible. Trudi was a new friend and when Jenny looked at her, she didn't think about the old days with Sue, or even the girls at the salon, she didn't think about what she had lost. She only thought about the possibility of a happy future.

'Hiya, Jenny! I got the invitation, thank you, duck, that's so kind of you!' Hannah came in, spreading cheer and positivity all around as ever.

Jenny's eyes lit up. 'Is that a yes then, Hannah?'

'Of course it is! I wouldn't miss it for the world! I've booked my mum to babysit and everything.'

'Oh great!' said Jenny, trying to hide an overwhelming sensation of giddy relief.

'Not that I'll have much to spend of course,' said Hannah. 'But I could do with a good drink.'

'Yes, just come and have a good drink and a laugh,' Jenny assured her. 'You don't need to buy anything, love. Just turn up, that's all.'

She left working feeling elated. Good old Hannah.

As she was walking up Manor Lane in the heat, Lonny sent a text from the train. They were both coming home. Ryan's dad was a no-show.

CHAPTER 17

Heat

Ryan's dad, Alan, was prone to cancelling at the last minute. Lonny and Ryan arrived home weary but not complaining. The moment that Lonny had decided to get the train instead of driving to the pre-arranged motorway service station was, no-doubt, the moment that Alan decided he wasn't going to turn up, Jenny thought. He hated any kind of change of arrangements at the last minute. That is, unless he created them.

Ryan was happily strumming his guitar within seconds of arriving back. Jenny could feel his mental sigh of relief that the visit had not gone ahead. She was pleased too that it would probably be Christmas time before there was another attempt at a visit.

Robbie turned up to give Ryan his guitar lesson, as Ryan had messaged him to say he wasn't going away after all so the lesson could go ahead. Robbie was pleased; he needed all the money he could get now he had his new girlfriend Chloe on the scene. A new girlfriend who never shut up according to Ryan, who had met her briefly.

'She's a right blabbermouth,' he told Jenny.

'Tell me about it,' she replied.

Jenny wondered when Ryan would venture out onto the dating scene again. He had been with his classmate Ellie for a year but she had ended it last summer and now he seemed happy just to concentrate on his music. She often wished it was a bit more tuneful though, he seemed to be strumming for the sake of it half the time.

The next day, she got up early and, as she had a couple of hours before going to Bill's, she sat at Lonny's desk by the bedroom window, there being no peace in the garden due to Dawn, and made another weak attempt at starting her essay.

She wrote the title for the tenth time: Jenny Lonsdale: wife, mother, carer, friend... was that the right order? She looked up with a grimace as down in next door's garden Dawn sprayed her kids with a hosepipe and the shrieking that followed nearly shattered the windowpane. Maybe she should write a chapter called *neighbour* and get some of her disdain for Dawn off her chest. She could subtitle that chapter 'Dawn – the neighbour from hell' she thought wryly.

She wondered how much information she was supposed to give in this essay. Did the teacher really need to know all the ins and outs of her family? Wasn't she just being plain nosy? The chapter headings – or paragraph headings more likely – of the various roles in her life made it all seem so simple. After all, she didn't need to make anything rhyme and she didn't need to think of a story with a beginning, middle and end. Thank goodness. But still, what would she write? How would she describe Lon and the boys and all the people she looked after at work... and Sue? She thought of the inevitable tears which would fall, soaking the sheets of paper. Don't be a fool, she told herself, you have to type it on Lonny's laptop and then print it out, you can't expect Celia to read your scribble. Oh God, she was so behind in her ways. She wondered if Trudi would be having the same difficulties. Probably not. The brief time she had spent watching Trudi in the class, it was clear that she was enthralled with the whole writing thing and couldn't wait to get started on her first essay. After an hour or so of daydreaming and no writing at all she gave up and got ready for work.

At Bill's that morning she updated him on the news that Alan hadn't turned up. Bill was outraged on Ryan's behalf.

'He's bloody useless!' he shouted. Even well into his eighties he still managed to be outraged about lots of things. 'So how does that tie in with him trying to be a good dad?' he continued as she ironed his scraggy undies in the kitchen.

'It doesn't!' she called back.

'Well, I can see young Ryan not bothering with him further down the line.'

Good, thought Jenny. Thank you, Bill.

Then five minutes later he called, 'How're the party invites going, duck? I see I haven't received mine yet!'

'It's a make-up party for women, Bill. It won't interest you.'

'Won't it? I think I'll be the judge of that! I like a bit of company, me.'

Jenny tutted. She wouldn't put it past him to get in a taxi and turn up if he knew the exact date and time, he had his favourite taxi drivers to help him get from A to B. She would have to stop mentioning it.

'Lon's got his eye on your back wall, Bill.'

'Has he now?'

'It's south facing, you'd get lots of lovely tomatoes off it. Would you like that?'

'So long as he's doing the work, duck, I don't mind.'

On the way to Debbie's, rushing as usual, she thought about the probable scenario that the heatwave would still be ongoing at the time of the party and that Trudi would expect to sit outside at least for a bit, which would mean she may well witness shenanigans taking place in Dawn's garden next door. Kids running riot, Dawn shouting and screaming at them, using all sorts of foul language. Where was that husband of hers, the other half of the newlyweds? He seemed to be strangely absent when it came to the garden. She saw him come in and out of the house at the front sometimes but he never seemed to sit out in the sun. Most likely he wanted to get some peace too, she thought, but he was the one who married her so he bloody well needed to pull his weight and help look after the kids. She thought of their wooden fence. She hadn't given up on an extra foot or two being added. She would chase Lonny on that project when she got home. Meantime, she would just have to keep hoping for the best-case scenario for the party: wet weather and plenty of lovely women inside.

Lovely women where art thou, she thought as she arrived at Debbie's door. There wasn't one at this address that was for sure, unless you could count Freya as a woman, and you could hardly do that, she was only ten.

The front door of the bungalow was open as usual so she walked in and down the hallway. As she passed Debbie's bedroom she saw her attempting to get herself out of bed and into her wheelchair after her nap. She was hanging onto the disability rail, precariously swinging back and forth, her frail, twisted body unable to summon the strength to navigate the final heave-ho.

'Debbie, why didn't you wait for me?' demanded Jenny as she ran to help.

'You were late,' she said, 'as usual.'

'What? Debbie that's not fair, I'm hardly ever late, thank you very much! I've been late twice in all the time I've been coming to you. And that was because Bill kept me hanging on. And I sent you a text to let you know.' She plonked Debbie in her wheelchair, hugely annoyed. This woman was a prize pain in the backside; what on earth was the matter with her?

They looked at each other for a long moment, as they always did. Two cowboys each with a hand on their holster ready to draw and shoot.

'If I say two o'clock then I mean two o'clock, Jenny.' Debbie manoeuvred her chair out of the bedroom into the open-plan kitchen.

'Oh, excuse me, it's five past two! Five minutes! And you know I'll add it on to the other end, so what's the problem?'

'The problem is that I start getting out of bed at two o'clock thinking you'll be coming in at any second.'

'Well, you should just wait until I arrive. How do you know there hasn't been an emergency?'

'I'm the one who has the emergencies!' she shouted.

Jenny breathed deeply. 'OK, well I'm sorry, Debbie, I'll try not to do it again. I'll tell Bill that if he wants to go to the toilet just before I leave, then it's just too bad because Debbie up the road might be doing something stupid and I have to get there as soon as possible.'

She glared at her and started moving the dishes towards the dishwasher to load up.

'I can do that,' said Debbie. 'That's why we've got a dishwasher, so that I can do it. You can do the bathroom today please, Jenny. I had an accident last night and Freya didn't manage to clean it all. It went everywhere.'

Jenny tried hard to keep herself together. Accident in the bathroom my arse. How come that always seemed to happen just before her shift? She grabbed the cleaning products from underneath the sink.

'Don't forget your gloves,' said Debbie, looking somewhat happier. 'You'll need them.'

Debbie must have been a sergeant major in a previous life, thought Jenny as she made her way home. Always barking out orders, taking immense pleasure from seeing Jenny scrubbing the back of the toilet. At least if Jenny was doing it, little Freya didn't have to, she thought. That was some consolation.

She walked down Bramfield Drive thinking that it must be over 35 degrees; this heat was getting beyond a joke. The sun was so dazzling she could hardly see. At this rate they might have to start pulling the curtains and keeping every room in the dark, like Bill and Joyce did.

As she passed one of the sturdy birch trees on the opposite side of the road, she jumped. There was something moving in the tree. She looked up into the branches and could see long rope-like-things hanging down, like Tarzan might have used to swing through the jungle. She tried to look closer but the light was so bright it was dazzling her. But it did look like some kind of creature was hanging upside down from one of the branches. How peculiar.

'Hi, Jenny!' said the 'creature' and waved a hand. Jenny jumped with fright. Oh my God, it was Stella, Lonny's permaculture friend from the allotments. What the hell was she doing hanging out of a tree?

'You must be wondering what I'm doing hanging out of a tree.' Stella smiled, jumping down, her breasts and long dreadlocks bouncing as she hit the ground. 'I'm just seeing if it's suitable to put a tap into. Birch syrup is pretty much like maple syrup you know. Our street could have a little bit of syrup for free, how brilliant would that be?'

Jenny tried to smile, but really, she felt like she was face-to-face with a Martian. She needed Lonny to handle this.

'I'll be down at yours soon,' Stella continued, her joie de vivre managing to annoy Jenny quite a bit. With her sunburnt face and her crow's feet, her braless chest and her long dreadlocks, this woman shouldn't be so darned happy, but it just seemed to be bursting right out of her. 'I'm going to help Lonny with the solar panels!'

'Oh OK, thank you, Stella,' Jenny said, before jumping again as another part of the tree seemed to move.

'Oh,' laughed Stella, 'that's my sister! She's up there too!'

Now Jenny really had to go. She waved and smiled and got the hell out of there. Oh God, she thought as she hurried home, if Lonny had seen them talking he'd get his hopes up that they would be friends. But she didn't have anything in common with Stella or her sister. What was it with hippie white women and dreadlocks? They looked awful! At least they did when they were her age anyway. She stopped, suddenly remembering that Lonny had mentioned Stella was having a forty-fifth birthday party soon so she was in fact five years younger than Jenny. That doesn't mean anything, she thought, desperate to reach the house and hide before Stella arrived.

'That's good timing, duck!' said Lonny as she walked in. 'Stella will be here in a minute, she's going to help me –'

'Yes, I know,' she said, grabbing a quick glass of water and downing it in one. 'I just saw her in the street.'

'Great! Did you ask her to the party?'

'Of course not, Lon, she's not the type for make-up.'

'Yeah, but she might buy a bit of cream or summat.'

'No, she won't.'

'It's worth a try int it?'

'No, it isn't.'

'I thought you said it was organic plant stuff? Stella would be into that.'

'No, no she won't,' said Jenny, heading towards the back door as the bell rang at the front. 'Never mind about the party, you just get on with the stuff on the roof.'

'Well, she's here now, why don't you just ask her?'

'No, Lonny!'

'Why not? Where're you going?'

'To get some tomato plants for Bill, he's really keen.'

'Don't go in the greenhouse, it's an oven!'

'I don't mind!'

She left her bemused husband to open the front door and ran up the garden into the steaming hot greenhouse, pulling the door behind her.

Beady eyes followed her from across the fence. Dawn put a ciggy in her mouth.

The temperature that hit Jenny was as though she had just landed in Dubai in a heatwave. Oh crikey. She looked at the tomato plants for a few seconds before the heat made her kneel to the floor. Oh God this was intense, this was so intense, it was like a sauna gone berserk. How could people live in hot countries? How was it even possible? And they were getting even hotter. Oh my God. Oh my God. Those poor people, those poor people.

Dawn continued to gaze across the fence as the minutes went by. For the tenth time that day, she absentmindedly yanked up a bra strap which kept falling down onto the large tattoo of her eldest daughter, Shanelle. She inhaled on her cigarette and wondered what the friggin' hell Jenny was doing. Any idiot knew not to go into a greenhouse on a day as hot as this.

'Oi, Jenny!' she called. 'Are you alright, duck?'

Jenny staggered out, her face the colour of beetroot.

'Oh there you are! I thought you musta fainted or summat!'

Jenny was about to glare back over the fence but she was distracted by the sight of Lonny and Stella climbing up the scaffolding ladder onto the roof. She looked at Dawn and put her finger to her mouth in a hush sign and then, to Dawn's bemusement, scuttled down to the back of the garden and sat out of sight, by the compost bins, in the much-needed shade of the cherry tree.

CHAPTER 18

The soil

Jenny continued to sit in the shade of the cherry tree at the back of the garden, unwilling to contemplate moving until Stella had gone and it was safe to go inside. Stella and Lonny and now Stella's sister were all huffing and puffing as they fixed and checked the solar panels on the roof.

She wished she could like Stella more, after all, she had the same interests as her husband. But a woman who swung from trees and never wore make-up and never even shampooed her hair by the looks of it, well that made her nervous. You become who you spend time with, so the saying went, so she had better not start hanging out with Stella or her similarly dreadlocked sister, in case that triggered a freefall into the abyss. God Almighty.

Still, she was grateful to the two women for giving Lonny their help and advice. It looked like hard work and Lonny couldn't do it on his own. He kept lifting his t-shirt to wipe the sweat away. This heat was far too much in the shade, never mind on the roof.

Actually, being under the tree was by far the best place to be. The shade was so calming. That's what they needed more of these days, trees and shade, trees and shade. She closed her eyes and began to doze.

She thought of the Saturdays when she used to go horse riding as a little girl. Sue was always busy with her family on a Saturday, leaving a big gap in her life. How to get through a day without Sue? Dad had signed her up for horse riding lessons so although she didn't have her best friend, she did have her father to herself as well as a beautiful pony whose neck she loved to hug and snuggle. That pony was called Starry Night and as she dozed, she felt its solid body beneath her again and she could smell the damp Welsh air on its mane. It must have just rained, everything was so cool and misty and what British people called 'miserable', but she knew now to appreciate the dampness and chill, because the alternative blistering heat was so difficult to bear. The wooden slabs of the stable doors were cool to the touch. The moss at the side of the paddock looked like someone had left green velvet out in the rain. She rode Starry Night out into a lush field where every leaf and every blade of grass glistened with moisture and the trees at the edges bowed low with the weight of the extra water. Dad waved to her encouragingly and she patted the horse as he trotted round the field. Happy days.

She stopped dozing and the heat hit her with renewed force as she left behind those wet Saturday mornings from her childhood and opened her eyes.

Oh God, the heat.

Suddenly, she heard a noise from the field behind her. A cow was coming up to the gate at the end of their garden.

A cow.

Jenny jumped up. She looked up quickly to the roof where Lonny, Stella and her sister were still doing important things; at least, that would be her excuse as to why she didn't want to bother them.

The cow was looking at her. She wondered why it should be here, it couldn't be searching for more grass could it, when it had the whole back field to graze in. Maybe it was searching for shade, just as she had been.

With Starry Night still fresh in her mind, she couldn't help but look with sympathy at the cow. She loved animals and often found them easier to understand than people. Human beings were so selfish, they didn't give much thought to the way animals might be suffering in this terrible heat. Look at that poor dog outside Bill's.

She walked up to the cow and gave it a cautious pat on the side of its neck and then more of a stroke as the animal seemed to like it. Then, after a while, she put her arms round its neck and moved her head in for a nice nuzzle. Breathing in the animal's warm smell she wondered how she could be friends with a cow after five minutes but be surrounded by women she didn't get on with. Why was it all so difficult?

'Don't you be like that old doggie,' she whispered. 'You must look after yourself. Find some shade and you stay there, d'you hear me? Stay in the shade, it's very important.'

She glanced around the field, what she could see of it anyway. She couldn't see any more animals, just this solitary cow and a mobile home which had been placed at the top of the slope. That wasn't there before. She would have to tell Lonny that someone had moved into the field that he so badly wanted for his permaculture plans. Someone had beaten him to it. Someone with a mobile home and a cow.

She stayed with the animal a little while longer, until Stella had gone and it was safe to return to the house.

At dinner that evening she mentioned it to Lonny, who raised his eyebrows hopefully. A cow was a good sign, maybe the people who had outbid him at the auction were thinking along the same lines as him. He would have to get to know them – a steady supply of manure would definitely be a good thing for the garden.

'It will stink though, Dad,' said Nate, speaking for his mother and brothers too.

'We'll get used to it,' said Lonny. 'We can put up with a bit of stink when you think about the good it does for the soil – it's gold dust!'

He helped Jenny clear the dining table and then set up his laptop ready for a webinar with international soil expert and founder of Ecosystem Restoration Camps, John D. Liu. He wanted to find out more about volunteering not just for the camp in Spain but also for when they got back to the UK. There were people all over the world on the webinar, France, Germany, Spain, Denmark, Guatemala, Mexico, South Africa, Australia, the Philippines, the US. Lonny was thrilled.

'I just need to know what is the best thing I can do right here on the ground, John. I'm signing up for the camp in Spain in August, cos we're going over anyway to see the in-laws. But what about when we get back?' he asked when it was time for questions. 'We're in the middle of a heatwave here at the moment but generally speaking we're not short of rain so nothing looks too bad.'

'Where are you calling from?' asked the great John D. Liu.

'Stoke, duck,' said Lonny.

John thought for a moment and then shrugged and looked off-screen to someone who was suggesting Stokeduc might be in The Netherlands.

'Nah, it's the middle of the UK,' said Lonny.

'The situation in the United Kingdom is obviously not as bad as in some other countries, but there are still many large industrial farming areas where the soil is degraded and not functioning correctly,' said John. 'There are huge numbers of farmers in the UK trying to convert their land to a regenerative system, permaculture is gaining in popularity and many more farms are converting to the mob grazing system that Allan Savory advocates. All of these systems are excellent but we need volunteers to help set them up, many, many volunteers. This work is crucial now. As we know, it is only when the soil is restored to good health that it will drink in the carbon that we need it to. It wouldn't matter if all flights and car journeys stopped tomorrow, we will not be able to stop climate change unless the soil is restored. Are you on board, Lonny?'

'Yes I am, John, definitely. I can help with that,' said Lonny seriously, aware that all three of his sons were now sitting behind him and probably in the camera shot that John was looking at. 'How many volunteers are we talking about exactly?'

'Hundreds of thousands from each country. We're talking about an army of volunteers, an army from each country and we need them on the ground and working quickly to re-green the planet. This is what needs to happen the world over.'

'An army. Right.' Lonny winced but quickly tried to cover it up, as Solly leaned forward and asked, 'How are we going to do that, Dad?'

Later, when the webinar was finished, he showed the lads one of John's films about a project in China, where a huge piece of land the size of Belgium was restored by the local people. The film showed the before and after shots to great effect. This encouraged them and it encouraged him too because the word 'army' was pretty intimidating.

On his evening rounds of the garden, he walked down to the gate at the bottom to see if he could see the cow. A man was walking around the field and bending over every now and then to study what was on the ground, to look closely at the types of grasses growing, to see how he could help the soil improve. Lonny recognised those movements and that look, he had seen it on Matt and Stella and all their friends at the allotments, and he knew he had that look too. Maybe this 'army' of volunteers was already coming together, mobilising, ready for action, ready to reclaim and regenerate the land.

CHAPTER 19

Meltdown

The next day, when she was picking up *The Sentinel* for Bill at the newsagents, Jenny saw Lauren buying a packet of fags. She must be on her way to work at the pub she thought, seeing that Lauren was wearing a similar style shirt to the one she had worn before.

'Hi, Lauren!' She waved. 'Remember me?'

'Yeah, the lady who fell into my pub.' Lauren grinned. 'Of course I remember you. It's not every customer who does that you know Jenny. They normally fall out of the pub, not in!' She winked.

Jenny beamed as a sudden thought of staggering genius struck her like lightning. Lauren might look like the World Darts Champion in her work outfit, but she was a lovely person – after all, she had listened to Jenny's woes for an hour the other week. She should grab her for the party. She knew she had previously rejected the idea but time was marching on and she still needed three or four more people.

'On your way to work?' she asked.

'Nah, it's my day off.'

'Oh!' OK, that was unexpected. Lauren obviously didn't have many clothes. But still. She made up her mind. She would go for it. She knew that the heat might be affecting her ability to think clearly but she would go for it anyway. 'I'm going to ask you something,

Lauren,' she said, 'and I want you to think about it, you don't need to give me an answer now.'

Lauren raised her eyebrows.

'How much do you reckon on average you spend each month on make-up and skin care?'

'Zilch.'

'Sorry?'

'Nada. Nuthin.'

'Don't you ever wear make-up?'

'No.'

'Ever?'

'Nope,' said Lauren, taking out a cigarette and lighting it.

'But you must wash! Don't you use skin care products? Cleansers and toners and moisturisers? Facial peels? Scrubs? Facial oils?'

'No, none of that, duck. Soap and water.'

'Really?'

'Yeah. I can't be bothered with anything else. It's all bullshit.'

'Oh, OK,' said Jenny, backing off, her mind being forced to release the brilliant idea she had just had. Release it and re-label it as a completely stupid idea. 'No worries.'

'Why?'

'Well, it's just a little party I'm having, a make-up and skin care party.'

'Sounds like my worst nightmare,' said Lauren, wincing as she took another drag.

'OK, no worries!'

'I'll be seeing yer, duck,' she winked. 'Come and fall through my door again sometime.'

'Oh, haha,' said Jenny, waving. 'I will!'

Stupid idiot, she told herself as Lauren walked off. Stick to your own type. After all, nice as Lauren was, what on earth would she be doing at a make-up party with beautiful people like Trudi and Emily? It would be a joke.

She handed Mrs Holdcroft the money to pay for Bill's local paper *The Sentinel*.

'How are you today Jenny, duck?' the newsagent asked.

'Great, thank you, Mrs Holdcroft. That's a strong fan you've got in here, it's much better than mine!'

'Oh, it's high-tech, duck,' she said. 'God knows we need it these days.'

'We certainly do.' Jenny was about to turn away when she noticed a nice flash of pink on the newsagent's lips.

'You look nice today, Mrs Holdcroft. What a lovely colour lipstick.'

Mrs H blushed. To get a compliment from someone like Jenny was praise indeed. 'Well, I like to wear a bit of make-up sometimes, duck. It's nice to make an effort now and then isn't it? You always look lovely, Jenny, I must say.'

Jenny pounced like a leopard on a gazelle. She scrambled in her bag for an invitation.

'Mrs Holdcroft, I'm having a little make-up party soon, just a few friends over at mine. Why don't you come and join us?'

Mrs Holdcroft smiled and took the invitation and said she would love to attend.

It was that easy.

Hallelujah, thought Jenny, now all she needed to do was find out her first name before she got introduced to Trudi.

Coming out of the shop with a triumphant look, she noticed Mark, the other half of the newlyweds, going into the Windmill pub. So that was where he was hanging out. I bet you need a drink living with that one, she thought, but you shouldn't have married her should you? You must have known what you were getting into.

Lonny was outside in the garden when she got back. In the garden and at the fence talking to Dawn, which he often seemed to be doing these days. He was encouraging her not to swear no doubt. Every time she let rip he rushed over to the fence and called her over, careful that her daughters wouldn't hear him. 'Dawn, Dawnie! What yer playing at? Yer can't talk to the kids like that! In a couple of years they'll be saying it back to the teachers at school and it'll get 'em into no end of trouble. Control your language, duck! Come on, Dawnie, you can do it!'

And with it coming from Lonny, she would grin and blush and beam and laugh and take it.

'Have you got any tomato plants you can give me, Lon? I fancy growing some by the kitchen wall.'

'Yes, duck, I certainly have,' Lonny said, thrilled. 'And I've got a few peppers and chillies if you want them too?'

'I dunna want any chillies, I hate 'em.'

'What about cucumbers?'

'Go on, alright then, I'll try one. All in pots yeah? I onna doing any digging.'

'No, that's alright, just get yourself some bigger pots from the car boot sale, you'll need them in a few weeks.'

'Have I got to pay you, duck?'

'Course you haven't, Dawnie, I'm your neighbour.'

He put his arm across the fence and pulled her closer. 'Your *fucking* neighbour.'

Dawn roared with laughter; she adored Lonny.

'Not in front of the kids though, Dawn, see what I mean?' he winked.

'Yeah, I get it,' she said and whispered back to him. 'I *fucking* get it, alright?'

Now it was Lonny's turn to roar with laughter.

Jenny looked on disapprovingly. She had to admit that Lonny certainly did have a lovely way about him, whereas she would have come across as snobby and patronising if she had told Dawn to stop swearing. Dawn would have no doubt just told her to fuck off and mind her own business. She knew she didn't have Lonny's gregarious nature. However, Dawn should make the most of it because when that extension was built on top of the fence all this nonsense back and forth would end once and for all.

She set up the ironing board in the kitchen to finish their outfits for this evening's gig. Maybe tonight would be the best time to tell Lon that she didn't want to do it anymore. He would just have to find the money for his food forest somewhere else. She had left Marie Osmond behind a long time ago. But she would miss singing, that was for sure. She loved to sing more than anything. And these days she hardly sang at all apart from at the Topsmonds gigs. Not even listening to the radio or walking to work. She just didn't. Oh God, she wished she could jump to Monday and the creative writing class so that she could see Trudi. A good couple of hours with Trudi, that's what she needed more than anything.

She stopped ironing and wiped the sweat off her brow with her t-shirt just as Lonny had done on the roof. This heat was incredible. Even inside.

She hung her dress on the patio to air. As she clipped the peg in place she could feel eyes boring into her back. She swung round to see Dawn grinning at her over the fence.

'Hi, Jenny, have you washed your nice dress again?'

'Apparently so.'

'Well, it's the right weather for it, int it?'

Dawn was pleased to see something resembling a smile and a nod of agreement coming from Jenny. This was promising. In general, she was pretty nervous when she spoke to Jenny. It was like speaking to a social worker or a cop. One wrong word and she might regret it forever. But she persevered. She was drawn to her like a moth to a flame. She would try and keep the conversation going. Maybe ask her why she was sitting up by the compost heap for so long yesterday. Or hugging that cow. Then again, better not. She took a slow drag on her cigarette. Actually, Jenny was looking a bit weird today. Like she was all clammy and sweaty. Her hair at the front looked soaking wet.

'Are yer alright, Jen? Yer look all clammy and sweaty.'

'I beg your pardon.'

'Yer hair is all wet, duck. Are yer having a hot flush or summat? My mum had them all the time. The sweat used to drip right off her face into the dinner.'

Jenny looked all around as though she needed a witness to Dawn's audacity. This woman was unbelievable! She glared at her. 'I don't have hot flushes actually, Dawn.'

'Oh? I thought you would by now 'cos you're older than Lonny aren't yer?'

'Am I?'

'Yeah, course. Unless you're the same age but looking a bit rough,' she chuckled. 'Nah, I'm only joking, duck, take no notice!'

Jenny went in and slammed the door, leaving a bemused Dawn at the fence yet again. What on earth? That woman was incorrigible! And how the hell did she know her age? Had Lonny said anything? It was one thing having that misogynistic bitch Miranda to dinner but at least they would never have to see her again. Dawn was just next door! Right there under her nose every time she went into the garden.

165

She couldn't stand it any longer. The sooner that fence was raised the better. Lonny should get the wood and prioritise it. She didn't mind if he was up half the night putting it all together. She would help him. She would bloody well take up carpentry and do it herself if she had to!

But when they were driving to the gig that night, Lonny wasn't having any of it. He said he had no intention of making the fence higher. He liked Dawn and although she would often turn the air blue, she didn't mind him reining her in a bit. He said Dawn needed their help, she was married to a prat and skint as a church mouse, it was tough for her, it was –

'I don't care two bloody hoots how tough it is!' said Jenny outraged. 'Didn't we have it tough too? We didn't have money to buy food sometimes but we never sank to her level did we? She uses the C word at her husband, Lonny, the woman's a monstrosity!'

'Well maybe he deserves it, he sounds like a complete dickhead. Come on, duck, I've had enough of this *Daily Mail* mentality! Where's it coming from? You've turned into such a snob.'

'I'm not a snob. How dare you!'

'*How dare I?* Listen to yourself, Jen! Dawn's your neighbour, you should always be friendly towards a neighbour unless there are extreme circumstances.'

'Well there are! There are extreme circumstances! The extreme circumstances are that she's absolutely foul! She's rude to me, she's always telling me I look old for my age, she told me I was having a hot flush today, cheeky cow!'

'She's nervous with you 'cos she knows you don't like her. If you were nice to her she wouldn't be so on edge.'

'Lonny, you cannot look at her and then look at me and say it's my fault. Look at her, just look at her! She arrived in a disgusting old van with bin bags for suitcases! She called her husband a cunt! She tells her kids not to be little shits! She's an awful person. I admit she's not quite as bad as bloody Miranda but that doesn't say anything. And I want that fence going higher. If you don't do it then I will!'

Lonny snorted. He knew that in this state he would only be adding fuel to the fire if he said anything at all. So he said nothing. But he just kept snorting as he drove.

The gig was up in Hanley at The Pilgrims Pit. They had played there many times before and were always a hit. At least the men were. Lonny parked and they entered the pub in a subdued mood, which was very unusual for them. Jenny avoided the other guys even though she had planned to speak to Jackie to see what had happened after the dinner with Miranda. But her eyes were barely managing to hold back the tears. It was awful. She and Lonny never rowed and of all things to row about, why did it have to be bloody Dawn? She sat in her crappy little dressing room aka the broom cupboard and tried to check her make-up while the men were doing a sound check. She felt so awful she wished she could die, just float away and be with Sue. The thought made her eyes flood with tears. How ridiculous; she could never leave Lon and the boys. Oh God, oh God, how was she ever going to do this stupid gig? How was she ever going to get through it?

Lonny came in and stood there for a moment as she wiped her eyes, her awful sore eyes. She seemed to spend her whole life crying at the moment. He sighed.

'OK, duck, I don't know what's going on, it seems to be one step forward and two steps back dunt it? Come 'ere, you know I love you.'

He hugged her and kissed the top of her head.

'I love you too,' she said quietly, unable to look at him. She felt ashamed, but why? She was sure she was in the right.

'Good luck,' he said. 'Why don't you come out and watch us? Don't stay in here on your own.'

'I will,' she said. 'In a bit,' she added, the tears resurfacing. Lonny left and she was alone again looking at her miserable reflection in the mirror. She had about twenty minutes before she would be on stage singing 'Paper Roses'. She knew everyone would walk out of course, but even so, she couldn't arrive on stage looking like she did now, like she'd been bawling her eyes out. She heard Lon and the guys singing 'Love Me for a Reason' and she heard all the drunken women beginning to sing along and shriek occasionally when Lonny would bend down to someone on the front row just like Donny did when he was fourteen. They finished the song to an almighty appreciative roar, like Stoke had just won the FA cup or something. The audience cheered and clapped and whistled and threw bottles and stamped their feet and downed yet more alcohol.

Jenny did that thing that unhappy women everywhere do in toilets when they look in the mirror and force a smile and then another and hold it in place and breathe and stretch their face until it aches, until it is eventually convinced that things are not too bad. It helps the tears dry up. But everyone knows it's a temporary fix, just like the make-up Jenny was hastily reapplying.

The guys had just started singing 'Let Me In' and she knew that she needed to get out there because if she stayed much longer in the cupboard with the brushes and mops it would just start all over. She needed to get out into the wings where she would see other people and she wouldn't allow herself to cry any more.

She stood up in her beautiful pink dress and curled hair with a paper rose in it and walked round to the side of the stage, behind the curtains and still out of sight of the audience, where a young man was operating the sound system. She pulled back the curtain just enough to see the crowd. God, they looked drunk tonight. She felt grateful that they would disappear as soon as she came on, disappear to pee or smoke or message someone and tell them to get their arse down to the pub as it was a great night. A great night for everyone except her. She could see Lonny and the boys in the white jumpsuits that she and Sue had had made especially for them. No one-size-fits-all fancy dress outfits here, these were proper bespoke costumes, white and bejewelled and tasselled and open to the waist and clearly sending the women wild. Women of every age, shape and size, all with a common bond: they were plastered and screaming adoringly at a bunch of middle-aged black men singing Osmond songs.

She looked on as the excitement in the crowd intensified and a 'bride' from one of the many hen parties near the front heaved herself up onto her friend's shoulders and started taking her top off. Good God, what a state to be in. The top was off and she was waving it around like she was in a Parisian strip club. Drunken cow. What was she doing now, unhooking the bra? She'd better not be. Oh my God, she was.

And the tits were out.

Right.

There was a switch saying 'Emergency shutdown' above the young man's sound desk. Jenny pressed it down with a furious prod like she was poking someone's eye out. The music stopped. The electricity went out. Only the lights of the bar illuminated the room.

She stormed onto the stage.

'Why don't you save them for the poor sod you're gonna marry, you stupid fat tart!' she hollered, pointing aggressively at the topless woman.

There was a gasp from the crowd and a groan from the men on the stage.

169

The bride-to-be grabbed her veil to cover herself.

'Oh Christ,' said Lonny.

Jenny stood there for what seemed like an eternity, panting and angry and then slowly realising what she had just done. This was it, she had crossed the line. It was the point of no return. Her madness was out in the open. A hundred mobile phones were pointed right at her. Her craziness and loneliness and grief were all out in the open for everyone to see and nothing would ever be normal again.

'Fuck off, duck!' shouted someone from the back.

CHAPTER 20

Nina not Marie

Shoppers at *Aldi* in Meir Park couldn't help but notice Lonny as he and the boys arrived on foot, through the gap in the hedge surrounding the car park. The vast majority of people of colour in Stoke were of Pakistani heritage; very few were descendants of the Windrush generation who had settled in other cities in the Midlands but for some reason not The Potteries. So as one of the very few British Caribbean men in the area, Lonny often got noticed. But today it was more the stressed-out look on his face that was causing some people to stop and stare. He looked like he was about to blow a gasket.

Matt was outside telling staff how to organise the vast collection of summer plants that were threatening to take over the car park.

'Alright, Lon?' he said, as Lonny thundered towards him. 'What's up, duck? What happened?'

'Ah, man,' said Lonny, hardly able to put his words together. He knew he couldn't speak openly because the boys were in earshot. He didn't want them hearing the full story of what had happened last night. They didn't really know what was wrong at this point because Jenny had remained in bed.

He spoke quietly and tried to remain calm. 'It's not good, it's not good. She's not coping at all, she's lost on her own, without her friends. She's going bloody nuts.'

'Ah shit. What about the party? What about her new friend, Trudi?'

'I dunno, duck,' Lonny shook his head, a wince of pain never far from his face. 'I dunno if it's going ahead or what. She hasn't heard from her and that's not helping. It's like her whole happiness is hinging on a friendship with this mysterious woman and I don't know who she is, where she lives or anything.'

'Maybe Trudi isn't real,' suggested Solly, poking his head into the conversation, a bit in awe of Matt, as usual, with his muscles busting out all over.

'Course she's real!' snapped Lonny. 'I just don't know why she's in such a state about her. I never even met the woman!'

'Well, we need to find her, that's a priority,' said Matt, repeatedly slapping his right fist into his left palm like he meant business.

'Shall we call the police so they can track her down?' asked Solly.

'Don't be daft, get out of here,' snorted Lonny. 'Go play.'

He and Matt walked off to get a bit of privacy.

'She had a meltdown at a gig last night, right on stage. It was terrible, man, terrible.'

Now it was Matt's turn to wince. 'Oooh. That dunt sound good. Maybe she shouldn't do any more gigs for a while.'

'No, she can't do any more, it's out of the question.'

'It's too stressful for her.'

'Far too stressful. She's on her own out there and she hates it.'

'Yeah,' said Matt, staring off into the middle distance. 'When I came to the gig that time I could see that she wasn't having as much fun as you guys. The audience didn't pay her any attention. I felt like shouting at 'em, "Listen to this woman yer dickheads! Listen to that voice!'"

'Well,' said Lonny, looking at his friend and wondering if he had just a little bit of a crush on his wife, 'she's not well enough for any of that now that's for sure.'

'But she must still sing, Lon,' said Matt concerned. 'She loves to sing dunt she? If she stops singing she'll get even more depressed.'

'Yeah, it's funny, she used to sing about the house all day long; she doesn't do that any more.'

'That's her depression getting the better of her int it. Try and get her to sing at home every day, that will help. Meantime what about we try and find Trudi and get the two of them together? Where does she live?'

'I dunno, duck, I dunno anything about her except she's on the same writing course.'

'OK, when's the next class?' Matt winked.

'Monday evening.'

'Let's hope she turns up then. Maybe you need to be there to pick Jen up, then you can offer Trudi a lift home, help things along a bit.'

'That's a good idea, cheers, Matty,' said Lonny, slapping his back in appreciation. Out of all his friends, Matt was the one who Lonny could talk to about Jenny's depression this past year. Their mutual love of gardening and permaculture had developed into a firm friendship.

Back at home, Jenny was reluctant to wake up. She lay in bed for a while, slowly remembering the scene last night. Poor Lonny, he must have been mortified. She herself was beyond it though. Beyond humiliation. Beyond caring. She felt numb.

She lay on her side and thought of Sue lying next to her like they used to do when they were teenagers sleeping over. Recounting the gossip and stories of the day, making each other laugh till they cried. She remembered just how much Sue used to make her laugh. She would be on the brink of wetting herself, she would snort like a pig, she would be in pain with laughter. Because Sue wouldn't just tell the story once, she would run it through a myriad of times, each time adding a bit more nonsense on top until Jenny was a wreck. A laughing, snorting wreck with hands clutching her crotch to stop the wee.

'I wish you were here, hon,' she said out loud. In her mind's eye she could see her best friend lying next to her. Beautiful Sue with her dimples.

But the Sue in her mind said, 'Come on, Jen, this isn't funny anymore.'

'I can't help it, I'm lost without you.'

'I know, but you need to get a grip now.'

'I can't do it.'

'You can, Jen.'

'I'm trying but I can't.'

'You can, hon, you can. You have to. You know what Lon says, *It's all hands on deck.*'

'I'm no use to anyone now though. I've lost it completely. Look at last night.'

'Don't worry about that, babe, it will be forgotten in five minutes,' said her lovely friend. 'Come on, Jen, it's time to get your act together. You need to start living your life again. There are some brilliant times ahead of you. Come on girl!'

'I don't want any brilliant times without you though.'

'Well, you have to, you have to let me go now. How d'you think I feel watching you be so miserable and not being there for the kids and Lon? I want to see you happy like you used to be. Even happier. Wonderfully, gloriously happy. That's what I want for you.'

Jenny sniffed.

'Did you hear what I said?' asked Sue. She laughed loudly just like she used to.

'Yes, but I don't know how I'm going to do it.'

'Just do the opposite of what you're doing now! Seriously, babe, it's not rocket science, just make sure you have a little fun every day. Don't worry about friends, they'll come soon enough.'

'OK,' said Jenny. 'I'll try.'

'That's it. Now come on, get up and let's get you outside in the sunshine.'

Jenny reluctantly turned over to sit up and get out of bed, knowing that the spell may then be broken and Sue would be gone.

Sure enough, when she turned back the bed was empty.

She noticed that the numbness had vanished. Instead she felt a little bit better – awful and terrible, but she supposed that was still better than being numb. She wondered if it was true what Sue had said. Could there possibly be brilliant times ahead?

She made her way downstairs and out into the garden. It was all quiet this morning as she walked down the path past Lonny's many raised beds. Just a bit of birdsong and a lovely breeze making the trees and plants flutter and move like they were in an ongoing dance between lovers that we humans could only comprehend a fraction of.

She saw a few flowers dotted about. Together with a couple of early yellow roses, they would make a lovely little bouquet. She picked up a pair of secateurs and thought about the night before as she cut the stems. Surely last night she had reached the bottom. It had to have been the bottom. The shame, the humiliation and the knowledge that no doubt there was now plenty of footage on social media showing the abrupt transition from sweet-singing Donny to finger-jabbing, battle-axe Marie.

God Almighty. It was the pits. She was at the bottom of a great big pit and it felt terrible. She bent down over one of the vegetable beds, which appeared to be just soil with some straw on top, and laid out the flowers to assemble them. As she moved the flowers around, she pushed the straw to one side and ran her fingers through the soil, enjoying the sensation of it in her hands. She didn't see Lonny's label at the end of the bed saying that cauliflower seeds had been planted here last week.

Yes, things felt terrible. But at least now that she had hit the bottom she could look up. Before, she was falling all the time. She had been falling again and again till she had thought the pit was bottomless but it wasn't. She had landed now. She had finally landed. And now, hopefully, the only way was up. She imagined looking up out of the pit but the sky seemed an awful long way away. It was too far. She looked down at the work her hands had made: the flowers were beautifully arranged and laid above a heart drawn in the soil with the word 'Sue' inside it.

She felt an overwhelming urge to stop this right now. Stop it. Stop it. Stop it. She had to move on with her life, just as Sue had told her to. She stood up with a strong desire to see Amy and Alice. She needed to see them a lot more often. She needed to see them *today!*

She rushed into the house just as Lonny and the boys were coming in.

'I need to start having some fun every day to make me better, Lon! I'm going to drive to Cardiff and take Amy and Alice out bowling or something.'

'Whoa!' said Lonny. 'What, now? That's over a hundred miles! Have you phoned them?'

'Not yet but I'm going to,' she began to call them.

'Wait, duck, wait,' said Lonny anxiously, switching her phone off. 'I can't have you driving down the country after what happened last night, I can't have it, I'll be worried sick.'

'It's OK, Lon, Sue told me that I need to move on now, I need to have fun every day. She said there are happier times ahead for me. She said I would be gloriously happy!'

'That's nice, when did she say that?'

'Just now.'

'What? Ah shit,' he groaned. 'OK I think we need to get you to the doctor's today and then we can go and see the girls next week. Let's give 'em some notice. You can't just go charging down there like you're going into Hanley or summat. It's a long way.'

'You can take us bowling instead, Mum,' said Nate. 'We haven't been bowling for ages.'

'Yeah, Mum, take us bowling,' said Solly and Ryan.

'No, no, I'm fed up of you boys. I'm fed up of you men, picking your noses and farting and burping and saying dirty things. I'm sick of it! I want women around me, don't you understand? I want to look around this room and see nothing but lovely women! You don't want to talk about beautiful things or lovely music or amazing dancing or stylish clothes or funny films. You don't want to drool over a particular shade of paint on the wall, you don't want to stay up all night talking about boyfriends –'

'Yer've been married eighteen years!' snorted Lonny. 'What d'yer wanna talk about boyfriends for?!'

'It's the principle!' shouted Jenny. 'I want women around me. Women like me. I don't want people who would rather be killing everyone in a stupid video game. A horrible violent video game. Blood flying everywhere. How can you even do that? It's disgusting!'

'We can get rid of the Xbox, Mum, we wouldn't mind,' said Ryan sheepishly.

'Yeah we would!' said Nate, outraged.

Solly clutched at her waist. 'Shall I transition for yer, Mumma?'

'We could all try and be a bit more female friendly,' said Ryan.

Nate snorted. Lonny winced, exasperated. He took Jenny's elbow. 'Come on, duck, we can't have this. This is ridiculous. Come on, let's go to the doctor's. Don't make any fuss now.' He tried to usher her into the hall but she resisted and pushed him away.

'It's Sunday, Lon, they're shut!'

'A & E then. Come on, let's go to A & E, duck.'

'Don't be so daft!' Jenny pushed him away again. 'And have me queueing up next to people who've been in a car crash? There's nothing wrong with me. I'm just sad that's all and Sue's told me I need to start having some fun.'

'What kind of fun d'you want, Mumma?' asked Sol.

'Fun with women!'

'Like what?'

'Well, I'm going to see the girls and take them out somewhere. And I've got the writing class tomorrow when I'll see Trudi. Then I have the make-up party next weekend. That's going to be a lot of fun.'

'Is it?' asked Lonny.

'Yes, of course.'

'I thought you needed some more people for it to work?'

'Well, I do, but I'm sure I'll find them. I'll ask Hannah if she knows anyone who wants to come.'

Lonny nodded. This was sounding better. 'That's good, duck, that's good.' He suddenly remembered what Matt had said. 'What about your singing?'

Immediately, tears welled up in Jenny's eyes as the memory of her meltdown came flooding back. 'I don't think I'll be able to sing anymore to be honest. Not after last night.'

'Ah, Jen, come 'ere.' Lonny wrapped his arms around her as she sobbed silently into his shoulder for a minute. He mouthed to the boys, 'Go play, go on' and ushered them out with his hand.

'Jen,' he whispered into her ear. 'You're a great singer. Now you've got to get back on your bike straight away. Don't worry about gigs for now. I just want to hear you singing around the house like you used to.'

'In the house?'

'Yeah, like you used to, come on. Why don't you sing for me now? Just me.'

'Oh no, I don't feel like it, Lon. Not after last night.'

'No, forget last night, you're not Marie any more. You were never really Marie anyway, duck. You're much more of a Dusty or an Aretha or a Nina –'

'Nina's my favourite,' Jenny admitted, 'but not in public, I'm never going to –'

'No, no, not in public,' said Lonny. 'Just here, now, with me. Sing along with the record.' He kissed her and she smiled weakly. Lonny hurriedly picked a Nina Simone album from his vinyl selection. He put the record on at the first track and he kissed her again and said, 'Let's get you back on your bike, Jen. Forget all about Marie, you're no Marie, you're a Nina!'

The music started and Lonny carried on over the introduction, 'Come on, Jen, you can do it! Sing for me darlin', sing! Just for me!'

Jenny started to sing along with Nina's depressing opening, 'Ain't got no home, ain't got no shoes, Ain't got no money, ain't got no skirts...'

Lonny ripped the needle off the record. He could see where this was going, it would only be a minute before 'Ain't got no friends' came up. 'Hang on, hang on, not this one, let's do this one instead, sorry, duck, my fault.'

The next track started with a piano introduction. Lonny wiped the sweat off his brow. 'Come on, Jen, you can do it.'

Jenny closed her eyes and heard the song '*I wish I knew how it feels to be free*' and felt it sink deep into her soul, dragging it upwards from the depths of the darkness and the pit. The lyrics and melody perfectly encapsulated the pain and frustration Nina was feeling in her own life as a black woman in America in the sixties. Did Nina know how many women hearing it since would feel it was written just for them? Did she guess how many women would wish to break the bonds and chains of their lives or wish they could fly through the air like a bird and really feel freedom? Jenny sang the song, cautiously at first, then gaining power and momentum with each verse until she felt her heart begin to open again.

Lonny danced around her like he was coaching the kids at football. 'That's it, Jen, my beautiful woman! Sing, sing!'

The boys looked on furtively from the kitchen, grinning, trying to push spoons into a stolen tub of posh ice cream from the freezer, but finding it as hard as a brick.

CHAPTER 21

Rain

The next day, the heatwave broke temporarily and there was a thunderstorm and torrential rain. Lonny was thrilled as his system of second-hand tanks for rainwater collection, which wrapped themselves around the back of the house, would get a chance to refill. The growing vegetables drank and drank and Lonny smiled as he stood outside getting soaking wet, watching the way the huge drops of rain landed and cascaded down the leaves of the early brassicas. Mind you, he would have to be on slug alert later.

As the rain kept falling, the release of tension in the air was tangible. Kids ran around gardens screaming in delight, grown men stood outside with their hands held up in thanks. Women felt a release in their bodies like that of the first day of their period when all the built-up angst is diffused as the blood starts to flow. It seemed people only recognised the intensity of the heat they had been in when there was some relief from it. The rain poured down for twenty-four hours solid.

Jenny too felt some release in the rain, just as she had felt some release by singing Nina's song. But there was still a long way to go. In the afternoon, she sat upstairs at Lonny's desk in front of the open window trying yet again to begin her essay. The creative writing class was this evening. She had to get something down on paper so that she could talk about it with Trudi and also show Celia that she was at least making an effort. Of course, she didn't care about it really, but she had to go along with it till her friendship with Trudi was firmly established, then she could quit the class and just see Trudi on other occasions. Besides the 'friend' section, the other roles in her life – 'wife, mother, carer, daughter' – continued to daunt her too. She thought guiltily that she hadn't phoned her parents in a while. Then again, if she could be sure her father would pick up, she would be happy to phone every day. Why didn't he use the mobile she had bought him? He'd probably had it confiscated by her bloody mother. Oh God. She knew she had never got on well with her, but surely now that her mother was growing old, she should be a good daughter and phone her more often. But it was hard being a good daughter to a bad mother. So hard.

If she could just write most of it about her father, that would be easier, he was such a lovely man. There most likely wasn't a single person in South Wales with a bad word to say against him, and probably not in Spain either. He was always telling daft jokes, always having a laugh and cheering people up and taking care of them. He would do anything for anyone. She thought of his funny DIY projects, which appeared on a weekend – the dolls' house he made her, the child-box attachment for his bike which took so long to finish that she had outgrown it by the time it was ready, or any of the many pieces of furniture her mother demanded, usually something covered in mirrored tiles so she could look at her reflection.

Hmm, she doubted she would be able to keep her mother out of it. Still, what did it matter? She just had to get started. Finally, she wrote a few words and stopped, feeling exhausted. This was like pulling teeth. Hearing shrieks outside, she gladly looked up from the laptop to see what was going on. Dawn and Shenise and Shanelle were running around in the garden in the rain, screaming and jumping and slipping on the grass and generally behaving like lunatics. Dawn's clothes were becoming drenched, not the most flattering look for a woman of her size, stupid cow.

Immediately she heard Sue's voice in her head: 'What did I tell you, Jen? I said just do the *opposite* to what you're doing now, it's not rocket science!'

A pang of guilt erupted in her chest. Was she being too hard on her unruly neighbour? Was she being a snob as Lonny had said when they had that row? What was the opposite to stupid cow? Immediately she said to herself, *Dawn is a stressed out young mum who is managing to grab a few minutes of fun with her girls.* She was proud of herself for coming up with this, proud and pleased that she had done what Sue suggested. She looked again at Dawn and the little girls, who were now soaked and muddy. They were having fun in the rain, the kind of fun that she and Sue loved to have when they were little girls, the kind of fun that her boys loved too. Maybe Dawn was doing her best with the few resources that she had. Maybe, as Lonny said, life was tough for her, maybe her husband was a prat who gave her no support, maybe –

'Woh! Fuckin' 'ell fire!' screamed Dawn as she slipped on the grass and slid down the garden on her backside, kicking garden toys hither and thither. 'Fuck! Fuck! Fuck!'

'Fuck! Fuck!' shouted Shenise and Shanelle, in saggy nappies and soaking clothes. Jenny's scowl returned with a vengeance. Good grief, she thought, she is deplorable.

Lonny came into the bedroom to change his wet clothes. He looked out of the window and saw Dawn and her daughters.

'Wahey!' he said. 'Look at old Dawnie out in the rain.' He waved to her out of the window, enjoying seeing her laughing and having so much fun.

Jenny sighed. Lonny could see Dawn's charm but she couldn't. And that was the end of it.

'How're you feeling, duck? A bit better?'

'Yes thanks, love. I'm just trying to get started on my essay but it's so difficult.'

'What do you have to do again?'

'Write about the different roles in my life, you know, like, wife, mother, daughter, carer... friend.'

'Does it have to rhyme?'

'No.'

'Do you need to use a lot of clever words?'

'I don't think so, not really.'

'So, what's the problem?'

'Well, it's no problem really, I'm just not used to it, I only joined the class to meet Trudi.'

Lonny chuckled and kissed her. 'You and your Trudi, I hope she's as nice as you think she is.'

'Of course she is, she's lovely. You might meet her at the party, Lon. I'll try and get her to wait until you and the lads come back from the cinema. Only a few days to go now.'

'Have you got it all organised?'

'I still need a few more people but it's only Monday. I'm sure by Saturday night I'll have found some nice women.'

'OK, duck, what about booze and stuff?'

'Just a few bottles of wine, that will be plenty.'

'Sure?'

'Yes.'

'You don't want to –' he stopped. 'Never mind.'

'No,' said Jenny. 'What were you going to say?'

'Nuthin, duck, nuthin.'

'Yes you were, what were you going to say?'

'Just that we could go and see the doctor tomorrow maybe.'

'What for? You know he'll only want to put me back on anti-depressants.'

'Yeah, but there may be something else.'

'No there won't. I'm glad I went last time, cos he gave me the idea to go to college, but there's no reason to go again now, especially when I'm going to be so busy this week.'

'Alright, duck, alright.'

He kissed her affectionately and was just about to leave her side when she shrieked loudly:

'OH NO!'

An email had popped up on the screen: '*Due to flooding at the college, tonight's class is cancelled.*'

'Oh no, that means I won't get to see Trudi! How do I know if she's coming to the party or not?'

'Ring her, haven't you got her phone number?'

'No, I never got it. I never got her email address either!'

'The teacher might give it to you.'

'She won't, she'd give me a filthy look for even asking! Stupid cow!'

'Jen, stop it.'

'She's a right bitch, that one!'

'Jen, stop it! Stop talking like a bloody *Daily Mail* reader!'

She burst into tears. 'I'm not! Why d'you keep saying that! Oh Lon, I can't stand it, I can't stand it, I thought I was going to see Trudi tonight and now I won't! Why is it so difficult? It's not fair! Why won't anything go my way?'

Lonny sighed. 'Eight o'clock tomorrow morning, duck, I'm calling the doctor's and getting an appointment.' He puffed his mouth out like he always did when he couldn't quite believe what was happening. 'Bloody Trudi,' he muttered as he left the room.

Jenny curled up on the bed and started sobbing.

CHAPTER 22

Joyce's son

The intense sunshine was back the next morning. At 8am Lonny kept getting the engaged signal from the surgery so he gave up, knowing that any GP she saw wouldn't really have the solution to his wife's problems. If she would just get out in the garden a bit more and look at the wonders of Mother Nature maybe that would lift her spirits, but her intense dislike of Dawn was ruining the chances of that happening.

Earlier that morning, when he had been doing the rounds in the garden, he saw that something had messed up the soil on the cauliflower bed and no doubt scattered the seeds to the wind. He was just about to curse the cat from three doors down when he found the heart drawn in the soil. OK, well it was obviously still early days. Very early days. At least singing that Nina song had been a release for her, he thought, and he hoped against hope that the upcoming party would be the same.

Jenny was making breakfast and trying hard to shake off the feeling of impending doom about the party. Did Trudi say she would definitely come? That was how Jenny remembered it – but was that right? She tried to recall the specifics of what had happened in the classroom. She had given her the invitation and Trudi had said something like, 'Oooh sounds great! I'll definitely be there!' and then given her a big hug to seal the deal. Her phone number and email address were on the invitation so surely if she had changed her mind she would let her know?

Just at that moment, her phone buzzed with a message... from a new number. *'Hi Jenny, what a shame about the flood, never mind it will give us a bit more time to start writing, I still haven't written a word! I'm off to visit my in-laws for a few days but hope to be back by Saturday for your party, looking forward to it! Trudi X'*

Oh my God, hallelujah! She ran over to Lonny shrieking with delight. 'She's coming, Lon! She's coming!'

Lonny tried to smile but really he was wondering how long this high would last before the next low kicked in.

Jenny quickly sent Trudi a message saying that she too hadn't written a word and she was looking forward to seeing her at the party. How lovely it was to send that message. It was true what they say – the best things in life are the simplest things. She set off for work with Lonny's grandma totally in charge of her internal mantra. Hallelujah! Trudi was definitely coming to the party. Now she just needed to find some more women.

She brooded on this as she made her way from Bill's to Joyce's. Bill had been on automatic pilot this morning requiring only food and toilet help and the fan moving to a better position and not much else. Which was good because Jenny had a lot to think about. What if there were only Trudi, Emily, Hannah and Mrs Holdcroft plus herself, would that be so bad? Of course, Hannah had already said she had no money to spend, she was just coming for a night out. So that would mean the Neal's Yard woman would have only four potential customers. Sod it – she had said she needed seven minimum. She would have to ask Hannah if she had any friends who wanted to come, and try hard not to sound desperate.

She approached Joyce's drive and wondered at the nice new electric car in the driveway. She hurried to the front door in case the doctor was there.

Hannah opened it. 'Hi Jen, come in, duck, Ben's here, Joyce's son.' Jenny followed Hannah into the lounge where Ben, a smartly dressed man in his early fifties was sitting with Joyce, drinking tea. He stood up when Jenny came in, like the gentleman he was, like the gentleman that Joyce had inevitably produced, her being the classy lady she was.

'Hello, Jenny,' he said. 'Lovely to meet you at last, I've heard a lot about you.'

'Oh!' Jenny exclaimed. 'Has Joyce been talking about me?'

'No,' Ben said quickly, 'Hannah.'

'Oh, yes of course, sorry.' What a prat she was sometimes, of course poor Joyce couldn't possibly be singing her praises, she didn't know what planet she was on let alone who she was with or what their names were.

'I've just been getting up to scratch with everything, Jenny. I'm sorry I can't be here more often. It's difficult when you work in London. I always intend to visit every month but the weekends just get booked up with other commitments.'

'Oh, don't worry, we understand, Ben,' said Jenny. 'It's a very good team here anyways, isn't it, Hannah? Everyone loves your mum and we take good care of her.'

'Thank you, I appreciate it.' He looked at Jenny. 'Hannah said that you're a singer and that you're trying to help Mum sing again.'

'Well, it was an idea I had, I know it may not work but it did seem as though she might join in. I don't know if I'm dreaming though.'

'Yes well, she hasn't sung for many years now, many, many years, but she does certainly still love her music. You know, if there's a concert you think she would like at the Victoria Hall or even up in Manchester, if you want to take her somewhere, please do, just send me the invoice. I will pay for all the expenses and for your time of course. You can get an idea of what she likes from her CDs. It's not all Beethoven and Mozart, she loves the old musicals, Rogers and Hammerstein that kind of thing. And Gilbert and Sullivan of course.'

'Of course,' said Jenny. 'OK, thank you. I will have a look and see what's on.'

She thought what a nice man Ben was and what a shame it was for him to see his mum deteriorate like this. She felt for him.

'And she hasn't tried to run off anywhere recently?' he asked.

'No we don't give her any opportunity to,' said Hannah. 'She's never on her own except at night when she's asleep.'

'I do worry about that as well,' he said, 'but I can't really afford round-the-clock care until things go downhill and she has to have it.'

'Has she ever wandered off?' asked Jenny curiously.

'Gosh yes,' said Ben. 'She will head for the A50 given half a chance – remember when your predecessors caught her down there, Hannah? They just got to her in the nick of time.'

Jenny gasped in horror.

'Don't worry, she's not left alone for even five minutes,' said Hannah.

'Of all places to go to! Fancy heading for the A50!'

'Well there's a story behind that, it's not quite as random as it seems,' said Ben. 'My father and brother were killed on that stretch of road, a long time ago of course, but obviously my mother never got over it. Neither did I, for that matter,' he smiled sadly.

Jenny reached her hand out towards Joyce. 'Oh no, how awful. What happened?'

'We were all in the car, it was just one of those cases where the people on one side survive and the people on the other don't.'

'How old was your brother?' asked Jenny.

'We were sixteen at the time. He was my twin. My father had just had his fiftieth birthday.'

'Is that when Joyce stopped singing?'

'Yes, that's right.'

Jenny looked at Joyce with even more fondness than before. Poor, poor Joyce. She'd had to keep going all those years because of Ben and now that she was old she could retreat into a crazy Alzheimer's twilight where she didn't have to remember the sound of brakes screeching on that awful day.

'Hannah says it's you who has been going through Mum's wardrobe, Jenny, making more of an effort with her clothes and jewellery. Thank you for that.'

'You're welcome,' said Jenny. 'I just thought it was a shame for all those lovely vintage clothes to be gathering dust. They're back in fashion again! And she does seem to like wearing them.'

'Yes, she loved dressing up and looking nice when I was young,' said Ben. 'And anything with beads on is good for her to touch, it helps with her anxiety.'

Jenny noticed, not for the first time, that Joyce was playing with her bracelet, taking it off, putting it back on and feeling each bead like it was a rosary.

*

Back at home, sitting alone on the patio, Jenny ruminated on the contrast between Joyce and Eddie. Joyce must have only been in her forties when her husband died so she may well have had further opportunities for love but no, she understandably couldn't get past what had happened. Whereas Eddie seemed to be intent on

191

gallivanting back down the aisle with this teacher woman immediately his first year as a widower was up. How could he?

She was looking forward to seeing the girls the next day. She would take the train to Cardiff but not stay over, they would just go shopping and maybe somewhere nice to eat. If she didn't see Eddie that would be the best thing really.

The sun was beating down again and now, after all that rain, everything in the raised beds looked lush and green like a series of abundant oases in the garden. Lonny's plan was to eventually get rid of all the grass to make way for more vegetable growing. One of his books was called *Food Not Lawns*, which just about said where he was at. He wanted every corner of the garden earning its keep. He said the boys could play football at the park, they were too big to play in the garden anymore anyway. Jenny was just about managing to hang onto the rose bed on the border with Fusun's garden, behind the garage. She used to love checking them each evening through the summer, and she especially loved the divine smell of the yellow Buttercup rose bushes that had been in the garden since they moved in. Just the scent of those gorgeous flowers would be enough to send her into raptures. This last year however she hadn't been quite so attentive to them for obvious reasons.

A text sounding on her phone made her sit up straight when she saw who it was from. Her cousin Fiona in Cardiff. Uncle Pat had been moved into a hospice and wasn't expected to last much longer. Jenny stared at the message for a few seconds. Stared at it and then re-read it.

So he was finally dying. Good, the old creep. Maybe now she would be free.

For some reason, even though this was good news, that thought of freedom made her put her hand up to her eyes to catch a tear. Had she really not been free before now? Was it all depending on him? A man who had abused her more than forty years ago? When Sue was alive, she felt free, that was for sure. But now... now, she had to admit that it wasn't the first emotion to come to mind. More like depression, misery, bad temper and hate she snapped to herself in frustration.

Oh God, she didn't want to hate anyone, but now in her fifty-first year she seemed to be hating way too many people. Of course she had always hated Uncle Pat and really the sooner he was dead the better. But she knew that the feeling of acidity and bitterness that she had for people like Miranda and Dawn and Alan and even Debbie, well maybe hate was too strong a word, but she didn't like feeling that way, it was a horrible feeling. She was judging them, just like she was judging Eddie, but sod it, they deserved it didn't they? Yes, they bloody well did! Certainly Miranda did anyway. And obviously Alan did. And as for that nosy parker Dawn...

But when Sue was alive, she was never aware of anyone irritating her like this, she was a lot more like her husband in those days. Live and let live might have been their motto.

Oh for the good old days...

She lay back in her chair and began to doze in the heat.

She caught the scent of the yellow Buttercup roses, which seemed more heavenly than ever this year. Then a breeze brought her a smell of something delicious cooking in Fusun's kitchen, it wafted over the hedge from patio to patio and enticed her to relax further. The smell of the food and the sounds of young babies chuckling and birds chirping in the trees and her friend the cow mooing in the back field, they all began to soothe her and after a few breaths, she felt like she was stepping into a cool milky bath. She felt peaceful and good.

CHAPTER 23

The girls

Lonny drove Jenny to the train station the next day, still unsure of what he was dealing with: was she stable or unstable? Was it safe for her to go off on a day trip? What if the girls turned up at the station late? She could just wander off and anything could happen.

Don't be so daft, he told himself, her mental health couldn't be that bad, she was still holding down a job, well, the daytime one at least. The trouble was, he had no faith in any doctor sorting her out, he knew that she had changed when Sue died and she might never go back to the old Jenny, the one who was his rock, his best friend, his sexy, sassy wife and a fantastic mother to the boys. All of those pillars seemed to have been bulldozed and were collapsed in a heap on the floor and it was up to him to try and help her stand them up again. No doctor peddling anti-depressants would be able to do it. He had read that it was the small steps that counted as far as depression went. Rarely was there a big miracle cure or an overnight success. Of course, people liked to think there was, but in reality it was all about the tiny steps you took every day. Just like in the garden: mulching, composting, sowing the seeds, checking for pests, watering, feeding, then finally harvesting – and that was a lot of work too. Everything was a lot of work and these things had to be done, there was no getting away from it. The trick was to get it all on a schedule so you could take daily positive steps without even thinking about it. He wondered though if Sue's death had been the final straw after a series of negative small steps – losing the salon, her other friends moving away and maybe her perimenopause, which he knew she was on despite her telling Dawn otherwise.

Actually, he thought, these were all pretty big steps, any one of them on their own could cause some grief. He wondered what small actions he could do each day to support her moving in the right direction. Every day he would tell her he loved her, every day he would encourage her to get out in the garden and get her hands in the soil and be in touch with Mother Nature. Hopefully it would be when Dawn was indoors as she definitely seemed to be a trigger for Jen at the moment. And every day they must eat good food, fresh food that the boys could help pick and cook. What else?

He thought proudly of her singing that wonderful Nina Simone song. That was amazing.

The traffic was moving slowly as they approached Stoke station. When it ground to a halt at the lights, he turned to look at her. She was on her phone, reading another text from her cousin Fiona.

'Uncle Pat died last night,' she said.

'The old creep?' Lonny asked, reaching for her hand. She nodded. 'Well, that's good news, one less perv to worry about! Shame he lasted so long, int it?'

'Now who's talking like the *Daily Mail?*' she laughed, pleased that he had said it and not her. She began to read the message again, worried it might just be a dream. Lonny gave her a moment, then he said, 'Jen, come 'ere, look at me.'

'What?' she said looking up.

'I was just thinking of you singing that Nina song the other day.

That was awesome.'

'Thank you, darling,' she smiled.

He put his arm around her and pulled her to him.

'I love you, duck. If I told you five hundred times a day it wouldn't be enough.'

'Thanks, Lon, I love you too.'

When she got out of the car at the station and blew him a kiss he felt pleased that he had made an extra effort. This is what he had to do each day now. Small steps to help get her back on track. This is what it was all about. He'd been trying to do it before, but what with the garden and the solar panels and the activism, he knew he had been distracted. He must find a way of being able to focus on her as well as everything else.

Jenny boarded the train and walked through a couple of carriages looking for a seat as she hadn't managed to reserve one. With the news of Uncle Pat's death sinking in, she was beginning to feel exhilarated. The abuse had all happened so long ago, she hadn't expected to feel such utter relief. The news had made her spirits soar. She still had to deal with her mother though. Her mother would expect a call and a long chat, but that could wait. She was going to enjoy today with the girls, then she was going to enjoy the party with Trudi and then possibly after that, she would finally deal with her mother.

As she walked towards the next carriage, she could see that there were a lot of people in it, but hopefully she would manage to find a seat somewhere. As the doors opened, she was met with a barrage of young people with banners who were going to a protest in Birmingham, one of the many climate change demonstrations that were going on around the country. Jenny recognised the Extinction Rebellion logo from the poster that Lonny had in their front window. She remembered her caution last year when she heard that Alice and

Amy would be protesting in Parliament Square and potentially missing school for several days.

'They might miss out on something important though, Lon,' she had said. 'They might even get arrested. Imagine having a criminal record when you're trying to find a job.'

Lonny snorted. 'That's the least of their worries!'

Now, she found herself smiling at the young protestors and some old ones too. Thank God we have people like this in the world she thought to herself. She made her way slowly up the carriage and because she was looking at everyone in a friendly fashion it wasn't long before someone jumped up and offered her a seat.

'Oh, thank you very much!' she said and sat down right in the middle of them.

'Not at all,' said the young man, 'you're welcome to join the party.'

'My husband is a bit of an activist,' she said, beaming. 'He thinks we can save the world by growing our own food.'

'He's right!' said a young girl with a woodland scene painted on her face. That must be the kind of face painting that Chloe was talking about, Jenny thought; it looked great.

'Of course, it still leaves the fashion industry, industrial agriculture, fossil fuels...' said someone else.

'Well I've solved the clothes problem in our house,' said Jenny, on a roll. 'We can have whatever we like so long as it's second hand. I buy for the whole family on eBay. And we walk or cycle most places too.'

'What's your name?' asked a young woman.

'Jenny.'

'Jenny, you're awesome!' she said and high-fived her. Everyone laughed and the talk continued.

As the journey passed, Jenny observed that she was managing to keep up with the conversation and contribute every now and then. It was amazing what she had picked up from Lonny. She realised that she was feeling good, strong even. After a year of feeling so low, it looked like things were finally looking up. Well, at fifty-one, it was better late than never. A sudden thought crossed her mind: she wished she had stood up to Uncle Pat all those times when she was little. How her life might have been different if she had found the courage to defend herself. And how much worse it would have been if Sue hadn't been there for her when she was.

At Cardiff station, she ran towards the girls with open arms and the three of them hugged for some time. It was difficult for them not to shed a tear, it had been a while since they had seen each other — this was only the third time since their mother's funeral. Jenny was ashamed about this as it must be her fault — she was the adult with the money and the car, the girls were young and had recently lost their mother, she should be looking after them. But it seemed like it had taken her almost a year to realise this.

They went for lunch in a cafe where the food was from regenerative farms and then went shopping at a vintage fair to buy Amy's birthday present. They walked among the trees in Roath Park and Jenny told the girls, not for the first time, of the times she and Sue had played there, in the days when the park had a big long slide, and how it was so special that they had wanted to go there every day. Their talk wove in and out of life with Sue and without Sue and they cried and then dried their tears and felt full of hope and then cried again.

Overall, it was a lovely day.

Eighteen-year-old Amy was the one who looked most like her mum; her dimples mesmerised Jenny just like Sue's had done. She was feisty like her mum too. Jenny laughed when she heard Amy's tale of how her English teacher was giving her grief about being late for lessons because of the shifts she had to do at her part-time job. She loved how neatly Amy had put him in his place with just a line to bury him and then a smile to raise him up again and tell him that she would still be friendly. Jenny bet that all the teachers loved her just like they loved Sue. To have someone so eager to hoover up knowledge and excel themselves was a gift to the classroom. Jenny felt a twang of guilt about conning Celia, the creative writing teacher, into letting her study, when really all she wanted was to get to know Trudi. Should she tell the girls this, make them laugh? No, she didn't want to come across as moving swiftly on from Sue, like their father had done.

When the girls mentioned Charlotte, their soon-to-be new stepmother, they spoke kindly of her and felt for her coming into a family where they were all still grief stricken. Even Eddie, she was pleased to hear, had his moments when he still broke down and cried like a baby. Good. Jenny thought better of him for it. Charlotte had her work cut out for her but that was the way it should be.

When she heard about Alice's new boyfriend, she wondered whether she should say anything about contraception because surely Eddie wouldn't. Still, didn't teenagers know it all these days? A worrying thought crossed her mind. Had Sue put her in charge of this kind of stuff? She couldn't remember, those last few days at the hospice were a blur now. The talks they had had in those last days, the cuddles and kisses and hand-holding and the laughter breaking through the tears were all beginning to fade from her mind. That last bout of cancer had moved so rapidly that the medical staff expected it to be days not weeks. In the end, it was a fortnight. Lonny ran the show at home single-handedly while she doted on her friend, trying to be strong for the girls and Eddie but failing miserably.

199

When they were alone one time and she had caught Sue waking up and looking at her directly with sadness in her eyes, she had found herself taking her hand and repeating something she had read: that there is no such thing as time in heaven, which meant that Jenny would be there already when Sue arrived so there wasn't any need to be afraid. Everyone else they loved would be there too. 'Great,' Sue had smiled quietly. 'We'll have a party.'

'Now, I don't want to hear about any unexpected pregnancies,' Jenny blurted out clumsily to the girls before adding, 'You've got to do your mum proud. Study, study, study, then marry someone fantastic.'

'Things aren't really like that any more, Jenny,' Amy laughed. 'No one expects to be with someone forever these days.'

'Well you never know, you might be lucky and meet someone like Lonny,' Jenny said, which for some reason made the girls roar with laughter.

'My commitment is to Mother Earth,' said Alice.

'Mine too,' said Amy.

'Good girls, there you are, that's just like Lonny!' She laughed and together they set off for afternoon tea at a local restaurant, Jenny in the middle with Amy and Alice on each side of her, linking her arms like they used to with Sue.

Afterwards, when Eddie insisted on coming to pick up the girls so that he could say hello to Jenny, she hugged him and noted that the grief was still showing in his face and in his newly grey hair. She saw his fiancé, Charlotte, in the front seat of the car and managed to smile and wave at her. Such a young woman, she couldn't be more than thirty. Jenny was surprised that she felt nothing but compassion for her. Charlotte didn't realise the quality of the woman in whose footsteps she was walking. She didn't realise it at all.

CHAPTER 24

The boys

When she got back, she was both exhilarated and exhausted. It had been a long day, with two tiring train journeys and a big dose of quality time with her favourite girls in the middle. They wouldn't be able to come to the party of course, they were far too busy, but that didn't dampen her spirits. And never far from her mind was the happy news of Uncle Pat's death. She was stretched out on the sofa with her head in Lonny's lap, telling him the girls' news, when Solly ran in exclaiming squeamishly, 'Dad, there's a girl on Nate's phone talking all sexy! She's got no clothes on!'

'What?' Jenny jumped up instantly.

'Nate!' roared Lonny. 'Get down here!'

He ran to the bottom of the stairs. 'Nate! Get down here now! And bring yer phone!'

Silence.

'Bring it I said!'

Ryan came downstairs giggling. He picked up his guitar and started plucking it.

'What's going on, Ry?' Lonny asked.

'I dunno, Dad.'

'Has she got no clothes on?'

'I didn't see anything, I dunno.'

'Nate! Nate!'

Lonny lost patience and charged up the stairs, quickly followed by everyone else.

Nate was in his room rapidly making things disappear off his mobile.

'Gimme that phone!' Lonny grabbed it before realising that he wouldn't have a clue where to find anything anyway. 'Where is it, what app is it on?'

'There's nothing there,' said a sheepish Nate. 'It was only a joke anyhow.'

'For you it might have been! It wasn't a joke for that poor woman though was it? Eh? It's no flippin' joke for her! Imagine her life, Nate. You're just looking at her body, you're not seeing the true picture. She's being exploited and you're part of it! I'm disappointed in you, son. Haven't you listened to anything I've told you about respect for women?'

'You should be ashamed of yourself, Nate!' Jenny wagged a finger.

'I anna dun nuthin!'

'Don't give me that!' Lonny snapped. 'Why else would a woman out in bloody Romania or somewhere be taking her kit off for a fourteen-year-old in Stoke? She's desperate for money int she? She can't eat because of the corrupt fucking capitalist system keeping everybody down! She's got her low-life pimp on one side and her starving kids on the other! It's disgusting, son. You're taking advantage of a desperate woman!'

'She's not desperate!'

'She is!'

'She inna, Dad! And she's not from Romania.'

'How do you know?'

'Cos she sits next to me in History,' Nate blurted forlornly. Ryan punctuated his brother's confession with a good strum of his guitar.

Lonny and Jenny both looked like they were catching goldfish.

'Wha?' Lonny spluttered.

'She's in your class?' Jenny grimaced. 'Right. What's her name? Give me her name, the little tart!'

'Duck!' Lonny groaned. 'What have I told you about that attitude?'

'It's Polly Holdcroft!' grassed Solly and promptly got a clout from his brother.

Jenny gasped and put her hand to her mouth.

Lonny said, 'Which Holdcroft is she? Is her old man the one at the allotments?'

'No, the other one,' said Sol. 'Her mum's at the newsagents.'

'Mrs Holdcroft?' Jenny wailed. 'Oh, no! She's coming to the party! Oh, Nate, what have you done?'

Lonny snorted, exasperated that they couldn't go five minutes without panic about that bloody party.

'I anna dun nuthin!' roared Nate. 'I never asked her to do it!'

'Didn' yer?' asked Lonny, peering into his son's eyes to try and establish the truth of the matter.

'No! I'm as shocked as everybody else!' said Nate. Ryan strummed his guitar hard again, trying his best not to laugh. Jenny wrestled it out of his hands.

'What have I told you about playing that guitar – play a tune or don't play anything!' she snapped.

'Nate, tell me the truth, duck,' said Lonny.

'Come on, young man, talk!' said Jenny.

'Are you guilty or are you innocent?' shouted Solly.

'Fuck off!' said Nate, shoving his brother.

'Nate!'

'He's guilty m'Lord,' interjected Solly.

'No I'm not! I'm fuckin' innocent.'

'Nate!'

'Did you encourage her to do it?' asked Lonny.

'No! Course I didn't! I dun even know who she is! I never even sat next to her till last week.'

'Well, why did you go and sit next to her?' asked Jenny, anxious that it be her son's fault and not the daughter of her party guest. 'Who said you could do that?'

'The teacher. He moved us all about.'

'And then what?' said Lonny. 'Yer started talking to her when you should have been studying?'

'No way Dad, she was talking to me!'

'And then you talked back, right?'

'No way! I never! I never spoke to her!'

'Well, you were looking at her then?'

'No, never! I never even looked in her direction!'

'Well you should have talked to her, Nate,' said Jenny. 'And you should have looked at her! Then she wouldn't have to be doing all this stupid nonsense just to attract your attention.'

Lonny raised his eyebrows like he couldn't quite believe what his wife was saying.

'Jen! For crying out loud!'

'What? It's the truth!'

Lonny turned back to Nate. 'What's wrong with the girl? Dunt she know how dangerous it is to post that stuff online? All the pervs'll be after her in no time!'

'It's not online, Dad,' Nate corrected him. 'It was a message just for me.'

'A message just for you? Hasn't she heard of bloody texting?'

Lonny asked. 'Listen, Nate, just tell me the truth. Did you encourage her in any way?'

'No. I never.'

'You sure now?' said Lonny.

'Yeah, Dad, I swear.'

'OK, OK. I believe you. Good lad, good lad,' he muttered, hugging him and kissing his cheek.

Jenny couldn't help but breathe a sigh of relief. She patted her son's arm. 'Good boy, Nate, good boy.'

'You've done nothing wrong,' continued Lonny. 'She's obviously a bit forward or summat. We'll have to speak to Mrs Holdcroft about it. Right. Come on, let's get up there now, the shop'll still be open –'

'NO!' shrieked Jenny, standing with arms outstretched to stop him passing. 'No, no, no! Lon, please don't speak to her, she'll be embarrassed and she won't come to the party! Please, I'm begging you, don't speak to Mrs Holdcroft!'

Nate turned away, catching Ryan's eye, both of them trying hard not to grin.

'Bloody 'ell, duck! Course we've got to speak to her.'

'Not till after the party.'

'What? No way, we've gotta tell her now!'

'It was only a bit of fun, Dad,' said Nate. 'It won't happen again.'

'See?' said Jenny. 'It won't happen again, Lon. It was just a bit of fun.'

'You just called her a little tart!'

'Well I was being too judgemental. You're always telling me off for that aren't you? We can tell her after the party.'

'Bloody 'ell,' snorted Lonny. 'We either do it now or we don't do it, Jen. You can't invite her to have a nice time at the party and then tell her afterwards.'

'Why not?' said Jenny, exasperated that the numbers on the party list were coming down faster than they were going up. 'Are you sure she's Polly's mum?' she asked the boys. 'Are you sure she's not her nan? If it's her nan at the shop, we don't need to tell her, surely?'

'No, she's definitely not her nan-ar,' said Solly, pronouncing the last syllable strongly, the way they do in Stoke, where three nan-ars make a police siren. Nan-ar, nan-ar, nan-ar.

'But she's so old!'

'She's same age as you, Mum!' said Ryan.

'But she wants everyone to call her Mrs Holdcroft, that's so old-fashioned.'

'That's the way she is, she's dead strict,' shrugged Nate.

Lonny snorted. 'That's working out well, int it?'

*

Later, when Jenny was in the shower, Lonny thought he would ram home a bit of relationship education while she was out of the way and unable to twist everything to be about that bloody party.

'I just don't want you lads messing your lives up, you've got to be so careful,' he said to Nate in particular, who was sitting next to him on the sofa while Ryan was further up and back to plucking on his guitar. Solly lay across his dad's lap, occasionally moving towards Nate's, where his head would end up in his brother's crotch.

'You've got to go nice and slow,' Lonny advised. 'Get to know them first, get to be good friends, find out about her family, what they do —'

'Who they vote for,' said Ryan, laughing.

'Yeah that's true, Ry. You can laugh, but these things are important.'

'Dad, there's no time to do all of that stuff,' Nate said, shoving Solly's head out of his lap.

'You've got to make time,' said Lonny. 'First and foremost, you want to make sure she's a nice, decent person. That's the most important thing. You've got to ask yourself, "Is she nice? Is she decent?"'

The three brothers looked at each other like they couldn't quite believe what their father had just said.

'Oh man,' said Nate, hardly able to contain himself. 'She's decent alright, I know that much, Dad!' He dissolved into high-pitched hysterical laughter.

Ryan strummed his guitar loudly to punctuate the line.

'Oi!' Lonny laughed and grabbed Nate's knees and thighs and proceeded to tickle him hard. 'Get him lads!' he shouted to the others and they all piled high on top of Nate.

CHAPTER 25

Tapestry

The next morning was Friday and only one more day before the party. Jenny slept in Lonny's arms and just before she woke she dreamt she was looking at a huge tapestry. It was so big that it hid most of the wall it was hanging on. She was one of many women looking at the different colours and shades and textures that were present in the tapestry. Everyone was remarking just how exquisite and how beautiful it was and how rich in substance. There was nothing plain about it, it was so intricate and there was so much detail it could take someone a whole day to view it.

Jenny looked more closely at the large dark patch in the middle out of which the other lighter areas seemed to emanate. There was probably just as much light as shade and yet it was the murky, inky area in the middle which attracted her attention. Everything was being fed from this large bleak centre and when she looked closely she could see not just a black or grey weave but hundreds of different colours weaving in and out of each other, many of them bright in colour. The darkness was an illusion and, in fact, the lightness was also an illusion in the other areas that were pale. It seemed the only truth was that there were thousands and thousands of different colours and textures making up the whole picture.

She tried to focus her eyes and stand back so that she could see the whole tapestry but she couldn't. So she turned to one of the other women and asked, 'I can't make out the whole picture, is it abstract? What does it mean?'

But the woman just smiled.

Jenny woke up with a start when the alarm started to holler. Lonny immediately got up and stretched and started singing a happy tune as he went into the bathroom.

Jenny wondered what the dream had meant. She went over it in her head so that she could remember later. A big tapestry with lots of women looking at it and a big dark patch in the middle that was actually, when you looked closely, made up of tons of different colours which were not all dark at all.

She thought of the lovely day she had yesterday with the girls. She would ask Lonny if they could take them on holiday this summer with the boys. Either to Wales or over to Spain to see her parents. The girls would be a nice distraction from her mother.

She heard Lonny take a phone call as he raced downstairs. 'Yeah, we can do it,' he said. 'I'll confirm it in ten minutes when I've spoken to the lads. I'll get back to you, duck.'

It sounded like a last-minute gig. A shot of panic ran through Jenny as she automatically thought that she would have to do it too. Then she remembered with a sigh of relief. The Marie Osmond days were over.

After a super quick shower, when she both collected the water to feed the plants and put off shaving, she went downstairs and saw Lonny already out in the garden doing his chores. She made them both tea and toast and took it out to the patio.

'We've got a gig tonight up at Macclesfield, duck.' Lonny came down the garden. 'Someone's dropped out. Is that OK with you?'

'Of course, love, it's fine. What happened anyway, why such short notice?'

'The old Elvis dude had a heart attack.'

'Really? He wasn't that old was he?'

'He was eighty if he was a day, duck!'

'Oh. Oh, I must be thinking of that other one we met up in Chester that time.'

'No, not him, I'm talking about that old dude who looked like he might have been homeless.'

'I don't remember.'

Lonny sat down and took her hand just the way he always did. He gestured towards the garden.

'Look at this eh, babe? The Garden of Eden! Talk about lush.'

She smiled. 'Isn't it beautiful? I love this hot weather, just walking around the garden seeing the bees and the flowers and all the veg, it's wonderful.'

'Good for your depression an' all, Jen,' said Lonny. 'They say the more contact you have with Mother Nature, the better for your wellbeing.'

'I'm not so depressed anymore I don't think. Maybe I am still a bit wobbly, but nowhere near as bad as I was.'

'Good,' he said as he kissed her hand. 'I think seeing the girls did you some good, dint it?'

'Yes,' she said. 'I love them so much.' She told him she wanted them to come on a holiday with them every year, that she wanted a lot more contact with them. She had been afraid that seeing them would spark utter grief, like it had done in the first few months, but they seemed to have got past that and yesterday had been a lovely day for all. From now on, she wanted to always have a date in the diary for when she would next see them.

'Good idea,' said Lonny, kissing her some more. 'Come 'ere you gorgeous woman,' he smooched as he dragged her over onto his lap. 'Come 'ere a minute.'

The morning sun hit the garden and the young apple and pear trees lining the fence threw a dappled light onto the remnants of the lawn. Through the branches, a pair of hands held onto the fence posts; swollen, carb-fuelled hands, bloated from a lifetime of eating barely legal, industrially produced, processed poison, fingernails bitten down to nothing. Dawn's bloodshot eyes watched the tender love scene and her usual confused grimace became a smile. Part of her wanted to back quietly away and not say anything, but the other part of her, the rash, sugar-fed, impulsive part of her, couldn't resist. She picked up an old piece of storm-damaged wood from the dried-up flower border.

'Boo!' she shouted, bashing the patchwork fence to make a racket and making a section of it slip to the ground.

Jenny tutted loudly.

Lonny looked up. 'Oi, Dawn, what have I told yer? Watch me fence!'

'Sorr - eee!' said Dawn, laughing and being anything but.

Jenny climbed off Lonny's lap. 'Honestly, she hasn't got a clue, Lon! Now you see why I want that fence going higher?' She walked inside, banging the door.

Lonny sighed. He had been hoping that she had forgotten about that blinking fence extension. Trouble was, he was beginning to see his wife's point of view: Dawn just didn't know how to behave.

'Dawnie,' he shouted to her. 'Come 'ere, I want a word.'

Dawn came back over to the fence grinning. 'What?'

'Listen, duck,' Lonny said. 'A word of advice. If you ever see a couple doing a bit of smooching and cuddling and such like, just back right off. Don't say anything, don't disturb them. And don't spy on them either!'

'Sorry, Lonny,' Dawn giggled. 'I don't know how to behave, me.'

'Yes you do,' said Lonny seriously. 'Deep down, you do, Dawnie.'

'Mark always says I don't,' she said, her face clouding over.

'Well he's confused about a lot of things, int he?' Lonny said, his face clouding over too. 'But I'm telling you that you do know these things, you just have to learn to listen to the quiet little voice inside you.'

'I can only hear the big loud voice telling me to do something stupid,' she said, grinning at the same time as her eyes began to water.

'Well, next time you hear the loud voice, maybe you should tell it to shut up so you can begin to hear the little voice,' said Lonny. 'Come 'ere a minute.' He put his arm around her and pulled her to the fence so that he could whisper quietly. 'Tell it to shut the *fuck* up!'

Dawn roared with laughter; she loved Lonny playing this joke with her, it was great. She never tired of hearing it. Plus, the way he pulled her closer to whisper in her ear, she liked that too. He was a good man and he was pulling her closer. She liked that so much.

Inside the house, Jenny tried not to despair at the thought that, since Dawn moved in, there had hardly been a day when she could totally relax in the garden. God Almighty, was this the future? Constant interruption? Noise, swearing, kids, disgusting laundry on the line and now spying? She felt like phoning the council's noisy neighbour department, only she had to begrudgingly admit that Dawn might not be classed as antisocial in the way that the Stevensons over the road with their non-stop classics blaring out could be. Maybe she should bypass the council and just phone Myrtle's son and let him know exactly what kind of tenants he was letting the house to. But he was up in Scotland now, he wouldn't come down just to sort out this kind of issue. No, she just needed to work on Lonny so that he would make that dratted fence higher. Sooner or later, she was sure that he would agree with her.

She put her make-up on, kissed Lon goodbye and set off for her early shift at Bill's, leaving Lonny to get the boys off to school. She never minded doing the early shift with Bill, it was often easier to get him up and ready for the day than it was to get the three boys up, fed and out the door.

While Bill was eating, she started her to-do list for the party. Food and drink. Crisps and – no, not crisps, it must be healthy. Trudi was so trim, she surely wouldn't be wanting to eat junk. OK, she could make her own hummus and pesto for dips, crudites, nuts, proper nuts not salted, some nice cheeses maybe and she could make a salad from the garden. What else? Three or four bottles of organic red and white wine from *Aldi*. She would ask Lonny to go down and get them so that he could see Matt. There was no way they would drink more than that surely? And she would need some soft drinks too.

'How's Miss Trudi then, duck?' asked Bill, finishing his boiled egg.

'I won't know until she arrives tomorrow night,' she told him. 'I wonder if she'll be early or late? Most people are either one or the other aren't they, Bill?'

'She's not the type to be late,' Bill assured her.

Bless you, Bill, thought Jenny. You don't know what you're talking about, but your heart is in the right place.

Which was more than she could say for miserable Debbie. She was trying to get up and out of bed before she should have been, as usual, and was precariously hanging onto the bedside rail. 'I knew you'd be late,' she moaned. 'You're too busy thinking about Trudi and that bloody party!'

'I am not late at all!' Jenny shouted anxiously, glancing at the clock

213

and rueing the day Debbie had extracted the details about the party from her. She had been trying to cheer her up but with so little going on in Debbie's life, it had done the opposite.

'Have you thought about what's going to happen if she doesn't get back from her in-laws in time?' she jeered.

'I have that all mapped out, Debbie love, I will get blind drunk!' Jenny tried to remain in control, having not considered that for one moment.

'I bet you will an' all,' scoffed Debbie.

'Now,' called Jenny, as she quickly grabbed the cleaning bucket, 'would you like me to start in the toilet today or should I just get down into the sewers and start there?'

In the kitchen, Debbie's frown broke and she chuckled.

In the bathroom, Jenny muttered, 'Give me strength' as she snapped her rubber gloves and started to put them on.

Then she heard Debbie in the kitchen call, 'That's a good one, Jen.'

Jenny smiled and got on with her work.

That evening she found herself alone because Lonny was at the gig and the boys were out. There was nothing on the box so she went online to see if there were any snack recipes that would be good to try for tomorrow evening. But she decided she didn't want to get stressed about trying anything new, she just wanted to do what was easy so that she could relax and enjoy herself. It was going to be a bit stressful anyway because the numbers were low and she would have to use her second credit card to buy enough products so that Cheryl the make-up lady didn't get the hump. Hannah had told a couple of her friends and hopefully they would both come but they might not. Plus, of course, she had to make sure she didn't slip up with Mrs Bloody Holdcroft. She still had to find out her first name – it would be ridiculous to introduce her to Trudi without knowing it. But overall, she felt positive. Damn it, this was her first little event in many a long time, and she was going to make sure that everyone who turned up had a great time, including herself.

She went upstairs to check what she would wear. She had an old favourite long summer dress that never failed to impress. It was a print with different shades of pink and orange and red. And the white in the pattern really lit her up. Jenny held it up against her skin, wondering if she should wear it yet again and then thinking of course she would. Emily may have seen it before but Trudi and Hannah certainly hadn't. She must remember to do her nails as well, it had been weeks, maybe months, since she had done them properly. This last year it just hadn't seemed important.

She hung the dress up by the window to get some fresh air. The summer evening was still light even though it must have been close to ten. She wondered how much longer the boys would be out with their friends. They had a ten o'clock deadline which they were always pretty good at sticking to so they should be walking through the door at any minute. She wasn't used to this level of quietness in the house.

She looked down at Lonny's garden, the veg and flowers and fruit trees and shrubs all growing in abundance. And the field beyond, where she could see the cow in the distance. She noticed small trees had been planted which perhaps would eventually develop into an orchard. It really was going to be a Garden of Eden, it was absolutely beautiful.

Stepping away from the window, she sat on the bed for a moment with her notebook and pen to see if there were any last-minute things she could think of for the party. She was thankful that she wasn't at the gig, singing 'Paper Roses' to an empty room. She felt she had really moved on since that disastrous night. This time tomorrow,

Trudi would be here and they would be talking and laughing and getting to know each other and becoming friends. Yes, things were really changing for the better now and the party would be great fun, no matter the small numbers attending. She had done the right thing in arranging it – after all, Sue had nudged her into it, so it was bound to be a success. She wouldn't need to rely on the writing class alone now, she was much happier now that she was being more proactive. Maybe still a little nervous, but overall much happier.

She lay on the bed and began to doze. As she slept, she dreamt for a moment that Alan was in the room and shouting at her in a vicious, drunken voice.

'It's my fucking money!'

She woke then and realised that it wasn't a dream about Alan at all. The shouting was real and it was coming through the wall from the newlyweds' bedroom. She groaned. Really? At this time of night? For God's sake, she could hear them as clear as day.

'Give me the money,' Mark said. 'Give me the fucking money, Dawn! It's my money, where the fuck have you put it?'

'It's not your money, it's our money! Our money for food so you can fuck off!'

God, they sounded like they hated each other. Why the hell had they got married then? And he sounded like a right thug, not such a quiet bloke after all. Well, if they kept her awake tonight she would be extremely cross. The noise faded for a minute and she curled up on the bed, hoping that was the end of it.

But the row continued as they came back into the bedroom. They were shouting at each other like there was no tomorrow.

'I know you've got it, you cunt!'

'Fuck off!'

She heard some knocks and a scuffle and a loud thud.

Jenny gasped. She sat up and looked towards the adjoining wall behind the bedstead. It sounded like they were wrestling each other. She stood up and took a step towards the wall, just in time to hear the sound of a big slap and someone's head being bashed.

'Fucking cunt!' she heard Mark roar on the other side of the wall.

She gasped again, 'Oh my God!'

She froze, her hand at her mouth.

Then she heard Dawn moaning.

She reached out and touched the wall for a second till another thud made her jump.

She heard Dawn cry, 'Get off me, you pig! Fucking pig!'

Jenny's eyes flooded with tears.

All thoughts left her head and she went into automatic pilot.

CHAPTER 26

Allegiance

Jenny rapped sharply on the wall between them, shouting loudly, 'Dawn! Dawn! Are you OK?'

Silence. That was something, she'd obviously disturbed him.

A door slammed.

She ran into the bathroom where there would be a better view of Dawn's front garden – the scaffolding was blocking the front bedroom window completely. She opened the window just in time to see Mark walking quickly down the path and off into the dusk.

She ran down the stairs and out of the front door, along her path and around through Dawn's front gate, past the rubbish and bin bags and up to the front door. She rapped on it sharply.

'Dawn? Dawn?'

She heard one of the little ones begin to cry but then there was a hurried silence.

Jenny knocked again and looked through the letter box. The light was on upstairs but there was still no sound.

'Dawn! Are you OK?'

Still no sound.

She knocked again. 'Dawn!'

The light went off upstairs.

Jenny continued to look through the letter box. 'Dawn, if you don't come down here, I'm going to call the police!'

She saw a shadowy form at the top of the stairs. Dawn was slowly making her way down.

'Dawn, will you open the door, please, love?' she asked.

'Nah,' said Dawn when she reached the bottom. 'I'm alright, Jen.'

Jenny put her fingers through the letter box. 'Come here, darling, give me your hand.' Dawn reached out to touch Jenny's fingers. She was crying.

'Are you alright, lovey?'

'Yeah, I'm good.'

'Are you sure?'

'Yeah.'

'How long has this been going on for?' she asked. 'Has he done this before?'

'Yeah,' Dawn admitted reluctantly, her tears gaining momentum now. 'He's an arsehole.'

'He is, isn't he? He's a complete bastard.'

'Yeah.'

'Do you want to talk about it?'

'Nah.'

'Shall I phone the police for you?'

'Nah thanks, Jen.'

'Are you sure?'

'Yeah, I wanna go to bed now.'

'OK, well maybe we could meet up tomorrow for a cup of tea. Would you like that?'

'Yeah maybe.'

'OK, lovey,' Jenny said, reluctant to go. 'Are you sure you're alright?'

'Yeah, thanks, Jen.'

'Goodnight then and I'll see you tomorrow.'

'OK, duck.'

Jenny went home and sat in the encroaching darkness for a while, hardly able to believe what had just happened. Still in shock, she told the boys when they got in. Ryan reminded her that the boys had often heard arguing on a Saturday night when Jenny and Lonny had been out doing their gigs. They had mentioned it to Jenny on more than one occasion.

Yes I remember, Jenny thought, deeply ashamed that she had turned into some kind of excruciating snob just like her mother while her neighbour was being beaten by her own husband.

She slept fitfully, as though on red alert for more thumps and shouts coming from next door. But she heard nothing and when Lonny came back from the gig and slid into bed beside her, she thanked God – not for the first time – that she was married to him and not some messed-up brute who had to take his frustrations out on his wife. Then, just before she got up, she realised she had told Dawn that she would have a cup of tea and a chat tomorrow. But this was the day of the party and she would be running around like a blue-arsed fly. She would have to make time for her though, she must.

Before that happened though she would ask Fusun if she had heard anything this last month since Dawn moved in. She found Ahmed eating breakfast with the babies on the patio while Fusun was up the garden putting a wash out. Jenny waved and called her over to the fence.

'Hi, Fusun,' she said, 'I just wanted to ask you something. Do you ever hear anything from Dawn's at night-time at the weekend? Lon and I are normally out, but last night I was in and they had a big row and I heard him hitting her. I'm not sure if it's happened before though. My boys have said that they often hear them arguing, but they weren't sure if there was any violence. What do you think? Have you heard anything?'

'Oh, Jenny I'm so glad you asked me this, I suspected something was going on but I couldn't be sure. I've heard them rowing and I've heard the fear in her voice and I've been very worried to be honest. What happened last night?'

'I was in the bedroom and I could hear them as clear as day. They were having a row about money and then I heard him hitting her and I started shouting and whacking the wall to interrupt him and he must have heard me because he ran off.'

'Oh my goodness, this is exactly what I thought was happening.' Fusun shuddered. 'What an awful man he is. The last two Saturdays, I heard them shouting their heads off and she ran out into the garden and gave me a look as if to say, "I'm glad you are outside so you can be a witness". That's what I thought anyway. And now you've confirmed my suspicions. I'm so glad that you heard it, Jenny. I know you like to keep yourself to yourself but I'm so glad that it's not just me.'

'Maybe he gets drunk every Saturday and that's when it happens. Then again, last night was Friday –'

'It's whenever he gets drunk, Jenny, he acts up as soon as he gets back. She's often in tears, poor girl. She's having an awful time with him.'

'Oh God, he's a pig, isn't he?'

'He absolutely is.'

'Can we have coffee tomorrow to make a plan about speaking to her?' Jenny asked. 'I've got something on tonight so tomorrow is better for me.'

'Yes sure, that's fine. Let's try and be good neighbours and help her, I think she needs it.'

At that moment two other women came out onto the patio, dressed similarly to Fusun in their veils and long dresses and tunics.

'Jenny, meet my mother Nehir and my sister Zohal. They're staying with us for a few days,' said Fusun.

'Oh hello,' Jenny waved.

'Hello, how are you, my dear?' said the mother as they both waved back.

'Very well thank you.' Jenny looked at both the sister and the mother, who couldn't have been much older than herself. They were both wearing make-up and jewellery.

'Aren't they beautiful?' whispered Jenny, half to herself and half to Fusun. 'They're so glamorous.'

'Well, that's because they haven't got baby twins to look after day and night!' laughed Fusun. 'I used to be glamorous too but all of that has gone now. I can barely make time to go to the toilet!'

Jenny smiled. Out of nowhere, she suddenly got an urge to lean over the fence and hug Fusun, the young mother she had barely made any effort to get to know this last year. But Fusun had turned around to speak to her family as they called to her that one of the twins wanted another feed.

She looked back to Jenny. 'Let's have coffee tomorrow then, Jenny, about eleven? We'll try and get this mess sorted.'

'OK, good, thanks love,' she waved to her and to her family on the patio and then walked back down the garden.

And to thoughts about the party that night.

But while she was cleaning the house and making breakfast and writing a shopping list for Lonny and ironing her dress and trying her utmost to think about Trudi and how she would impress her and how they would become good friends after this event, she found herself instead thinking of poor old Dawn next door. To think that

Mark was some kind of vicious thug who had been beating her all this time was unbearable. How could she have missed it?

Then she thought of how she had underestimated Fusun. She had been a prison officer just the same as Ahmed before they had the twins; that must have been how they met. Jenny wondered how old she was, or rather how young because she may not be thirty yet. Her mum looked only a few years older than Jenny and seemed like a nice lady. And how beautiful was her sister? Why hadn't she made more of an effort to get to know Fusun and her family? Lonny was good mates with Ahmed by now, he chatted to him over the fence on a daily basis but blokes being blokes, they hadn't arranged any barbecues or meals out or anything, they hadn't taken it any further. Plus, of course, their babies were so young they wouldn't have time to do much beyond look after them. She should step in and organise something, get them round for a meal or a get together of some sort during this gorgeous hot weather. She quite fancied getting to know Fusun better.

She stopped suddenly. What an idiot she was. The make-up party might be right up Fusun's street – it might be a way of her getting some me time, only a minute from home, while Ahmed looked after the babies. And it wasn't just Fusun, there was her mum and her sister too. That would be three women. Three extra women. But she hardly knew them. What if one of them was a Miranda type and embarrassed her in front of Trudi? Surely, though, Miranda was a one off! In all her fifty-one years, she had never met another woman quite like her. Thank God. Dammit, she would invite them. She would invite them all before she could change her mind.

So she ran out and did just that. Very gracefully and charmingly over the fence as if the previous year of avoiding Fusun had never taken place.

'Neal's Yard Organics,' said her mum. 'Oh, I love their stuff, count me in!'

Ahmed agreed to look after the babies and Fusun's sister Zohal ran over and said, 'We do drink you know Jenny, in case you're wondering.'

'I don't, I'm feeding!' said Fusun, laughing.

'Well I do!' said Zohal and winked at Jenny and Jenny laughed and told her not to worry – Lonny was going to get the drink this afternoon and he would get extra now that Zohal was coming. And everyone laughed.

Jenny ran inside, thrilled to the core. They were all so lovely – and they had been there right under her nose all this time. She felt like she had stumbled on a veritable treasure trove of jewels and gold and sparkling tiaras. Then her negative side kicked in as it always seemed to do and said steady on, you don't know what kind of people they are really, they could have all sorts of customs and habits you don't agree with.

And instantly she found herself saying to this voice '*Shut up!*' just as she had heard Lonny tell Dawn to do.

When Lonny woke up, she told him all about it and he was pleased that she had finally realised that Fusun was a nice woman and worth getting to know.

'What are we going to do about Dawn though?' asked Jenny.

'I'll speak to her first,' said Lonny. 'I'll try and find out a bit more. There's no point calling the police and then her saying that nothing happened.'

'No, Lon,' she said. 'I'll speak to her, it's better coming from a woman.'

'OK, duck,' he agreed. 'You know best.'

He helped her put the outdoor fairy lights up and then the indoor ones from the Christmas decorations box. She went to take her phone off charge and noticed she had new messages.

Emily's said: *'Sorry, Jen, my flight has been cancelled! People protesting on the bloody runway! Will miss your little party, so sorry! Will call soon to catch up, lots happening here as usual lol! xxxx'*

And Hannah's said: *'Sorry, Jen, Kym is sick and can't do this eve's shift with Joyce so muggins here has to do it. I will either have to cancel the party or bring J with me?! Is that poss?!'*

Jenny felt the blood rush to her head. She let out a wail and sat down. What was going on? Why was it all so complicated? She had been looking forward to seeing Emily so much – she knew her and Trudi would get on well and now it wasn't going to happen. And much as she was fond of Joyce, an old lady with Alzheimer's being centre stage at the party was not what she had in mind when she planned it. She just wanted Trudi, just an hour or two with lovely Trudi. And now, after all the drama with Dawn, she felt she wanted it more than ever.

'Emily's not coming, Lon, and Hannah can only come if she brings Joyce with her! For God's sake, why is it so difficult?' she cried.

Lonny sighed. 'Don't worry, duck,' he said wearily. 'We'll get it sorted.'

CHAPTER 27

Last-minute panic

Matt was at the end of a call to *Aldi* HQ when he saw Lonny's car come into the car park way too quickly, with a screech of brakes, almost knocking into a recycling bin as he pulled up to park. It was so unusual to see Lonny driving his petrol car. He was usually on foot or on his bike and with the boys and their pals on the way to play football. And he was rarely stressed, he almost always had a smile for everyone. Now here he was screeching round the corner like a boy racer, scowling and looking like he was close to the edge. Matt and his assistant, Janet, looked at each other and raised their eyebrows.

'Blimey!' said Janet and they both rushed outside.

Lonny came thundering towards them.

'Lon, what's up, duck?' Matt asked.

'Nuthin, I just got the party to sort out.'

'Is the party on? Is Trudi coming?'

'I dunno –'

'Well, who's coming then?'

'Any bloody woman I can drag off the street,' said Lonny, marching into the store.

'Lonny, head office are saying they will meet you to talk about the pesticide campaign. They want you to be...' Janet shouted after him.

'Don't bother him now, he has to sort out the party first,' advised Matt hurriedly, trying to catch up with Lonny. 'What are you after, Lon?'

'Booze. Booze for the ladies,' said Lonny. He looked like he had aged ten years in the last week.

'OK, does it have to be organic for Jenny?'

'Anything, anything, just give me summat cheap and strong! I've got fifty quid and it's got to buy a lot!'

'OK, Lon, don't panic. Try this and this and this,' said Matt, selecting several wines, a bottle of gin and some tonic and a bottle of vodka and some juice. 'That should do it. Now take this,' he grabbed a bottle of Baileys Irish liqueur. 'This is for Jenny to have a nightcap with Trudi when everyone else has gone. My treat.' He winked. 'And find out if she's single.'

'Cheers, Matt, I will,' said Lonny as he pushed his trolley to the checkout.

'Have you signed my petition to reduce the size of car parks yet, Lonny?' shouted the woman he had met previously.

'Not yet, duck, not yet,' said Lonny as though only half hearing the question.

'Here, Lon, come here,' called Matt and he opened up a checkout so he could serve him straight away and he wouldn't have to wait in the queue.

After he had put everything but the Baileys through the till, Matt stood up and hugged him.

'Don't worry, Lon, get any group of women together with a load of drink and everything will be fine.'

'It's not the other women I'm worried about, it's just Jen,' said poor old Lonny as he walked off.

At home, Jenny realised it was already 5pm. The Neal's Yard lady was arriving at 6.30pm in order to set up for 7pm. It was too late to cancel. It was too late to do anything except hope for the best. What was the best that could happen she thought as though hanging on to a cliff edge above a large pit of doom. So much could go wrong tonight but what could go right? What good could come out of it?

She racked her brain, but it didn't feel like anything good could come out of it; it felt like she was walking into a disaster zone. *Try harder,* she forced herself. What if it was only Trudi and Fusun and her mum and sister? What if Mrs Holdcroft had spotted the video on her daughter's phone and thought maybe she shouldn't turn up after all? That might well happen. But it could still be decent, couldn't it? Maybe Fusun and her mum and sister would go home early because of the babies, and maybe the Neal's Yard woman would have to go early too for some reason and wouldn't mind at all that it was such a small party. Maybe she would say, 'Don't worry about a thing, Jenny. I'm not interested in making money, I just want people to have a nice time!' And there would be no pressure to buy more, to make up for the missing guests. And then maybe she could tell Trudi about how her other friends hadn't been able to make it and Trudi would laugh and say, 'All the more booze for us then, Jen!' and glug down an extra bottle of wine.

Tears came into her eyes. This didn't sound like Trudi at all.

Trudi looked so fit and healthy she might well be teetotal.

In any case, it didn't feel good relying on alcohol to save the day, but that seemed to be the only strategy she could come up with. And the knot of anxiety in her gut wasn't helping, it twisted and turned and kept coming up with more and more negative scenarios.

When Lonny came back with a box full of booze, it repelled her. Seeing her watery eyes and depressed demeanour and that she was still stuck in the chair, he plonked it down with a bang on the kitchen counter.

'Jen!' he said, 'I'm at my wits' end here! What are you doing? You're still going ahead with it, yeah?'

'I don't know, Lon,' she sniffed. 'Shall we go ahead with it? Shall we?'

'It's not *we*,' said Lonny. 'It's *you*. It's your party, duck. I can help you now but at seven o'clock, me and the boys are off out, it's all arranged. I've got tickets for *Spiderman*.'

'They've already seen it!'

'It's another version int it. Twice as crap as the last.'

'No, you have to stay and help me, Lon, please!' She jumped out of the chair. 'You're so funny, you'll make everyone laugh.'

'Not today I won't!' he snapped, tired and irritable. Surely you could organise the friggin' Olympics with less stress than this?

'But I haven't got enough people, I need numbers! I need bums on seats!'

'Why? Four is enough int it?'

'Not when three of them are from next door and I've only spoken to them a couple of times! What will Trudi think? What about the make-up woman, she wants people to buy stuff. I need more women!'

'What about Julie Holdcroft?'

'Julie?'

'That's her name, I Googled the newsagents. She's the proprietor.'

'Well, she never told me that, she might get the big hump if I call her —'

'Just give her a fucking drink and call her Julie!' snapped Lonny.

'Lonny stop swearing! You're supposed to be helping me!'

'Bloody hell fire, Jen, I told you I'm getting it sorted, just get everything ready. I'll tell people to be here at seven right?'

'Lonny! Who will you get?'

'Nice women, that's what you want int it? That's who I'll get then!'

'Don't get anyone horrible please, I'm begging you! I'm trying to impress Trudi!' she said, sliding down the wall.

Lonny snorted and went out, banging the door behind him.

CHAPTER 28

The guests arrive

When Lonny drew up outside at 6.45pm with Debbie in the front seat and Freya in the back, Jenny nearly collapsed. In the preceding hour, driven by sheer panic, she had worked hard to get the house lovely and tidy with only the nice stuff on show, anything else being banished to cupboards or under beds. In the kitchen, the wine was chilling, the buffet was laid out on the table and the fairy lights were on, while in the living room, Cheryl the make-up lady was busy laying out her Neal's Yard goodies. If only Trudi and Fusun's family were to attend the party, which would amount to just four people, Jenny was completely sorted in her head for what she would say and how she could interpret events in a positive manner. Petrified but sorted. Additionally, she would have to buy tons of beauty products from Cheryl to make up for the lack of people. Tons. Her second credit card was out and ready for the occasion. No doubt Lonny would go mad because they were on a tight budget these days, but she would cross that bridge when she came to it. She would ask Hannah for some extra shifts with Joyce.

Meantime, she would just have to face up brazenly to the shocked looks that Trudi and Fusun might give her when they saw that she had only invited one friend she'd just met and three neighbours she barely knew. Plus possibly the local newsagent who didn't want anyone using her first name. Surely they would wonder why, if some friends had cancelled, she hadn't just invited some more? How she wished she were in that fortunate position. Instead, what had she got? The arrival of the enemy.

She hid behind the living room curtain and looked on, horrified, as Lonny helped a cooing Debbie out of the car. Good God Almighty, how could he be so stupid? Debbie was her arch nemesis, didn't he remember? Hadn't she told him they fought like cat and dog? It was only because of lovely little Freya that she didn't dump that job; it was a lot more trouble than it was worth. Bloody Debbie, what a prize pain in the neck, trying to flirt with Lonny, how embarrassing. See, even little Freya looked embarrassed. Oh God, what were they doing here? What would Trudi think? She didn't mind Freya coming at all, but Debbie, *Debbie*?

Debbie noticed Jenny looking out with dismay from behind the curtains. What on earth was this lovely hunky guy doing with that bloody misery? Of course, she was good looking but looks aren't everything. She had met Lonny a few times before when he had very kindly come round to fix something; what a lovely, generous-hearted man he was. And how masculine! She had never found a man to be so attractive, oh goodness, he took her breath away. And when he picked her up and carefully placed her in the wheelchair, she got a real thrill being so close to his body and smelling his masculine scent. God, he was so strong and manly; he was delicious.

'Come on, Mum,' said Freya. 'We have to go and help Jenny.'

Debbie sniffed. Lonny's story of how Jenny needed help because her friend had died and she was depressed had obviously had an effect on Freya, but she wasn't quite convinced herself. Maybe Jenny was depressed, but aren't we all, she thought. In any case, surely she was so miserable that she was beyond the kind of help a little party might bring. Surely she needed some drugs in her system.

'It will be good fun,' said Freya. 'We'll be able to try out all the make-up and stuff.'

'That's right, duck,' said Lonny. 'You'll have a great time.'

As he escorted them into the house and down the hallway he caught sight of Jenny dashing off into the kitchen. What the hell?

'Just take your mum into the living room, Freya, Jenny will be with you soon.'

Then he called up the stairs, 'Lads? Come on! Time to go!'

Suddenly Jenny slid up behind him, whispering in his ear. 'I can't do it, Lon, you have to stay and help me. Trudi will like you, she'll think you're –'

He immediately headed for the hallway. 'No, duck, we're going out, it's all arranged. You'll be fine.'

'No, I won't be fine,' she hissed, trying to pull him back.

'You will, Jen!'

'I won't! I'm begging you! Don't leave me here!'

'Jen, get a bloody grip! Trudi will be here soon and I've got a few others coming an' all. Look, you've got Debbie in there already, go talk to her!'

'I can't! I hate her!'

'Jen, stop talking like that! I'm not having it!'

The boys came downstairs and tried to file past, somewhat bemused to see their parents scuffling in the hallway.

'Jenny, can I have a drink please?' shouted Debbie.

'Go on, get in there, you can do it!' Lonny shoved her towards the living room.

'Come on, let's go lads,' he said quietly to the boys, ushering them out of the front door, leaving Jenny clinging to the wall.

'You can do it, Jen, come on, duck!' he whispered.

Then he left, leaving Jenny right in it. Which was the best thing he could do really because she had to either sink or swim.

She was contemplating which way to go when Lauren arrived to take up her place.

As security.

At 5.30pm, Lonny had rushed into the Rough Close Tavern and up to the bar, and asked her if she was Lauren and if she was, did she remember Jenny, the woman from the running club. Lauren had replied that of course she did, and that she had seen her just a few days ago too, up at the shops. Lonny had asked her to please come to the party this evening and she had said no chance, she'd already told Jenny a make-up party would be hell on earth for her. Then Lonny had looked at her with this weird kind of look, wincing like he was in pain, suffering from piles or summat. He looked well stressed.

'Are you alright, duck?' she had asked him, wondering if there was something in the water at Meir Heath which would cause both husband and wife to be out of sorts.

'Yeah I'm fine, duck,' Lonny had said. Then he said, 'Sorry, I didn't make myself clear, Lauren. I don't want you to come as a guest, I want you to be there on the door as security.'

He slammed a £20 note on the bar and said, 'Two hours work duck, seven to nine o'clock, cash in advance.'

Lauren had immediately put her finger on the note and said, 'And what am I doing exactly?'

'Just make yourself useful, make sure it dunt get too crowded, that kind of thing. There might be some people in wheelchairs, old ladies, kids, babies. Make sure everyone is OK, make sure no one is out the back treading on me plants!'

'OK, I get the picture. Who's doing the music?'

'Oh God, I dunno, no one.'

'What?'

'Nuthin, I just hadn't thought of that yet.'

'Well don't worry, I'll take care of it.' She winked and showed her phone. 'I'll bring me speakers an' all.'

'Great. Cheers, duck.' Then he said feebly, 'Of course, if for any reason the numbers are low, you might have to stand in and let them put some make-up on yer face... or summat.'

'I told Jenny I don't touch any of that shit,' said Lauren as though she was talking about heroin.

'OK, duck, whatever you say, you're in charge.'

Then he pushed the note towards her and fled the pub and five seconds later she heard a screech of brakes as his car departed from the car park.

'Terry,' she called to her assistant manager. 'I'll be off out for a few hours this evening. Can you manage, duck?'

'Course, Boss,' said Terry, looking around at the empty seats.

*

'I thought you didn't like make-up?' Jenny asked Lauren at the doorway, somewhat unnerved at the sight of her power stance, darts player's shirt and reflective sunglasses.

'I'm on security,' she said. 'Don't worry, Jen, Lonny's already sorted out the money.'

'Well, aren't you going to come in?' she asked, confused and thinking that Lauren's presence at the door would not be the best welcome for Trudi.

'I'll come in to do a quick recce, but I'll be at the door as the guests arrive.'

Lauren followed Jenny in, clocking the decor and the photos everywhere and then the dreaded make-up woman – best to keep

235

well away from her, she thought. She nodded briefly as Jenny called, 'Oh, Cheryl, this is Lauren, she hates make-up so we've got to try and win her over tonight!' Lauren noted the strain in Jenny's voice; what was all that about?

In the living room, Jenny introduced her to a woman in a wheelchair who looked as miserable as sin. Debbie.

'Have you got a downstairs toilet for Debbie, Jen?' Lauren asked.

'Yes, it's right at the back of the kitchen.'

'Will we get the chair through?'

'Well –'

'I won't need the toilet thank you,' said Debbie emphatically. 'You don't need to worry about me.'

'Yer what, duck?' demanded Lauren, hands on hips.

'I won't need the toilet.'

'Everyone needs the toilet at sometime or other, duck.'

Debbie snorted. 'I'm wearing a pad!'

Cheryl looked up from her mixing of potions. Good God, this do was getting less glamorous by the minute. When she had first seen Jenny in the Potteries Market she had thought, what a beauty, I know that type, all her friends will be just as gorgeous as her. And sure enough, when she came in and saw all the photos of beautiful women all over the walls, she felt confident that it would be a wonderful evening. Maybe it would be, but none of the beauties had arrived yet that was for sure.

Jenny took a bottle of wine from the fridge and poured herself a quick shot. Her stomach was sick with nerves and dread like she was just about to be shot by a firing squad. It was as if she had just eaten her last meal and now she couldn't think of anything but the walk from the table to the yard and the wall where she would stand before being gunned down. And it was too late now for any reprieve from on high, like in the movies. She would have to go through with this awful, awful event. The best that she could hope for now was that Trudi would be a no-show, yes that would be the best thing by far. Then maybe she could get drunk with Fusun's sister possibly. OK, that wouldn't be too bad. But it wasn't likely to happen, was it? It was more likely that Trudi would turn up any minute and walk into Debbie and Lauren arguing about incontinence pads.

That thought catapulted her back into feeling sorry for herself and she was sinking fast as the sound of a car hurriedly parking suggested another guest had arrived. Oh God, she hoped it wasn't another of Lonny's surprise invites. But no, it was Hannah and Joyce. Joyce had come to the party. God Almighty. An eighty-two-year old lady with Alzheimer's would be centre stage eating bloody flowers and God knows what else. But at least Hannah was here too.

'Oh, Hannah, I'm so glad you've arrived, come in,' she said in greeting. 'Hello, Joyce darling.'

'I'm so sorry, hon,' said Hannah, grabbing Jenny's hand and putting Joyce's firmly in it. 'I've got to take Jake up to A&E, he fell off his bike. I think his nose is broken.'

Jenny looked down the drive to see eight-year-old Jake in his mum's car, holding his nose with a tissue and sobbing loudly. 'Come on, Mummy!' he demanded.

'But I've got the party,' Jenny said in disbelief. 'You can't leave Joyce here!'

'I'm so sorry, Jen, but I can't take her to A&E, I can't risk her wandering off. I'll pick her up soon, I won't be long.'

Hannah drove off in a flash. Jenny and Joyce stood hand in hand looking at each other for a moment on the front path as Mrs Holdcroft arrived. Jenny chickened out of calling her Julie and said, 'Hello, Mrs Holdcroft, how are you, love?' Giving her another opportunity to say 'Call me Julie' but she didn't. She never would. Dear God. How could she introduce her to Trudi?

'Everyone inside now,' said Lauren. 'Cheryl wants to get started.'

Then in rushed Robbie's girlfriend, young Chloe, who was already dolled up to the nines, lashes like spiders and obviously determined that she would be dishing out the make-up and not receiving it.

'I thought I'd do you like a rainforest, Jenny cos Robbie says you're all eco in this house!' she said at her usual mile-a-minute pace.

'Oh, yes we are.'

'So how's about some rainforest trees and a monkey and a parrot, stuff like that?'

'On my face?'

'Yeah, it'll be dead good, I'll show you on YouTube,' she said, running in.

Jenny followed her, dragging a reluctant Joyce. No sooner had she gone in and plonked Joyce next to Debbie than there was another stern instruction from Lauren.

'Just down the hallway on the left, move along now.'

Jenny rushed out to the hallway. 'Trudi?'

But it was Dawn.

The sight of her neighbour wearing heavy pancake make-up, to hide what had happened last night no doubt, made Jenny reach deep down into her gut and pull out some human decency and kindness like a rabbit from a hat. And as though, in return for this effort, her phone immediately sounded a message from Trudi that she had been delayed with the in-laws and wouldn't be able to make the party.

Jenny breathed a sigh of relief. *Trudi would not be here tonight. Hallelujah.*

'Hello, Dawnie,' she said. 'Don't you look nice. Come in, come in.'

And Dawn followed her in.

CHAPTER 29

The party

There was a minute or three when Dawn, Debbie, Freya, Joyce, Mrs Holdcroft and Chloe were sitting awkwardly looking at each other, and Jenny was handing out drinks to her guests and Lauren was hovering between the hallway and lounge in a semi-threatening manner and there was nothing but silence. Joyce clearly hadn't got a clue where she was and the other women were looking at her with some trepidation given that Jenny had hastily introduced her as 'Joyce with Alzheimer's.'

'There's always someone worse off than yourself, Freya, just remember that,' muttered Debbie to her daughter.

Then the atmosphere became like a hot and heavy blanket. Jenny found herself filling the silence by doing stupid things: offering a glass of wine to ten-year-old Freya, then giving it to Joyce instead and having to wrestle it back off her because of her medication, while Debbie insisted that there would be no harm done, she knew about these things. Of course she did.

It was the kind of three minutes that might take you three years to get over. But at least Chloe was checking her phone and hadn't started talking yet. When that happened, God help them all.

Jenny checked her own phone for the time. Ten past seven.

Nearly there, nearly there she thought. Only three hours to go before it was all over. Now that she knew Trudi wouldn't attend, she felt a lot more relaxed. Sod it, she might even enjoy herself tonight. In fact, the pure relief of Trudi's no-show was making her practically giddy with joy. How funny, given that she had spent the last three weeks unable to think of much else beyond how she and Trudi would bond at the party. But now what did it matter? There was still time to bond with her at the writing class. The main thing was, she thought as she scoured the unusual array of guests, thank God she hadn't turned up.

She had whispered to Cheryl earlier that she'd had some cancellations and quite frankly she didn't know who was going to attend tonight. Emily, then Hannah and now Trudi were all no-shows. So, in the silence with the five guests shy and not speaking, Jenny looked at Cheryl and Cheryl looked back and winked and they knew they were both thinking the same thing: this party was going to be so diabolical that it could actually be great. Unwittingly, Jenny had become something of an expert on this type of occasion. She had watched everyone attending their gigs hadn't she? Not that this party would have the golden oldies music as it seemed Lauren's playlist was much more hip-hop orientated. However, she certainly had enough booze to help things along.

She took another quick glug of wine and then remembered she was in charge of Joyce, so actually at work in effect. So she put her glass aside and waited, thinking once Hannah was back from the hospital she could down several large glasses in quick succession.

And then in waltzed Fusun, her sister Zohal and her mum Nehir, bringing with them a load of delicious smelling food plus the two babies because Ahmed had to work for a couple of hours; he would pop in later to pick them up. The smell of the food and the sight of the babies, who were on top form, gurgling and laughing away like

240

two little bundles of joy, immediately got rid of any shyness in the room. Now everyone seemed happy and even Joyce was enjoying watching the little ones.

Then Cheryl got to work on Nehir's face, massaging it and explaining what type of skin she had and what products she would need. Nehir declared that she meant business and was ready to buy up whatever stock Cheryl had as she loved these products and was there anything on offer today?

Hoorah! Jenny was elated. Hearing Nehir talk about how much she was going to spend let her off the hook as far as Cheryl's earnings went. She could now focus on her guests: she could take care of Joyce, she could try and make Debbie laugh, she could fuss over Freya, she could chat to Fusun and her sister and she could involve Dawn in everything, like she was her best pal and she hadn't noticed that she had come to a make-up party wearing a base of foundation that would take a plasterer's knife to chip off. How many bruises was that hiding, she thought, glancing at Fusun to confirm that they would both be speaking to Dawn about it later.

The atmosphere was good but not brilliant. Lauren was strutting around looking threatening. Cheryl couldn't really keep everyone's interest in the beauty products despite working hard cleansing and toning and moisturising and massaging, especially since she took such a long time on Fusun's mum, knowing that this was where the money lay. Meanwhile, Chloe had started talking ten to the dozen so Jenny quickly put her to work 'painting' Freya's face, as Debbie insisted that she wasn't old enough to have normal make-up.

Dawn was a bit subdued although she was clearly enjoying seeing inside her neighbours' house and the pictures of Lonny and Jenny and the boys and loads of other good looking people everywhere. They must have so many friends, their photos were all over the walls, although none of them seemed to be at the party. These must be local friends. Secretly, she was pleased. If all the women had been the same type as Jenny it would be really hard work. Still, she had been very kind to her last night, although she couldn't help wishing that Lonny was there.

While Joyce munched on a plate of Fusun's snacks, Debbie sat looking at one of Lonny's *Permaculture* magazines as though she was in a doctor's waiting room, totally oblivious to any of the beautification that was going on around her. However, Freya, bless her little heart, was very interested. Whenever Chloe had to rush outside to take a phone call, which seemed to be every five minutes, Freya would jump up and watch Cheryl and the way she worked the creams into Nehir's skin.

'Does it matter what order you do everything?' she asked Cheryl.

Cheryl and Jenny both looked pleased; what a little darling she was.

'Yes it does, duckie, and one thing I would say to you is, you're doing the right thing starting young. I tell you, I wish I had had the opportunity to. Start young and always use the best products.'

Debbie tutted and raised her eyebrows: as if that was going to happen. Their budget couldn't stretch to food half the time so it was hardly likely to include beauty products for a ten-year-old.

'You can make your own too, Frey,' said Jenny. 'I've done it lots of times. I might still have some of the base creams left over if you want to use them, shea butter and almond oil and then you add a few drops of lavender or geranium.'

'Yeah, but it never turns out like it should, does it?' said Debbie.

'Oh, I don't know, I'm sure Freya could have a good go,' said Jenny.

'It's all a big waste of money if you ask me,' moaned Debbie.

'You wait till I've finished with you,' said Cheryl, winking at her.

'You're going to look ravishing, duckie.'

Debbie laughed, pleased that someone had paid her some attention at last, because she knew Jenny didn't want to really. Pleased also that there was plenty of real food from Fusun's being passed around and not just the nuts and dips that Jenny had to offer. The food in fact was amazing and was the main factor in putting a smile on people's faces. Delicious patties and pastries and seemingly hundreds of them, all home-made.

'Oh my God,' said Debbie. 'I'm in heaven!'

'Duck, is there any magic ingredient that we need to know about?' Lauren queried. 'Anything from India or whatever? I always think I don't like spicy food, until I taste it cooked by someone who knows what they're doing.'

'I'm from Turkey, Lauren, so my influences are more Mediterranean than Indian,' said Fusun, smiling at the compliment.

'Oh, right,' said Lauren. 'Well, it tastes good anyhow, duck.'

Joyce finished her plate of food and began to shuffle on her seat. Lauren thumped Jenny on her arm and nodded towards the old lady.

'Are you alright, Joyce?' said Jenny. 'Do you want the toilet?'

'Yes, the toilet, that's right. Do you want the toilet, dearie?'

'No, I don't,' said Jenny, 'but you might, Joyce. How about I take you to the toilet just in case?'

'Would you like the toilet, dearie?' Joyce whispered sweetly to Debbie who was sitting next to her.

'No, I'm alright, Joyce, I'm wearing a pad!' Debbie shouted as though, because she was old, Joyce must also be deaf. 'You go! You go to the toilet with Jenny!'

'D'you want me to carry her?' Lauren stepped in.

'No, no, no!' Jenny took Joyce's arm firmly. 'Come on Joyce, I'll show you the way.' She wondered whether Lauren should go back outside on security even though she knew there was no one left to come; she was finding this new Lauren, in her reflective sunglasses, to be more than a bit pushy. She took Joyce slowly to the downstairs loo, which was at the back of the kitchen. No stairs to climb, thank goodness. And although the back door was open, the whole garden was enclosed and secure and there was no way she could wander off. She knew Joyce would take her time so she left her in there and came back to the party to find Dawn hesitating about taking the chair. Nehir was finished now and looking absolutely amazing, eyes as big as saucers in dark make-up and any bags or wrinkles firmly disguised. Her lips were ruby red and she looked at least ten years younger.

'Oh, Mum, you look gorgeous,' said Zohal. 'I wish this make-up would stay on for a few days. I've got a date on Tuesday night!'

'I'll show you how to do it. You can all do it yourselves once you know how – and with the right products of course,' Cheryl said, beaming, because Nehir had just bought at least a couple of everything she had used, from facial scrubs to eyeliner.

Now it looked like it was going to be Dawn's turn because she was sitting next to Nehir.

'Go on, Dawn!' called Debbie.

'Move along, you're next,' advised Lauren.

Jenny and Fusun caught each other's eye. 'Well, Dawnie you've already got a nice foundation on,' said Jenny. 'Maybe you could just work on top of that, Cheryl?'

'No, we need to start with a good cleanse,' Cheryl replied. 'Not being funny, love, but there could be all sorts hidden under that pancake stuff you've got on. Do you normally wear it that thick?'

'You had a reaction to the pollen didn't you, Dawn?' said Fusun, putting down the babies and coming up to stand with Jenny so that the others couldn't really see. 'I noticed you were a bit sore around your eyes yesterday.'

She touched Dawn around the cheekbone and said quietly to Cheryl, 'You should go very gently around here, not too heavy.'

Cheryl looked from Fusun to Jenny, who was giving her a knowing look.

Dawn's eyes filled with tears.

Thankfully, Cheryl got it.

'Oh, those allergies can be nasty can't they? Well don't worry, we'll just work on top of what you've put on. We don't want to give you another reaction do we, duck?'

Chloe came back in, curious to see what the problem was with Dawn. 'How about I do the rainforest on your face Dawn instead of Jenny's? I can do trees and monkeys and stuff, would you like that?'

'Yeah, I would,' Dawn said, eager to look and feel totally and utterly different for one evening at least.

'I'm just finishing Freya, duck,' said Chloe. 'Come over 'ere and wait, I won't be five minutes.'

Dawn moved to sit next to Freya, watching as a turquoise sea with dolphins on it appeared on the young girl's face. Chloe was obviously really gifted at face painting and fortunately her concentration was such that she couldn't talk while she was doing it, she was too busy going back and forth from the tutorial on YouTube.

Jenny sat down next to Dawn and linked her arm. 'I tell you, we're all going to look so stunning at the end of this that Lonny will think he's in the wrong house!' Everyone laughed politely, it was nice of Jenny to pretend that she wasn't easily the most stunning person in the room. It was nice of her to pretend that she was just a regular woman and not as pretty as a picture.

'Jenny, the photos of you and your friends are beautiful,' said Zohal. 'Why aren't they here this evening? Do they live far away?'

'Yes, Emily is in Lanzarote, although I thought she would be home in time for tonight, but she's not, never mind. Annie went to uni in Bournemouth, and Kate got married and she lives in Jersey now. So they're not in Stoke anymore, unfortunately.'

'And what about this lady here,' said Nehir, pointing to one of the many pictures of Sue. 'What a beauty she is! With her dimples, she's like the black version of you, my love!'

Everyone laughed.

'Yes, Sue was my best friend... but she died last year sadly.'

There was a big gasp. 'Oh no, what a tragedy, and what a loss for you, Jenny,' said Nehir.

'Was it cancer?' Fusun asked.

'Yes,' said Jenny. 'She fought it for a long time but...'

'Oh no, I can't bear it,' said Fusun. 'When are they going to cure this awful disease? Why is it taking so long with all this money and with all this studying and research?'

'There's big money to be made out of it int there?' said Lauren.

'Don't say that, dear,' said Cheryl. 'They're doing their best.'

'Yeah, but if there's a cure that's cheap and easy, we'll be the last to hear about it!'

'Oh no!' said everyone, more sad now that Lauren had voiced her opinion.

'Well,' said Jenny, 'I'd better go and check on Joyce, she might be finished by now.'

It was nice that people had been so sympathetic about Sue, she thought as she left them, but of course they would be – why wouldn't they be? It made her realise she wasn't used to mixing with people much these days, she had been so isolated, the kindness coming at her was a bit overwhelming.

She approached the back toilet through the kitchen. The door was open.

'Joyce?' she said, pushing the door open to double check. It was empty.

She went out into the garden – Joyce must be out there, it was so warm and inviting on this gorgeous summer's evening, she must be out there on the patio.

But she couldn't see her anywhere. She ran up the garden to look in the greenhouse. Nothing. She looked at the back gate which led into the field, it was still locked.

She ran back to the house. Oh God, oh God, oh God.

She ran inside and up the stairs.

'What's up?' shouted Lauren. 'Where's Joyce?'

Jenny checked all the bedrooms. *Oh God, oh God, oh God.*

'Quick, Lauren, she's gone, she's gone. Joyce has gone!'

CHAPTER 30

Escape

Jenny belted down the street towards the junction with Manor Lane, moving far more quickly than she had with the Running Sisters. She looked right and left, panting heavily. Could Joyce have got this far? Wasn't she just out in the garden somewhere and she had missed her? Surely they had only been talking for a few minutes. Then she remembered taking her time with Dawn and making sure she felt comfortable, then everyone got talking about the pictures on the wall and then Sue. It must have been then, when they were looking at the pictures, they had their back to the door and she must have slipped out. Oh God, what if something happened to Joyce? She would have to break the terrible news to her son Ben; he would be furious that they hadn't taken better care of her and both she and Hannah would lose their jobs. Well, she would lose her job anyway. But that was the least of it.

'Wait, Jen!' called Lauren. 'Come back and search the house and garden first. We need to do that properly – how do you know she's not hidden in a cupboard or summat?'

'She likes to wander off,' wailed Jenny. 'She's reached the A50 before, apparently.'

'She hasn't had time for that, duck. If she was walking down

Manor Lane we'd be able to see her,' said Lauren firmly. 'I've been on the door most of the time, I'm sure she couldn't have got out so quickly.'

'But you were talking to us! You were supposed to be doing security and you left the front door wide open!'

'But you never told me she was likely to wander off, did yer?' Lauren shouted back.

She rushed back to the house leaving Jenny looking at the main road and all around but there was still no sign of Joyce. *Oh Joyce*, she worried, *where are you?*

*

In the back of a taxi bringing him home from the pub, Bill's eyes widened as he saw Joyce getting off a bus by *Tesco* and *Aldi*, close to the flyover junction for the A50.

'Slow down, duck,' he said to Ali, his regular taxi driver.

'What are you looking at, Bill?' said Ali.

'See that woman? That's Joyce, one of Jenny's old ladies. She shouldn't be out here on her own, she's got bloody Alzheimer's. She's off her nut. Hang on, duck, I'm going to ring Jen.'

'OK, Bill,' said Ali pulling over. 'Do you want me to do it?'

Bill handed him his mobile phone. 'Yeah you do it, duck, you're much quicker than I am.'

Ali got the call going and handed it back to Bill.

'Hiya, duck?' said Bill to Jenny. 'Where are you?'

'I'm busy, Bill,' shouted Jenny from outside somewhere. 'I'll have to call you back later.'

'I've just seen Joyce outside on her own,' said Bill. 'What shall I do? Who's on duty tonight?'

Back up in Bramfield Drive Jenny jumped. 'What's that? Where is she, Bill? Where is she? Stop her please, she's escaped!'

'She's just got off a bus at *Tesco*.'

'Don't let her go near the big road!'

She ran back into the house and screamed, 'Joyce is at the A50!'

Immediately, Fusun was with her. 'I'll drive, Jenny, I'm the only one who hasn't had a drink.'

'Oh, Fusun, be quick, please be quick.'

'Don't worry, I'm an advanced driver. Wait, let me get the keys.' She ran home and came out with the keys.

Jenny hopped into the passenger seat. 'Go, go!!'

*

Meantime, Bill and Ali were quickly losing track of Joyce as they were caught behind other cars at the traffic lights to the flyover.

'It'd be quicker to get out and run,' shouted Bill.

'I can't get out here, I can't stop. Where's she gone? Can you see her, Bill?'

'There she is!'

'Who's that woman? Is she with her? Is that the carer?'

'No, no, Jenny's the carer and she's lost her! She's on her own, Ali!'

*

Fusun turned the car into Manor Lane and quickly reached forty miles an hour going down the hill.

'Did he say whereabouts at *Tesco*?' she asked Jenny.

'No, let me get him on the phone again.'

*

Joyce's mind was contained in a moment in 1973 when her husband and sons were heading off to a Stoke City game at the old Victoria Stadium and she was packing them a flask of soup each. The talk was about whether Jimmy Greenhoff would play today because he had been injured last week and there hadn't been a firm confirmation in *The Sentinel*. The boys wanted to buy a hot dog at the stadium instead of eating Mum's home-made dumpling soup. Ben was having a little paddy about it – all his friends had hot dogs, he had never had a hot dog. Dad said he could have a hot dog, why was Mum saying he couldn't? Ben was so funny, he looked like he wouldn't say boo to a goose, but underneath that veneer, he was quite a determined boy. Joyce could see Fred looking slightly awkward, her husband knew that he shouldn't have given permission without speaking to Joyce first. She was always in charge of these kinds of arrangements. Still, it was only a hot dog. Joyce knew that she was sometimes a bit too worried about money and how much things cost. She had turned down lucrative engagements which, if she'd taken them, would have meant a lot more money for the family, but then it would have meant a lot more exposure too and Joyce couldn't imagine anything worse than her face being recognised in the street. She was happiest on the stage of a concert hall, that was her home, not on the television giving her endorsement to some second-rate washing powder.

Ben and his twin brother Luke awaited her answer regarding the hot dogs. She could see the anxiety mixed with fury in their faces: why did Mum have to spoil things sometimes? It was because she was worried about money, Dad said. Joyce saw their big eyes and wondered why they were shining and moving like they were coming towards her, coming towards her again and again, so many faces, they couldn't all be Ben and Luke's, there were too many now and they were big horrible faces. Someone was screaming, what were they screaming for? They were only talking about hot dogs for goodness sake.

She felt the cold touch of a sharp metal edge and something told her to grip it and hang on to it, to hang on to it for dear life.

Fusun certainly was an advanced driver. She zoomed down Manor Lane, turned onto the Meir Park estate and towards *Aldi* and *Tesco* without having to stop once – she was reading the other drivers at a distance and could judge their speed accurately. Within two minutes she was on the large roundabout which crossed the A50; she swerved past the turn-off roads for Stoke City Centre and Blythe Bridge, coming full circle till she could see Bill and Ali both on their feet and pointing down the one-way slip road. With Jenny screaming in her ear, she had to think quickly. Joyce must have walked down the slip road and got on to the A50. She could see the traffic was moving more slowly than normal on the road below; horns were blaring and lorry drivers were gesturing out of their cabs. She made her decision, shifted into reverse gear and backed down the one-way slip road at speed. She stopped at the bottom with a screech of brakes.

Jenny jumped out.

Joyce was holding on to the metal fence in the central reservation. She must have crossed when there was a gap in the traffic. What were the chances? Now her face was as white as a sheet and she was muttering furiously to herself as though just becoming aware of what she had done.

Jenny saw the cars and lorries moving a little more slowly, all drivers and passengers now looking at her, the latest addition to this moment of madness on a sunny evening while driving through Stoke. And it would all be on social media and Signal Radio's travel news within the next half hour no doubt.

Jenny knew she had only moments to save Joyce. Reaching down into her gut for the second time that evening, she found courage and determination. She held her hand up to the cars like she was a lollypop lady and began to flag down the traffic. As the first lane came to a complete halt and allowed her to cross, she saw Joyce raise her leg and begin to climb over the metal barrier; she could see she was crying and distressed. Oh God, if she reached the other carriageway, she didn't stand a chance. Jenny became more animated in her movements to flag down the cars and the second lane slowed with a screech of brakes. She ran to Joyce and put her arm around her waist, pulling her back from the barrier. 'Hello, lovey! I've been looking for you!'

She kept an eye on the traffic behind her, nervous about how long it would stop for.

'They've gone to the football and I never let them have a hot dog!' said Joyce.

'What's that, Joyce?'

'I never let them have a hot dog.'

'OK, lovey, do you want them to have one?'

'Yes, I do.'

'Shall I phone them and let them know they can have one?' asked Jenny, kissing her forehead.

'Can you do that?'

'Of course I can, Joyce, I'll phone them and let them know they can have a hot dog.'

'Will you, darling?'

'Yes, lovey, I can easily do that, don't worry at all. Now, let's get you home shall we?'

She began to escort Joyce back over the road. Several people had got out of their cars in case she needed help but she managed to do it herself, and got Joyce to where Fusun was waiting with her car at the bottom of the slip road.

Once they had made it to safety and Joyce was in the back seat, Jenny turned with a wave to thank the drivers and passengers who had got out of their vehicles and then gave another wave to thank the cars and lorries further back who had stopped and had their journey delayed.

Their reply came back, a loud chorus of beeping horns and applause.

CHAPTER 31

Friends and neighbours

At the cinema, Lonny was having a hard time. Taking the boys to see this kind of movie felt like a remnant from the days before he got woke and it was impossible for him to relax. Before the film even began, he had shouted out loud, 'I didn't pay fifty quid to watch flippin' car adverts! What century are you living in?' which got a quick round of applause and some similar shouts from other angry people. When the film started, his stress was barely reduced by seeing the amazing special effects. If as much effort went into restoring the soil and the ecosystems as went into a Hollywood blockbuster, it would be job done, he thought.

On the bus journey home, he got back to worrying about the party. Blimey, a lot was hinging on this woman Trudi turning up and being as nice as Jenny hoped. If she wasn't, it could be a disaster. But as he and the boys made their way down Bramfield Drive in the evening heat they heard the faint but encouraging sounds of women singing happily coming from the other end of the street. Their end.

'Whoa, Dad,' said Ryan. 'Is that the party?'

'Might be, son,' said Lonny, as they rounded the bend in the road. He could see their house now, and it looked different somehow. There were people milling around the front door and he recognised a few neighbours who he regularly conversed with about gardening and permaculture hanging out with a beer like teenagers. Inside the front window he could see a crowd of women singing their hearts out to 'Somewhere Over the Rainbow' with someone warbling the final top notes like a veritable Nightingale in Berkeley Square. Wow. They approached the gate as the singing ended and everyone started to dance to 'Hot, Hot, Hot'. Unbelievable.

'Alright. Geoff? Dave?' he nodded to friends as he came up to the front door.

Then Lauren came out.

'*Fucking 'ell!*' said Lonny with an unfortunate slip of the tongue. Lauren's full mask of make-up, including beauty spot and cupid bow mouth, had flummoxed him for a moment.

'Alright, duck? You look great!' he corrected himself. 'Top marks for entering into the spirit of things.'

'I had no choice,' said Lauren with a glare.

'How's it going then?' Lonny asked nervously, still unsure how this fantastic party atmosphere had happened. Or maybe it hadn't. Was it safe to go inside?

'Yeah, it's been great. Not without its little moments though, bound to happen when you mix babies and the disabled and Alzheimer's with a ton of booze.'

'Oh yeah.' Shit, he hadn't thought of that. Surely there hadn't been that much booze?

He went into the house and the boys followed, eager to see what was happening. It was only Lonny who was cautious, worried that Jenny was sloshed on a sofa somewhere with babies crawling all over her, or maybe drunkenly baring her soul to the long-awaited Trudi in the back garden and letting the party take care of itself. Maybe Dawn had got her mates round. Maybe Debbie had turned out to be a laugh a minute and had got everyone in the party mood. Maybe –

'Lon!' Jenny screamed, throwing herself at him, an English oak forest painted on her forehead with fairies on her cheeks. 'Lon, you'll never guess what happened! Joyce escaped and got on to the A50! And I rescued her! I stopped the traffic and I rescued her!' She flung her arms around him as though she had never been happier. 'Fusun drove like a maniac! Oh Lon, she's such a good driver! She drove backwards down the slip road!'

'Whoa!' Lonny exclaimed. 'What the –? Joyce on the A50? What happened?'

Jenny told him of the evening's events and how she had stopped traffic to get to the central reservation to persuade Joyce to come back across the road and how once they got Joyce back to the house, she had started to sing – just out of nowhere – and they had all joined in singing all the oldies that they thought she would know. For whatever reason, Joyce sang and sang. Cheryl suggested that it was because everyone was so tarted up that she must have thought she was at some function or big party where she was supposed to sing. And so she did. And her son would be so pleased.

'Oi, don't forget about my contribution,' shouted Bill, who had got Ali to drop him off at Jenny's once he knew that this was the night of the 'do'. He had walked in with his stick and the first person he saw was an exotic beauty by the name of Nehar and she was joined by her two daughters and he had exclaimed, 'Who's this – the Three Degrees?' and they had all laughed and started singing, 'When will I see you again?'.

'I saw Joyce getting off the bus down at *Tesco*. I said to my driver, "That's Joyce, Jenny's old lady," I said. "She's got Alzheimer's, she can't be wandering round on her own, duck!" So we phoned Jenny and her neighbour here, she drove like a maniac, backing down the slip road onto the A50 where old Joycey was in the middle hanging onto the barrier! To be honest, Lon, I thought I was in an episode of *The Bill*. Hair-raising it was, bloody hair-raising.'

'Wow, that's amazing!' Lonny replied. 'Is Joyce alright? Where is she?'

'Yes, she's fine, there she is,' said Jenny, pointing to the sofa where Joyce was beginning to nod off, her worry bead bracelet in her hands. 'She was singing her heart out for a good half hour!'

'By the way, Lonny, did your dad work down the pit at Hem Heath?' asked Bill. 'Did he drink at The Potters Arms?'

'No, duck, he always drank down Meir at The Kings Head. And he worked at Royal Doulton.'

'Did he? Are yer sure?'

'Yes, duck,' laughed Lonny, as this was quite a regular occurrence. All the old guys thought they had worked with the only black man in Stoke, so Lonny must be his son.

There were a lot more people at the party than he had expected and everyone was enjoying themselves and dancing or chatting and drinking. Stella and her sister and their partners were there. Robbie was there, dancing with Chloe, who was talking ten to the dozen as she danced, describing what she had painted on everyone's face and why she had chosen that scene, and what she would choose next time if she got another chance maybe.

Lonny winked at Robbie. ''ey up, Jimi Hendrix!' Robbie laughed.

Chloe laughed too. Then she said, 'Jimi who? What's he on about?'

Lonny recognised other neighbours who had all come round to hear the story because Jenny had knocked on everyone's door in the search for Joyce. Even the Stevensons were there to investigate the top-rate operatic warbling they had heard, and they remembered Joyce from her prime so that was nice. And now everyone was in their house and the atmosphere was celebratory and it couldn't get much better than that.

'Which one is Trudi?' Lonny asked, looking around.

'Oh, Trudi couldn't come,' said Jenny matter-of-factly. 'Probably just as well, there's been so much going on!'

Hannah returned with her young son who had been attended to in A&E and was now feeling a little happier. Jenny told Hannah what had happened and she screamed and hugged Jenny and said she was a hero for saving Joyce's life. Jenny introduced her to Lonny and she whispered to Jen, 'You never told me your husband was such a hunk!' which Lonny heard while he was drinking a glass of wine down and he laughed and grabbed Jenny and they danced in the middle of the crowd.

Then Mrs Holdcroft, who had a wonky necked swan painted on her face due to Chloe finally running out of steam, approached Lonny, shouting above the music, 'Hello, Lonny, do you recognise me? It's Mrs Holdcroft from the newsagents!'

And Lonny immediately quipped, 'That's right, Julie int it, duck? How are yer?' He saw the tiniest flinch cross her face for a moment. She looked him straight in the eye but he looked straight back.

Eventually backing down, she turned to Jenny and pointed to a girl by her side. 'Jenny, this is my daughter, Polly. I hope you don't mind, I rang her and told her to come, seeing as there's other children here –'

''Old up!' Lonny interjected. 'Is this Polly who sits next to Nate in History? Eh? I've heard a lot about you, Polly Holdcroft –'

'Dad, shurrup!' said Nate at his elbow.

'Yer going down a very dangerous route, duck,' he told her, wagging a finger, to the bemusement of her mother. 'That is the road to ruin, young lady!'

Polly chewed her gum like she couldn't give a shit. If there was a chance it was a road leading out of Stoke she would take it.

'Do you hear me?'

'Dad!' Nate exclaimed.

'What're you talking about? Don't you think they should do History?' said Mrs H.

'I don't think your Polly should, no!'

'Come on, Nate,' Polly said, 'let's go out the back.'

'Oi! Oh no, you don't,' said Lonny, thumbing towards the door. 'Front garden only – where Julie can keep an eye on yer!'

Then Dawn, who looked simply stunning with a rainforest, monkey and parrot on her face, went and got her clippers from home because Solly said he would let her cut his hair. Which was unbelievable to his parents and when Lonny asked him why he said, 'Cos she didn't tell me off when I hit the ball into her bra.'

Everyone roared with laughter and Jenny's eyes widened as she saw Solly's oversize Afro coming off bit by bit. So Dawn had been a hairdresser before the children came along it seemed, something else she hadn't realised about her neighbour.

'There's enough hair to stuff a duvet there!' called Debbie, who was having a fine old time meeting lots of interesting new people and hiring Hannah as her cleaner because she said she loved cleaning and needed extra hours. That would leave Jenny with the other work, the kind she didn't mind. Jenny gave her a big kiss and apologised for not being a better cleaner herself. Debbie said, 'That's alright, Jen, I don't want to torture you with it any longer,' and they both laughed and knew that their relationship would be so much better now.

Then gradually, after much merriment and much talking and dancing with people she had ignored or overlooked this last year, Jenny's party finally came to an end. Everyone gave everyone else lifts or escorted them home so that Jenny and Lonny could stay put.

Jenny whispered to Fusun as she left, 'We never got a chance to speak to Dawn, did we?'

'Tomorrow,' said Fusun. 'I'll come round in the morning and help you tidy up and then we can make a plan.'

'OK, thanks, lovey,' said Jenny and kissed her new friend goodnight. How thoughtful and kind she was, and how stunning she looked in her new make-up. But once Fusun was gone, Jenny regretted that the whole evening had passed without a real chance to speak to Dawn about what had happened. Through the French windows, she saw her over the fence, lighting up her last cig of the evening. She went out into the garden to speak to her.

With everyone now gone and the boys slumped down in front of the tele, Lonny surveyed the scene with a grin as wide as a Cheshire cat's. The place was a complete mess but he couldn't care less. Jenny had pulled it off. Not only throwing a great party but heroically saving Joyce's life into the bargain. His beautiful, gorgeous, caring, kind-hearted wife was back in full force.

He saw her out the back having a word with Dawn over the fence. He could see her reaching out to hold Dawn's hand and patting it as she spoke to her. He could hear her saying that she and Fusun wanted to speak to her tomorrow, it was very important that they did this. Then it looked like Dawn was getting tearful so Jenny said, 'Why don't you come over now, lovey, and we'll have a little nightcap. Come on, come over now. I'll go and get the drinks sorted.'

And Jenny came back into the kitchen and Lonny's eyes were filling up as he looked at her and understood the journey she had been on. He was so proud of her, his chest was bursting. He had to blink quickly to make sure the tears didn't fall down his face.

Then a movement in the back garden caught his eye.

Dawn was climbing over the fence. Her arse was straddled across it, her legs were kicking and the patchwork pieces were beginning to split under the weight.

'Watch me fucking fence, Dawn!' he roared, the tears vanishing in an instant. He ran out into the garden just as Dawn brought the whole section down on top of her.

'What the fuck?'

'She told me to come over!' said Dawn, getting up from under the wood and looking confused.

'She meant come round!' shouted Lonny. 'Come over means come round!'

'Well I dinna know did I?'

'Fuckin' 'ell man!!!' He looked down at the busted fence in exasperation.

Then a loud snorting sound distracted them both. Jenny was leaning against the back door clutching her sides and laughing hysterically. Tears began to roll down her face.

She snorted like a pig.

Then she screamed, 'Wooh!' and clutched her crotch in surprise. Dawn and Lonny watched for a moment.

'She's pissin' her sen, Lon,' Dawn said.

'Bloody 'ell,' said Lonny in disgust. He looked at Jenny, who was getting more hysterical by the minute.

'Get a grip, woman!' he told her, but that only made it worse as she snorted some more and held onto her crotch for dear life.

'You're like a pig, Jenny,' said Dawn with a giggle. 'She's like a pig, Lon.'

'Sort yourself out, Jen, come on, get to the toilet!' Lonny ordered but Jenny waved him away and staggered towards Dawn. She threw her arms round her and kissed her. Dawn giggled some more and hugged Jenny back.

Lonny's frown vanished when he saw them together. 'Come here you two,' he said and hugged them both. Short-haired Solly looked on from the doorway with a grin as the three adults hugged.

'Now, how about a nice glass of Baileys and ice for a night cap, courtesy of our old pal Matty?' Lonny asked as he followed Solly back inside.

'Can I have it with ice cream?' asked Dawn. 'I love Baileys and ice cream!'

'I said a night cap not a pudding! Bloody 'ell, don't you know what time it is?' moaned Lonny.

'Wha?' said Dawn.

Jenny began to laugh hysterically again. She shouted after her husband, 'Oi you! If she wants it with ice cream she can have it with ice cream!'

She put her arm round Dawn as they went into the house.

CHAPTER 32

Closure

The landline rang the next day. Jenny had been expecting it.

'Hello, Jennifer,' said her mother. 'How are you, dear? Have you heard about poor Uncle Pat?'

'Hi, Mum,' she said, feeling the usual knot of anxiety tighten inside her. 'Yes, I got a text from Fiona in the week.' She waited. She knew that her mother would be expecting her to ask why she hadn't phoned immediately she got the message. But she didn't care. She wasn't going to talk until she was ready. She wasn't going to just fill the air with lightweight small talk claptrap like she usually did. Small talk to distract them from what they both knew had gone on.

'Well, God rest his soul, at least he didn't suffer for too long. And what a ripe old age, eighty-five, who would have guessed it?'

Jenny remained quiet.

'I need you to go to the funeral in Cardiff for me, love. They haven't got the date fixed yet but it will most likely be in a fortnight or so. I can't leave your dad and fly over. These days I'd be worried about getting back into the country.' She laughed faintly.

Jenny remained quiet. She pressed her feet into the floor and took a deep breath. The knot began to unravel.

'Are you there, Jennifer? Have we got a bad connection?'

'Yes we have, Mum,' she said finally. 'We've always had a bad connection.'

She heard her mother take a sharp intake of breath. 'What did you say?'

'I'm not going to the funeral Mum. Uncle Pat was not a nice man. He abused me for a long time when I was a little girl and I'm only just now managing to get over it. And the worst thing was, Mum, you knew about it and you sided with him over me.'

'Don't be so ridiculous!' her mother snapped. 'God Almighty, you are such a drama queen. You're talking about an old man for goodness sake!'

'He wasn't an old man then though was he, Mum? He was in his thirties and I was only six or seven. Think about that.'

'Yes and you were a little liar weren't you? You'd say anything to get a bit of attention!'

'No, that was you, Mum. That was you.'

'Jennifer stop this nonsense! I need you to go to that funeral and represent me.'

'We'll be over in August for a short visit,' she said firmly. 'I want to spend some quality time with Dad. I don't get a chance to talk to him normally because you never let him speak to me on the phone do you?'

'I beg your pardon! I never –'

'Then we're all going off to a camp to help restore the ecosystems.'

'You what? What on earth are you talking about?'

'We're going to do things a different way from now on, Mum. It'll be much better for all of us.'

'Jennifer!'

'I'll ring you nearer the time.' She swallowed hard and lifted her head up. She had done it. She had finally done it.

'Goodbye, Mum.'

*

Jenny stood at the bottom of the scaffolding ladder looking up to where Lonny was standing on the roof. The extra solar panels were finally installed and he wanted her to come up and see it all and look at the view before the scaffolding got taken away.

'Come on, Jen,' he said, 'you can do it.'

She was about to start climbing when she saw Dawn's husband Mark come out of their house and walk down the path. He stopped to reluctantly drag the bins to the front road for pick up.

Jenny called up to Lonny, 'Hold on, love.'

She turned towards the fence. Towards the man who carried an aura of toxicity.

'Hello, Mark, can I have a word?'

The nerves in her stomach churned into that familiar knot of anxiety. The same old feeling that she was walking towards her execution. But she knew she had to do it. She knew it the night she heard Dawn cry out, the night when all thoughts of having nothing in common with her neighbour were erased. Because once upon a time, she was just like Dawn, and Sue had arrived like an angel in the night and rescued her from Alan when Ryan was just a baby. Her whole life had turned upon that one night. Not that she could remember anything beyond the first punch.

She never knew what sixth sense had made Sue come running down the street to her rescue. The two women had been speaking on the phone when Alan came in, drunk of course, and the fear must have shown in her voice. She hadn't meant to lie to her friend, she just didn't know how to tell her about how bad her husband's behaviour was getting. When she came to, she was lying in the ambulance and she could tell by Sue's face that she must have looked

266

pretty bad. She remembered Sue holding her hand, Sue talking to the paramedics, Sue telling her that it would be OK, that Eddie was going to look after baby Ryan. And Sue telling her that from now on, Jenny would have to come and live with her, she could never go back into that house again. She wouldn't take no for an answer. Flashing lights and sirens going full blast and then stopping as yet another police car arrived. The expressions of shock on the faces of grown men as they saw what she looked like.

Yes, there was no doubt about it, Sue had been an angel in her life. She had rescued her on many occasions, some big, some small. And now it was time for her to do the same for someone else. Dawn.

She felt the ground beneath her. Each step she took towards Mark she could feel strength flooding in through the soles of her feet and rushing upwards. She felt that her whole life had been moving towards this one moment. Everything Sue had given her, her love and friendship and her unshakable confidence, she now had at her fingertips.

Lonny looked down from the rooftop. Fusun and Ahmed came out into their front garden. Dawn pulled back a curtain to watch as Jenny approached Mark.

'Hello, lovey,' she said, 'how are you settling in?'

'Good thanks, duck, still a fair bit to do,' he said, somewhat bemused. He looked around and was aware of faces watching him.

'I just wanted to have a word, Mark, because there seems to be a bit of a misunderstanding going on. I know about what happened the night before last with Dawn – and I just want you to know, we don't allow that kind of behaviour around here.'

'What? I dunno what yer on about, duck. What yer talking about?' He waved away a fly that was buzzing around his face.

'You were hitting your wife.'

'No way, I never touched her. She just says things to get attention, take no notice.'

'I heard you hitting her, Mark. I heard it.'

'No way, I said I never touched her!' The fly got swatted violently.

'I'm afraid I don't believe you.'

'Oh fuck off,' he said, tiring of being nice. 'I'm in my own house, I can do what I fucking want! What you going to do about it? Call the police? They'll be round in two weeks' time.'

'That's true, the police have a lot on their plate these days.' She kept her hands on her hips and looked directly at him, still feeling as strong as an oak tree, her feet firmly rooted in the earth. 'So maybe I'll go straight to the landlord and get him to change the lock so that Dawn and the children can live on their own in peace. Then you can go and make your own way in the world, how about that?'

'Who the fuck d'you think you are?' he snapped. 'Why should he listen to you?'

'Because he's a very good friend of mine. I looked after his mother for many years.'

His cocky look dropped suddenly.

'If you want to live in a civilised neighbourhood, Mark, you've got to behave in a civilised manner. If you can't do that you'll be out on your ear. Do you understand?'

He looked stupefied as Jenny continued. 'I'm sure the doctor can get you fixed up with some therapy. And there's plenty of good men around who you can talk to if you need to. It's not up to us women to sort you out, we've got enough to do.'

He looked round at the faces watching him; it seemed like the whole street was watching.

'Fuck off yer cunts!' he said and stormed off.

When he'd gone, Jenny took a moment to breathe. Then she

looked up at Lonny on the roof. She wanted to get up there with him. She climbed the ladder, no longer feeling the nerves or disinterest of a month ago. As she climbed, she could hear Beethoven floating on the breeze from the Stevenson's open window. She smiled, she loved this one. It was the sixth symphony, she knew it from her dad.

Up on the roof, Lonny showed her the field with its new owners, and the countryside beyond, stretching right down to the A50, which wound through the greenery like a serpent on its way towards the city. In the other direction she saw the rooftops of Meir Heath, the dormant windmill of the Windmill Pub, the long thin line of Manor Lane and the smaller rooftops of the houses and bungalows of Meir Park Estate leading down to *Aldi* and *Tesco*. Everywhere she looked she could see that other people were having the same ideas as Lonny – the solar panels were everywhere, glinting in the sun, creating energy for each home. Newly planted trees were flourishing. Green roofs and walls were drinking in carbon and gardens were overflowing in abundance as more and more people were growing their own food. Every street had wildflower beds to link in to the city-wide bee corridor. Concrete was receding in all kinds of places and giving way to a lush green carpet of long grasses which would help restore the soil sponge so devastated by the ignorance of the twentieth century.

A song-thrush was singing loudly from the treetops and somehow punctuating the music. Stella and her partner Geoff walked along the road with a wheelbarrow full of compost. Lonny hailed them and Jenny found herself waving too.

'Great party, Jenny!' called Stella.

The boys were kicking a football in the street with their mates. The sun was beating down. Lonny put his arm around her and smiled and Jenny felt a peace in her heart that she had never felt before.

CHAPTER 33

The first draft

Jenny looked at the blank page in front of her. She had scrapped what little she had written before and now all she had was the title – her name followed by some of the roles she had accumulated on her life's journey: 'Wife, mother, friend, carer, singer, neighbour, daughter'. At least that was it for this essay anyway; she knew that there were even more roles that she couldn't think of right now, which she could drop and pick up whenever she had to. For the first time in her fifty-one years, she felt the joy of owning such a vast array of diverse experiences and it was all there at her fingertips waiting to be used.

It was 9am. Bill was at a hospital appointment with another carer so she had the morning off.

She began to write.

From time to time, she paced the room, looking out at Lonny in the garden and waving occasionally to Dawn or Fusun if they were also outside. She kept her written language simple and didn't try to be clever. She would think of some big words later perhaps. Unexpectedly, she found herself enjoying it much more than she thought she would. Maybe she was meant to go to the class for the actual writing after all and not because of Trudi. She blushed to herself at the thought of what a state she had got in while trying to be

Trudi's friend. How could she have been so desperate? She hadn't realised what a wealth of good women were around her, right under her nose.

She thought of the morning after the party when it became apparent that things had changed and she would never have to go back to her previous dysfunctional isolation. She started a WhatsApp group called 'Friends and Neighbours' and invited everyone from the party to join. Which they quickly did. Then they thanked her for such a great evening. 'Best party ever!' said Zohal.

'Lovely to meet all your friends, Jenny, thanks so much for the invite,' said Debbie and Lauren said, 'Great voices, ladies, you should start a choir, Jen!'

That suggestion hit home like a missile. A choir. For local women. How wonderful would that be? So she messaged back, 'Great idea, Lauren! Would anyone else be interested?'

And everyone said they would be and they knew other women who would be too.

Jenny wrote and wrote all morning and finished the essay, or at least what Celia would call the 'first draft', around 2pm. She found that as she was writing about her mother and Uncle Pat and Alan, and that she was eager to forgive them all. Not for their sakes, but for hers. Because forgiving them enabled her to let them go. She knew she had been carrying it all around for far too long and she didn't want that any more. Sue's death must have stirred everything up again but now she had settled it all and she could move on.

She emailed it to Celia as an attachment, which she knew she wasn't really supposed to do, but she needed some feedback, after all she hadn't really got a clue if she was doing it right. Once she got some feedback she could finish it later. The class was this evening and no doubt Celia wouldn't have time to read it by then, but it felt good to be handing something in. Possibly Trudi would still be away and would be a no-show again, but that didn't really matter anymore. It was funny how life sometimes led you down a path that you thought meant one thing but all the time it meant another. She was looking forward to Daz's latest poetic offerings; she really hoped he had got back with his boyfriend, he had seemed so forlorn the last time she saw him.

The day passed and she and Lon exchanged glances and smiled at each other like they had a little secret. The secret was that she was back on track. She felt like a newer and improved version of her old self. And Lonny couldn't keep his hands off her. After they had made love that morning, he had caressed her naked body and said how much he liked the natural look she was going for, like it was the 1970s coming back into fashion again. 'What d'you mean?' she had asked, before realising what he was talking about. Her body hair was running rampant. 'Oh my God I can't believe it!' she shrieked.

In the afternoon, when the boys were back from school and they were all outside helping Lonny with the garden, she went to each side of the fence to invite Fusun and Dawn and their families to a barbecue at the weekend. Later, as they ate dinner and she watched the boys eating homegrown vegetables, she recognised again that she had never been this happy.

And it didn't feel like this was going against Sue.

It felt in fact like Sue had been behind it all.

*

At 6pm, she arrived at the community college and went in, eager to find out more about how she should write. Surely there would be some point where it would all be explained. If she didn't know the proper way of doing things, it was just possible that she had done everything wrong and Celia may ask her to leave. But if that was the case, then at least she had had a go. There was no shame in failing if you tried your hardest. The shame was if you didn't try.

Daz was already there, looking quite bright-eyed and bushy-tailed. He winked at her as she sat down beside him. 'How are you, gorgeous?'

'Never been better,' she smiled. 'But how are you more importantly? Last time I saw you it was *The End of The Affair*.'

'Oh,' he shrugged. 'What can I say? We made up at last. Partly due to being so bored without him and partly due to him getting down on one knee and proposing.' He brandished his left hand and showed off a diamond ring.

'Oh, Daz!' Jenny screamed, forgetting that the class was filling up and was about to start. She hugged him. 'I'm so happy for you!'

Just at that moment, Trudi came in and Jenny noticed that the golden glow that she had obviously been projecting on to her as some kind of idealised friend was no longer there. Trudi was just a nice, attractive but thoroughly normal woman. She came and sat down on the other side of Jenny.

'Hi, Jenny, how are you? How did the party go? I'm so sorry I missed it!'

'Oh, that's OK,' said Jenny. 'It was great thank you, very busy!'

'Have you managed to write anything yet?'

'Write anything?' said Daz, leaning in so that all three were huddled together. 'She's handed in a first draft!' He swung round to the people behind him. 'Jenny's handed in a first draft!'

'Oh my God! Well done!' whispered Trudi.

At that point, Celia came over with the printed-out essay. 'Jenny, I'm so pleased that you sent me your first draft. I've printed off a few notes for you and I want you to go back and tackle these as you still have another week. But generally speaking, I was very pleased. I know this was your first attempt and it read very well. Very well indeed. So well done, Jenny, you should be extremely proud of yourself.'

'Thank you, Miss,' said Jenny shyly.

'Call me Celia,' said Celia, smiling and walking back to the front of the class.

'Wow, you've done so well,' said Trudi. 'I feel like I haven't taken anything on board yet. My husband and I are building a homestead on some land near Stone, and we've just had everything go wrong in the last few weeks, that's why we had to go away. It's been a nightmare.'

'My husband is making our house into a homestead,' said Jenny. 'Have you heard of permaculture?'

'Yes, we've done the design course!'

'Lonny has too, you should meet up with him, he might be able to help you!'

'Oh that's fantastic! Thank you!' said Trudi. 'Can you stay for coffee after class?'

'Jenny, Trudi,' said Celia disapprovingly. 'When you're ready please, ladies, then the class can begin.'

Jenny and Trudi tried to look shamefaced for a moment, but found themselves giving each other a quick glance and a smirk.

CHAPTER 34

Feeling good

Nina sings loudly on vinyl about 'Feeling Good' and we can see that Jenny and her family, on the edge of Meir Heath, which sits on the edge of Stoke-on-Trent in the centre of England in the north of Europe, one of the continents on Planet Earth, are all feeling good and living well. The cow poops in the back field and the cover crop grows quickly and the soil begins to heal. Nina sings about birds flying through blue skies and in Lonny's Garden of Eden, the harvest shows nature's abundance in all her glory: squashes, courgettes, pumpkins, potatoes, carrots, tomatoes, peppers, chillies, aubergines, cucumbers, raspberries, strawberries, spinach, rocket, lettuce, onions, leeks, celery, coriander, basil, oregano and beetroot, with parsnips and cabbage and cauliflowers on their way and roses and other flowers, companions to the veg, in every bed. Apple trees and pear trees and cherry trees bow their branches with heavy fruit, giving, giving, giving…

And down in the garden of the new café, where all the food will come from local growers like Lonny and Matt and Stella and many, many others, the opening event is very well attended. The chef prepares gorgeous food and knows that what he is actually doing is helping to regenerate the soil and the land which in turn will help alleviate climate change. Lonny is there talking to anyone and everyone. People are discussing how they too can grow their own food, or make their own homestead or live a more natural life without pesticides and plastic and all the other toxins left over from the twentieth century. Discussions are profound and deep as the axis shifts away from the short-lived glories and the long-suffered inequalities of the neo-liberal capitalist system. Something new is coming and everyone is feeling good.

And Nina's song is now being sung by a choir of women and we can see Jenny and Dawn and Fusun and Debbie and Freya and Lauren and Chloe and Hannah and Julie amongst many other local women all singing Nina's song and all feeling good. Trudi and Nehar and Zohal and the boys are among the crowd watching and Daz the poet is there with his boyfriend, grinning at Jenny and singing along.

And as we get closer to Jenny and witness her glorious happiness, we can see in a shimmer of golden light that Sue is dancing and singing alongside her.

ABOUT THE AUTHOR

Ruth Torjussen grew up in Stoke but now lives and works in Brighton as a Shared Lives Carer.

She is a passionate advocate of eating local food grown through regenerative farming as the answer to climate change.

Follow her on Twitter, Instagram and YouTube.

Printed in Great Britain
by Amazon